Advance reviews of *Being*

"Susan Jones has written a ma[...]
discussion set around two wom[...]
I love the way the book bravely [...]
dissects Scriptural verses. It coula nave been a rather heavy tome,
but it isn't. Susan has a deft hand exploring notions of God and
women in the Bible. Interspersed with the discussion is poetry
that glides and sings its way throughout. What a refreshing book!"

Rose Riddell,
author of To be Fair: Confessions of a District Court Judge

"It's marvellous! Susan has managed to distil numerous
theologians not to mention her own thought PLUS poetry with
humanity and elegance. The result is a book I didn't want to put
down till I'd finished. It left me looking for more."

Trish Patrick

"A super read. I gained a lot. Women are great. What the men of
the church have missed out on over the centuries."

Yvonne Wilkie

"At last, a pillar of the church, a Doctor of Theology, a scholar
and a life-long disciple of Christ, has gathered in one book, a
multiplicity of inspirational facts, lists of Biblical names, historical
details and research from a wide selection of writings, teachers,
theologians and Biblical scholarship. They reveal a perspective of
Being Woman in the World which honours both women and God.
I believe this book will give women hope for a better future for
their daughters and sons, and ultimately go far towards healing
our planet.

The magic of this book is that the style of writing is so totally non-
patriarchal! A local coffee bar, an inquiring student, moments of
humour, poignant, appropriate poems, heart-breaking insights.
And an author who gives us an insight into her strong caring,
compassionate connection to her audience, her beliefs, her God,
herself and to full disclosure of the truth of *Being Woman in the
World!*

Some parts may not be a concern of yours right now. But stay
with it, the next page could be a life-changer for you!

Bev Holt,
Manager/Trustee, Te Wahi Ora Women's Retreat, Piha

Being Woman in the World

Conversations in a Coffee Shop Book 3

Susan Jones

Philip
Garside
Publishing Ltd.

Email Susan at: jones.rs@xtra.co.nz
Follow her on: www.jonessmblog.wordpress.com

Paperback print-on-demand USA edition 2022
ISBN 9798358004177

Philip Garside Publishing Ltd
PO Box 17160
Wellington 6147
New Zealand
books@pgpl.co.nz — www.pgpl.co.nz

Cover photograph:
Photo 98865492 / Woman © Mimagephotography |
Dreamstime.com

Coffee cups line art:
Rosemary Garside

Contents

Basic Assumptions

1 – When her world changes, what's a girl to do?

The party is hopping. Jane, a postgrad student like I am, gives the best parties ever. My introverted personality shrinking from the noise and the prospect of many brief, chatty, witty conversations, I brace myself, at the door to Jane's eclectically decorated living room. I'm not sure 1960s orange wallpaper goes with her purple couch and the amber glass in her lighting fixture. But, the multicoloured room reflects Jane's colourful personality. I wonder sometimes how Jane and her first parish would get along.

Jane hails me as I turn, drink in hand, to find a quiet corner. She pulls me over to another ministry student from our class, Hazel. She's standing in the corner of the crowded room with a younger woman. The young guest is surveying the partying postgrad students with a cautious eye, while Hazel chats to one of the theology tutors.

"I've been wanting to introduce you! You know Hazel but meet Faith. Faith's in town for the high schools' Open Day at the University. She's staying with Hazel over the weekend before she goes back down south. Hazel's Faith's aunt, right?" The young woman nods nervously. Jane does rather overwhelm people at first meeting. She turns to Faith.

"Faith, this woman is also in my postgrad class. She might have an idea of how you are feeling." Jane introduces us, including a sidebar description for each of us. I am taped as a minister, now working part time while studying for a Masters' degree alongside Jane. I'm also described as formerly Baptist, now married into our common established national church. Faith is described as in her last year at high school, planning to study English and Philosophy with a side dish of Theology thrown in. "Faith was raised Brethren," adds Jane, lifting her eyebrows at me meaningfully.

I get the point. Jane and I have a conservative background in common. We have had many conversations about the jolt to a person's faith and identity when they hit both the secular and theological academic worlds from out of a conservative church background. It can be discombobulating.

Faith and I begin talking. She doesn't have a glass and I ask if she wants a drink. She says no, but I wonder if it is because most people are drinking wine. I remember the confusing times I'd had at social events having lived in a teetotal family all my life. "Would you like a lemonade?" I ask.

Faith looks relieved. "Would that be OK?" she responds, "I thought perhaps there weren't any soft drinks here."

"Oh yes, it would be poor hosting if there weren't. I can never drink wine all night. I wasn't brought up with alcohol in our house and I've been slow in getting used to it. I can take it or leave it. My Mum and Dad have been teetotal all their lives and they're in their seventies. Unlikely to change now."

I get a lemonade with ice and Faith gulps it gratefully. Poor girl, she must have been getting really dry in the hot room.

The noise of the party makes it hard to pick up each other's nuances, so after a few exchanges, we move out on to the deck in the early evening sun. The quiet garden atmosphere is a relief. As I encourage her to continue talking, Faith's story slowly emerges.

"I'm from small town Southland," she tells me. "Quite a well-off farming district. The local Brethren Assembly in which I've been brought up has quite a few farmers in its membership. It's often said there that when a man is prosperous it shows he is good with God."

I nod. Many Brethren church members did do well in business. I wasn't sure if it was God's influence or simply good, disciplined business sense. "Where do you fit into your local Assembly?" I ask.

"I got involved in the church as a youth leader. When my twin brother and I've done a few events together, I noticed the elders always talk with Mark and take his advice or opinions. If I come up with something, even if it is creative and interesting, it's ignored." I nod sympathetically and she continues.

"It was a shock for me when my aunt, who'd also been raised Brethren, started training for the ministry in your church. Hazel is very intelligent. She'd always been careful to do the right thing in our little Brethren Assembly. She went to Bible College which everyone approved of. From that experience however, she seemed to get other ideas about what women could do in the church."

"How do the local elders react to that?" I ask.

"They questioned it. I remember Hazel wrote a careful piece interpreting the New Testament passages about women in church. The elder she'd written it for kept it for 6 weeks without even reading it! She was furious, and hurt, I think."

"I know she went through a lot wrestling with whether or not it was right for a woman to take a leadership position in the church," I respond, thinking of the long conversations Hazel had had with several people involved in ministry training.

"Where do you go to school?" I asked. I knew the area Faith came from and was curious to know where she fitted there.

"I was home schooled for my primary years. Now I'm finishing up at an independent Christian high school." Faith named the school. It was one I knew well, popular with mostly conservative Christian families.

"What are your favourite subjects?' I ask.

"I love English and History. The curriculum we followed at home and now do at high school requires all our assignments to be related to the biblical story of Creation. We've had to be quite inventive at times to get it to fit. It was often a bit of a twist to link things together."

"Huh. I think it would be quite a task to do that!" I had heard of other schools doing that. My own relatives had attended a similar college.

"I'm not sure how it will be at uni. The Open Day today was quite a whirl. I liked what they said about English, but I wasn't sure if I completely understood all that Philosophy is about."

I nod again. "You won't be alone in that. I remember those first days in the undergraduate arts subjects I took. There were so many Big Ideas flying around in lectures. Some I'd never encountered and yet, they made sense of what I'd always questioned deep inside. I was particularly amazed at the variety of stances on the one topic. How could there be that many theories on women's place in the world, or the historical significance of the second world war, or on colonisation in New Zealand?"

Faith laughs. She is beginning to relax as we talk. "Yes, like the papers we heard about today. It seems in Philosophy 103 God definitely doesn't exist. In the second, Medieval Literature, it seemed God may exist and then just before lunch, when we were in the Theology department, God definitely exists, always has and always will!"

I laugh, "it does make you think, sorting it all out. I found it a shock too that what I had been taught as fact back home in my local church, was actually just one of a number of theories, depending on from which position or ideology the author was operating."

"Oh! It's good to know other people have felt the same way," confesses Faith, flushing a little. "This is all really interesting. I'd like to know more about all that. Who'd have thought a party would result in a conversation like this. This is better than the usual butterfly style conversations where people flit about and only stay talking to you for a while."

"Spoken like a true introvert. Extroverts like that kind of conversation. It's not meant to be a night for serious talking like this. I'm glad you're finding this interesting. I was just wondering if I'd got too carried away. Blame my own introversion. Introverts like to have deep meaningful conversations, not just brief cocktail party type encounters."

"Really? I must be an introvert then. I can't stand that bright chatty kind of talk. Give me this kind of conversation any day." Faith looks at her watch. "I'd better be going, though. Hazel said she didn't want to be late tonight. I think she has an assignment due."

She turns to me.

"I've really enjoyed talking to you. Thank you very much."

"You'll probably have heaps of other questions next year when you get into uni study. I often meet people in coffeeshops to talk things through. Here's my card. Get in touch if you would like to do that too."

"Oh. Well… thank you … I…"

"No pressure. Just if you want to," I reply.

"I really enjoyed talking with you. Now I'd better go," replies Faith. She turns and walks across the deck back into the still crowded living room.

Watching her go, I wonder if I will be 'damned if I did and damned if I didn't.' Brethren governance and theology is very disciplined and strict. If Faith'd been socialised in that worldview for the whole of her life this far, she might be resistant to any new ideas waiting for her.

If she decides to join a group which she had been warned against all her life, she will cause a lot of friction with her family. On the other hand, if she steps back from the challenge now, she might always wonder what might have been. It is always the way with the first call to journey deeper within yourself. You don't know what you don't know, and you certainly don't know exactly what is ahead of you. I remembered a poem I'd written about that, years ago. It was a process you only understood properly in hindsight.

But, in a person like Faith, there sometimes is this push from within to discover the new world she can only just glimpse ahead. I thought I could see the beginnings of that in her. When that happens, you feel urgently you need to go and find it, although you know at the same time it isn't going to be easy.... I always wonder whether it would be fair to warn people of how far one initial question can take them as one question leads to another and another and another and into different territory.

I think back over the young men and women I'd talked with during my previous few years in ministry. I met them in *The Cup,* a coffeeshop across the road from the church where I had been inducted some years ago. Some who stood out included Guy, trying to reconcile being Christian with being gay. I remembered Hope wondering why her beliefs didn't work anymore.[1] Charity had been upset by our church's attitude to LGBTQI+ Christians.[2] They had all found there were more questions within their initial questioning. Because they had embraced those further questions, they had grown as spiritual seekers as a result. I wondered whether Faith's investigations would do the same for her.

I hoped I would hear from her. Faith would need to talk with someone, whatever path she would choose in the end. I braced myself to re-enter the noisy room. Back to the light and trivial.

Yes

Often, I have envied Mary
her calm serenity
her saintly certainty
as she said 'yes'
to you.

But now
I read that maybe this divine mother
knew little of the other 'yeses'
that would be inside her first.

So, Mary too,
like me,
gave what she could at the beginning
little knowing to where it might lead.

Like peeling layers from an onion
you strip me slowly, God.

My first assent gave permission to deal.
In my innocence I assumed
one peeling would achieve your purpose
but you continue to claim me,
to seek my trusting 'yes'
for one more layer
and then another
and another.

So, I face the other 'yeses' that were inside the first
if I had known it.

A confidence trick? A con job?
Yes and no.
You asked me only
for what I could yield at the time
I can only handle this painful exposing
in stages.

My confidence in you builds as one skin is shed
I find I can cope and so can say confidently
The next 'yes'

That's the point
not the understanding or the amount yielded
but the continuing faithful readiness
to say the next 'yes' too;
to have the courage
to continue the job
having started;
to remain open and trusting enough
to shed the next layer
and not to fear what I will be
when all the skins have gone.

To be faithful
to the desire to find out what's next;
which promoted that first
most inadequate
and yet most important 'yes' of all

Yes, yes, yes,
continue[3]

2 – I need to talk

The years of postgrad study ended and that Christmas I returned full time as minister in the church across the road from *The Cup*. That might sound like a strange way to identify a church, but the students with whom I mainly worked called *The Cup* my 'other office.' I was often meeting them there, sometimes developing a service with one of the students for the alternative Sunday night café church we held in the side chapel. Many a creative worship idea had been teased out over cups of coffee and hot chocolate, with cheese rolls on the side, perhaps.

I knew from Hazel that Faith had settled into her classes quite well. She was enjoying the hostel experience and had a compatible roommate – something which wasn't always a given. She hadn't contacted me, though I had seen her in the distance a couple of times. I noticed she had slipped into both our contemporary and traditional church services on occasion, but never stayed for morning tea. Perhaps I had put her off the idea of discussing what was happening for her. I hoped she would find someone to talk with because I was sure she would encounter some bumps in the road sooner or later.

Then came the morning when I opened my computer and saw an email from Faith. It was brief, simply asking if I had meant what I said and could we meet sometime this week if possible.

"Of course, " I wrote back, "it's good to hear from you. I had been wondering how you were finding everything. Do you know *The Cup* on Wayfarer St? It's opposite the church where I work. Is that a convenient place for you? The under-thirties at my church call it my second office. We could meet there when it suits us both, any weekday except Monday. Why don't you email me a few times which suit you? We can arrange something which works."

So it came to pass that Faith and I faced each other over two hot chocolates the following Thursday, in the early afternoon.

"Hi Faith!" So nice to see you." I took a quick survey of her as I spoke. There were a few shadows beneath her eyes – some midnight oil had been burned then. She looked happy enough, still conservatively dressed mainly in navy blue with a plain skirt and plaid shirt with the generic navy puffer jacket.

Faith smiles shyly. "I have thought of contacting you several times," she admits. "Somehow I didn't get round to it."

That statement was evidence for me that talking over whatever was bothering her was something about which Faith was still ambivalent.

"What's on top of your mind," I suggest, "let's go with that."

Faith is quiet for a moment and then bursts out with, "It's all the different ideas!" She rushes on…

"When I think about it, when I was at home as a child, and then a teenager, most of the people I met came from the same background. Their theories about the world were all the same, more or less. That led me to the impression that if everyone agreed on something, it must be factually true. But here at uni there are lots of different ideas, even ideas which are different from subject to subject."

I reply "Do you mean that the people at home were operating out of the same worldview and not everyone has that worldview?"

Faith replies slowly, thinking it through as she talks

"You know, I hadn't worked that out till now! I've been so shell shocked at the different ideas and handling the different expectations I haven't had the time to sit back and work out why it is so different here, or perhaps I should say, why it is so different at home."

I smile at her, understanding what a big moment this 'aha' is for her, and add what I hope will be some wider context.

"Perhaps the most important thing I learned when I came to university was that there are many different worldviews knocking around about the human community. The one we come from is God-centred. A little like the argument Galileo had with the medieval Catholic Church, whether the sun or the earth was the centre of the universe. For Christians, especially conservative Christians, God is the centre of the universe and from God all ideas, principles and morals flow." Faith nods. She knows that worldview well.

"Obviously," I continue, "for atheists, it's not God at the centre. Secular people have a variety of different ideas at the centre of their particular universe. For capitalists, it's business and the pursuit of wealth. For communists, it's establishment of a society with a socioeconomic order based on common ownership and a classless society."

"Hmm, I don't know communist societies like Russia and China are achieving the loftiness of that goal!" Faith grins.

I'm glad to see that grin. She hasn't been totally swamped then!

"We read *Animal Farm* at high school, " Faith continued, "which taught me that in some communist societies the goal is power rather than economic equality of all. Sharing everything seems to be beyond human ability!"

"Not only in communist societies," I reply. "In capitalist societies power lies in having wealth, so perhaps power is the centre of both those universes, the communist one and the capitalist one, only exercised by different means. What would give you a totally different worldview from that?"

Faith thinks carefully. "What about if you approach the universe putting the poor at the centre? When you begin looking at the world through their eyes, it reveals a lot of cracks in the systems of our global community."

"Any of your uni subjects giving you a glimpse of that kind of worldview?"

"Yeah," answers Faith. "In Theology 101 we're doing an overview of different approaches to theology. I like the sound of liberation theology where South American priests and nuns began doing theological reflection in the real-life context of the poor. They discovered when you look at the Gospel from the underbelly of society you find different meanings in Jesus' messages. I'd never heard anything like that in the Gospel Hall back home."

"I agree. My home Baptist church didn't take that approach either, though some do now. I'll tell you another approach which gives you different results. That's when women are put at the centre of the worldview. That's the feminist worldview."

"Wow! Feminism! That's almost a swear word at home. My cousin Hazel used to use that word – not with the elders of course. I think they thought feminism was the work of the devil!"

"Has your Aunt Hazel talked to you about the interaction between feminism and church at all?"

"Yes, when we met up at Christmas and in College holidays, she talked about feminist theology a lot. That was when she was working through her own stuff about women's leadership in the church. Later, she ran workshops looking at how women in the Bible could be reinterpreted by knowing more about the context of the time and viewing their behaviour in that light. There was Bathsheba, I think, Mary Magdalene, Hagar, (who usually comes off pretty badly beside Sarah), and Rahab. They didn't get preached about much at…"

"…my local chapel!" I finished for her. We laugh together, recognising our common experience. I add another thought which has come to me.

"It took me a while to realise that some theologians look at any theology which has a qualifier in front and think of it as not 'real' theology – you know, feminist theology, black theology, liberation theology, rainbow theology… there are quite a few new contextual disciplines which have grown up since the 1960s."

Faith is nodding so I continue. "I like the way those contextual theologies get to grips with real-world issues. In contrast, when I listen now to a conventional theologian or biblical scholar, I find their world really a-contextual. It's as if they believe theology comes straight down from heaven untainted by earthly concerns. The way they view black spirituality, women, the poor and other groups is then not critiqued or challenged by what they study and teach."

"Oh it is so good to talk about this stuff. I knew I was getting twisted up inside, but I didn't know why."

"Glad to help. I'm glad you got in touch."

"Oh, " Faith flushes, "I hoped you meant it. It took a bit of courage to email."

"No problem," I reply. I wait, but she doesn't say anything more, head bent, her spoon also chasing marshmallows.

Tentatively, I ask, "if there was one key idea or concept that was threaded through all you want to know, what would it be?"

Faith's spoon follows a white marshmallow for a moment more while she ponders.

"I've decided…," she replies eventually, "….the common thread to a lot of my questions is being a woman in the world. I'm beginning to see in the university world – not just in the books I'm reading and the ideas in lectures, but the way students and teachers behave, that women are treated quite differently from what I'm used to in the Brethren community."

She ponders for a moment, brow wrinkled. "Now I've found there're many different ways of looking at almost everything, I guess there must be different ways of being woman in the world….. and that will include in church too …. I have a sneaking suspicion if we could follow that thread, I might find out heaps about God and church along the way. Perhaps some of the questions I suspect are lurking inside me might also get answered along the way."

She sat back. I thought she was a little shocked at being so open. Perhaps relieved too she had got it all out at once.

"Well, that's a big topic!" I respond with a smile. "Are you happy to come several times, because it might take us a while to deal with this really well?"

"Oh yes!" says Faith enthusiastically, "if you can be bothered, I would love to have a lot of conversations with you. Only if you have the time, though!"

"I have plenty of time for this kind of talk," I say. "We could make this time on a Thursday the regular slot, say every two weeks or so. If either of us have to change in any one week, then we could let the other know?"

"That would be good…. I think!" Faith was obviously pleased to have made contact and got started, but was still not 100% sure.

"Look, how about you think about it and then get in touch and tell me if and when you want to start talking. This is your journey and the speed of it is up to you."

"Thanks, I appreciate that," replies Faith, looking relieved at the offer of time.

I think that this is probably enough, and I concentrate on getting her talking about her papers. She describes how Thursday mornings are a series of three subjects where in the first, God doesn't exist, in the second God might exist and in the third God definitely does exist.

You'll need to keep your wits about you when you are writing assignments!" I comment. She laughs. "Yes, I'd been thinking that."

We talk on. It is good to make the connection and to see Faith relaxing, though I suspect she has a rocky road ahead of her on her own pilgrim's progress.

I don't know what to think!

Back home there was only one option:
God's way or the highway,
you could say.

God knew what-was-what.
We could too, if we had
faith
belief
trust.
If we obey,
trust and obey,
there is no other way.

But here there are heaps of ways!
I don't know what to think!
I don't know who I can trust with my confusion and fear
I need someone who won't scoff,
who's been this way before,
who knows I don't know what to think
because she's not known what to think once too.

3 – In the beginning

To my delight, Faith did email to arrange a meeting for the following Thursday. I wait for her in *The Cup*, with the noise of the coffee grinder in my ears and aroma of freshly brewed coffee teasing my nostrils. I remember Thursday is when she has three lectures where the existence of God varied from 'definitely not' to 'maybe' to 'definitely so.' She was a brave woman coming to talk with me on top of that kind of morning.

I wave as I see Faith crossing the street. I wonder if her headscarf was a Brethren thing or a fashion statement. It is brightly coloured, but conservatively worn, so maybe a bit of both. Faith's curly black hair flows out underneath the scarf.

"What do you want to drink?" I ask as we enter the café. "Hot chocolate, please," Faith replies, shrugging off her backpack on to the seat next to her. It was heavy with books and her laptop. I thought chocolate was a good option for me too. I'd had several coffees already today, time to turn the caffeine levels down a bit.

With our drinks in front of us, our spoons toying with the pink and white marshmallows which the child in me still loved, a small silence falls. Faith is the first to break it.

"So where do we start?"

"What about 'In the beginning'?" I grin back at her and sip some hot chocolate to prepare me to continue. "You remember 'in the beginning'?"

"You mean… 'In the beginning God created the heavens and the earth.' Sure do after all those creation-integrated assignments!"

"Yes, that 'beginning.' Do you remember what comes next?"

"Yeah…," says Faith slowly, thinking hard, "…something about darkness and deep waters and the Spirit brooding over them."

"Exactly." I take out my tablet and quickly bring up the verse. "This is the New English Translation: 'Genesis 1:2 Now the earth was without shape and empty, and darkness was over the surface of the watery deep, but the Spirit of God was moving over the surface of the water.'"[4]

"I remember," says Faith, craning her neck to see the screen.

"So, this isn't yet about human women being in the world, but even before the world is, there is the watery deep or *tehom*. This mysterious, dark deep is linked by some scholars to Mesopotamian creation myths in which the creation emerges from a so-called world-egg."

A sort of squeak escapes Faith and I look up.

"What?"

Faith is looking surprised and bursts out...

"There are other creation stories? Not just the Genesis one?"

I smile, reassuringly, I hope. "Almost every culture has a story of how they think the world began. There are remarkable similarities between them. The writers of Genesis would probably have known about quite a few different stories. Remember Israel was on the silk route connecting Asia, Europe and Africa, so there was a constant stream of various kinds of people coming through. It wasn't like they were locked away in a Jewish-only kind of ghetto."

I look up. Faith has the same puzzled look on her face.

"What?"

"You say 'the writers' of Genesis. Plural. Didn't Moses write Genesis and the next four books of the Bible?"

Cautiously, I reply. "Probably not. That is sometimes a surprise to people from conservative churches. They often haven't heard very up-to-date scholarship."

"When did scholars start thinking of more than one writer?"

"The idea of Moses having written the first five books, the Torah or Jewish law, was being debunked towards the end of the 19th century. For example, a Free Presbyterian Church professor in Scotland got into trouble with the conservatives in his church for saying that Moses did not write the first five books when he wrote the first ever entry on Moses for the original Encyclopaedia Britannica, 'M' for 'Moses' – around 1881 I think it was."

"Wow," says Faith. You can see wheels turning in her head.

"Is it too soon to tell you that probably Genesis wasn't written down until centuries after the events in it happened?" I didn't want to hit her with too many new ideas all at once.

"Not written at the time?" stutters Faith.

"Most histories tend to get written well after all the action has taken place. When people are in a settled kind of kingdom, then a ruler can act as a patron and command scribes and historians to write the history of a nation. That's what they think happened with Genesis and the other histories in the Hebrew Bible. After all, you can't write any history until the event is over and there's been time to reflect on it."

"I guess I've always wondered who was taking notes during all the action in the first chapter of Genesis, especially before there was light, or before there was pen and paper, let alone a laptop!" quips Faith.

"If we do accept that this account was written many years later, you can see that there will have been a lot of thinking in between the events being written about and them being written down. Lots of thinking and discussion about creation, about God, about the act of creating must have been done before anyone put a pen or stylus to any kind of writing material, (probably papyrus in their time). There was also a lot of telling of the story, re-telling it over and over in an oral tradition for many years."

"We have learned in Med. Lit. about oral traditions where stories were told as legends before being written down years later," offers Faith.

"Same thing here. That means this is not a simplistic, childlike account coming out of primitive thinking. The thought of the time was highly symbolic and used metaphor a lot – far more than we think. Our mistake is to read it all literally."

"Yes! A lot of people in my community do think of the world being created in 6 days and they really think it is 6 periods of 24 hours. I don't know when I started thinking of it as 6 'bundles' of time," Faith waggles her fingers to indicate speech marks, "perhaps 6 bundles of 1000 years or 6 bundles of millennia, or just a long time. I was quite young, about 10, when I first started thinking that."

"That's when I started asking questions in my head too. Didn't always ask the adults around me. That wouldn't have been a good idea!"

"No! Definitely not, in my case," Faith grins.

"So are you OK to continue with Genesis 1:2?"

"Yes please, this is making sense. Quite a lot falling into place already."

Fleetingly, I thought how resilient she seemed to be. Faith obviously had been doing a lot of thinking since she was 10. This information was confirming her scepticism. I continued, trying to keep it simple without patronising her.

"So, we were saying that the cosmic oceans or watery deeps mentioned here are thought by many scholars to echo Mesopotamian world-egg creation stories. That suggests this mysterious darkness is feminine, since eggs are the female contribution to reproduction. And the Spirit brooding over the waters is also feminine – in Hebrew *ruach,* a female-gendered word for wind."

Another squeak of surprise from Faith makes me pause. "What?"

"The Holy Spirit is feminine?" Faith's face is a picture.

"Well, in Hebrew she is, and in the Greek, the word used for Spirit is *pneuma,* breath, and that is neuter, so in the biblical languages, the Spirit is either neutral in gender or female. No reason to call her 'he' at all!"

"Wow!" breathes Faith, looking awed and scared at the same time.

"Do you want to talk about that?" I ask.

"No… not… not at the moment. Perhaps later," stammers Faith. "Wow," she mutters under her breath.

I continue, choosing my words. I was realising this was a lot to go down in one conversation. Starting at the beginning was important, however, to give a base line in assumptions which underlay translations and interpretations we would meet later.

"So, between verse 2, with the Spirit brooding over the deep, and verse 3 where apparently God says let there be light, a lot of emerging and engaging has been left out. Catherine Keller, who is a leading feminist theologian suggests this is because it's more congruent for the orthodox male dominated establishment to argue God is male and omnipotent, so can bring the creation out of nothing, *ex nihilo,* (Latin for 'out of nothing', ex = out of, nihilo = nothing)." I add.

"If you skip over verse 2 and get into the 6 days of creation work, you avoid God being a female entity who helps the creation to emerge from the feminine waters or egg which are there already."

"You mean the egg or waters are feminine and the brooding Spirit is feminine and verse 2 is suggesting they work together to bring creation forth?" asks Faith, her brow wrinkled slightly.

"Yes, that is what Keller feels verse 2 is suggesting. In the orthodox version, largely argued by male theologians over the centuries, however, the deep is seen as either nothing, or chaotic and disorderly and needing taming."

"In other words, they see the feminine as a nothing or as a negative thing which needs controlling?" asks Faith

"You've got it. Catherine Keller puts it like this – it struck me so much I bookmarked it." I scroll through my phone. "Listen."

> It is becoming evident that the reduction of female divinity to an idolatrous and chaotic matter underlies all orthodoxies. Indeed Barth's hypermasculine God imagery…cashes all too readily into his systematic argument for the subordination of women…the Barthian *tehom* designates "the barren, monstrous and evil cosmos."[5]

"Now that's hefty stuff," I continue. "What sense are you making of it so far?"

"Well!" says Faith, eyes intent. "That's different from anything I've heard preached on Genesis 1. Let me see if I've got it right." She concentrates, brow wrinkling, as I am beginning to see, it does when she is thinking deeply.

"The deep mentioned in verse 2 is probably an idea which is like the other creation myths in the area at the time. They refer to an egg bringing the world into being. So, by association, the *tehom* is feminine, like an egg. Right?"

I nod. Faith continues.

"In the Hebrew language, the Spirit is referred to as wind which is a feminine word in Hebrew. Hebrew must be like French, is it? Different genders for words we would not put a gender to?"

I nod again. "You're doing very well so far."

Faith smiles and continues. "So, this view of the creation has a female deep and a female Spirit working together to help the creation to emerge."

"Right," I nod.

"Other theologians, the orthodox ones (this Bart guy seems to be one of them) see it differently. They either ignore the female stuff and see the deep as barren and a nothingness or they see it as unruly and chaotic and needing taming. Either way, in these versions, a very powerful (male) God creates the world out of nothing or against the chaos of the deep."

"That's right. What significance does Catherine Keller see in that approach?" I slide the phone across with the Keller quote in it and Faith reads intently.

"The Bart guy's way of looking at it (Oh, he's Barth with an h) makes sure there is no female divinity and Catherine Keller reckons his thinking underlies a position of female subordination," says Faith slowly, obviously thinking it out as she speaks.

She looks at me.

"Wow. There it is, right in the first chapter of the Bible. The Bible has two viable entities, the deep and the Spirit which are feminine and obviously part of the whole mystery of creation. But, when the original writers and later theologians get going on the story, the feminine is seen as chaotic and unruly or as a nothingness. For them, God's male, and he created the world *despite* the feminine or *without* the feminine. The whole Bible interpretation begins with women **not** being in the world, or, if they are, they are a problem."[6]

"Yes," I agree. "One of the reasons for Barth's position is that he will have been taught Hegelian philosophy – the philosophy of Georg Hegel who lived from 1770 to 1831. Hegel was very influential. He included God in his philosophical scheme so was particularly influential for Christian theologians and philosophers after him. In fact, Barth called him the 'Protestant Aquinas'.[7]

Faith interrupts. "Aquinas?"

"Thomas Aquinas was a major Catholic theologian/philosopher in the 13th century. He drew on Aristotle's ideas and has influenced even modern philosophy and theology. His approach was very rational and logical," I reply.

"Feminists point out that Hegel's philosophy, in fact all classic philosophy, identified logic and rationality as most important and equated that with male thinking and the mind," I continue. "Women were identified with nature and feeling and the body and not thought of as able to think rationally. They were therefore regarded in classical philosophy as the Other which was either a nothingness or chaotic unruliness."

"Hmm," says Faith, looking thoughtful. "So Barth was creating his theology with that kind of philosophy as his underlying assumption – I suppose we could call it his worldview?"

"Yes. Also, if we can perform some mental gymnastics here (even though we are women) ..." I wink at Faith "...it's important to distinguish between what was actually included in the Bible and how it has been treated since."

"What do you mean by that?" asks Faith.

"You have to use a kind of detective approach, or maybe an archaeological approach, where you are looking for fossilised words trapped in the layers of time giving you a glimpse of what might have been."

Faith nods and I continue.

"But even if you don't distinguish those two (and most average pew sitting Christians don't) for most women and girls, their encounter with God and the Bible metaphorically begins with Genesis 1. Yes, Catherine Keller is saying that from the very first moment of time as it were, the feminine was there but has been ignored as nothingness or misrepresented as unruly, needing to be controlled. The second verse with its amazing implications is skipped over and we move on to the active Creator God, powerfully speaking the world into being, apparently all on his own."

"Mmmm," mused Faith, "So that's why the Trinity is father (male), Son (male) and Holy Spirit (called 'he', though actually female or neuter in the biblical languages). Seems heavily weighted on the male side."

"Well, that's if you take all three persons of the Trinity to be male. What about the Son-male and the Spirit-female and God either male or female? That would even things up."

"God male or female? But the Bible doesn't say that!" I've surprised Faith again.

"This is where you need to go fossicking for those scraps of fossilised language. Let me recommend a book by Virginia Ramey Mollenkott.

Yes, it's a bit of a mouthful that name, isn't it! She began her academic career as professor of English in 1995 and died in 2020. Mollenkott's known for her interpretation of *El Shaddai* – a Hebrew name for God – as meaning 'God of the breasts.' The book is *The Divine Feminine: Biblical Imagery of God as Female*. First published in 1983, it's been reprinted since." I reach for a napkin, rustle around in my bag for a pen and write the reference down.

"God of the breasts!" gasps Faith. "Oh my! I certainly can't imagine any of the brethren preachers tackling that as a topic!" She laughs till tears start trailing down her cheeks. Is this entirely her thinking it would be a joke at the local assembly to hear that phrase? Or is Faith feeling slightly hysterical at all the revelations she has been faced with today? Could be either. I smile as I watch her wipe her eyes. I sip my cooling hot chocolate quietly, scooping out the last of the melted marshmallow flavoured foam, giving her time to recover further.

"Wowee," gasps Faith bringing out a tissue to wipe her streaming eyes. "I'm imaging the elders' faces if someone read the Bible reading and said 'God of the breasts.' Oh goodness me! What else has been done in this area?"

I grin at her as I continue.

"In her book, Mollenkott lists other less controversial imagery used for God in scripture, like the mother eagle, a bakerwoman, a mother leading her child in a walking harness. Remember Jesus likens himself to a mother hen when he wept over Jerusalem? References like that. I think you'd find it useful. It's one of the books in my library which I've kept for years – must have been one of the first printing in 1983!"

"Susan Harrison is another American Christian feminist who, I've recently discovered, has been experimenting with using feminine images of God. She blogs about it. You might find that blog useful – one of her posts looks into the use of *El Shaddai* in the Bible."[8]

Faith is still wiping her eyes, but she recovers enough to say, "could you text me the reference for that book and the link to that blog? It would be good to look at them before we meet next time. Would I get the book in the university library?"

"You should do – or in the library of the ministry training college up the hill. They welcome university students joining up there and they stock the more specialised theology texts. If you can't find it, I can loan you my copy. How are you feeling?" I ask. "We've covered a lot of new ground today."

Faith pauses. An image flashes through my mind of her taking her spiritual/emotional temperature.

"How am I feeling? I'm not quite sure, it's a whole mix of things. But I feel kind of .... lighter.... I suppose. Like there might be a lot more to hear and learn, but I've got started. That feels better than having stuff whizzing around my head endlessly to no great effect."

I nod. I remember that lighter feeling myself. "I'll send you a link to a blog which uses Mary Oliver's poem 'The Journey' about setting out on this kind of pilgrimage. It might help to look at it from time to time. It begins: "*One day you finally knew what you had to do, and began...*"[9]

"That's how it feels. It's the beginning that seems like the point at the moment."

"Yes, it's also like a prayer I love written by Thomas Merton, a contemplative monk who lived in the US which begins with a male God title, but we could replace that with *El Shaddai*.... I have it pasted inside my journal so I can see it whenever I like."

I take out my journal and open to the front cover. "*El Shaddai*....

> "..., I have no idea where I am going. I do not see the road ahead of me. I cannot know for certain where it will end. Nor do I really know myself, and the fact that I think I am following your will does not mean that I am actually doing so. But I believe that the desire to please you does in fact please you. And I hope I have that desire in all that I am doing.
>
> "I hope that I will never do anything apart from that desire. And I know that if I do this you will lead me by the right road, though I may know nothing about it. Therefore, will I trust you always though I may seem to be lost and in the shadow of death. I will not fear, for you are ever with me, and you will never leave me to face my perils alone." AMEN[10]

Faith had instinctively closed her eyes as I read the prayer and now she raises her head, eyes sparkling with tears. "I needed that," she said quietly. "Thank you so much. See you same time, on Thursday in two weeks time?"

"Of course. Go well, Faith. Be gentle on yourself."

Shrugging on her backpack, Faith leaves the café, looking like a modern-day Pilgrim off on her Progress. I wish her well silently in my heart.

In the beginning

In the beginning
The Deep swirled and seethed,
bubbled and brewed.
She created through ovum
contributing the feminine touch.

In the beginning
the Spirit brooded,
swooped and sidled,
glided and glistened.
She created by laying,
adding another feminine touch.

So not only He,
but She also
created the heavens and the earth.

4 – Theology or Misogyny?

"So, I've been thinking," says Faith as we settle down with our iced chocolates. The weather has been unseasonably hot, and a cool drink is welcome.

"Good! That's how we get to work things out," I tease, and she smiles back before getting that serious-thinking look on her face which I am beginning to recognise already.

"That hint of a more female friendly attitude is already there in Genesis chapter 1 but is now buried in the usual orthodox view of the creation. So, are there equally hidden themes when it comes to the creation of people? What has been found in the creation of Adam and Eve and their story when you look at it through women-friendly eyes?"

"I suppose the first thing which might have been hidden from people in most pews is that there are two stories of creation. There is also a different way to interpret the creation of human beings, when you look at the original language."

"Aha, I thought there might be more to it than I've been told," says Faith with an air of triumph.

"What is the story you've been taught?"

"Well… let me see…. Adam, a man, (representing all men), is created. He names the animals but is lonely. So God creates a helpmeet, Eve, by taking a rib from his side. And that is why women are not to be above men because men were created first and she was from his side, so should be alongside him not ahead of him or above him."

"Hmm, let's see how much of that is in the Bible." I turn to my tablet and bring up the second chapter of Genesis, angling the screen towards Faith so she can see. "Let's see… the first few verses are about God resting on the 7th day. That's where our idea of Sabbath rest comes from…. Now, here's a heading 'The creation of man and woman'…. let's see what that says."

Faith takes over, scrolling down the page.

"There's nothing growing at all because there are no men to till the land then…"

⁵ Now no shrub of the field had yet grown on the earth, and no plant of the field had yet sprouted, for the Lord God had not caused it to rain on the earth, and there was no man to cultivate the ground. ⁶ Springs would well up from the earth and water the whole surface of the ground.[11]

"Ha, ha, that's funny, very chicken and egg isn't it! Nothing grew because there was no one to grow it, or were there no people because nothing was growing? It's quite tricky writing a story about creating a world that works, isn't it!" Faith is chuckling to herself as she scrolls on.

"Here it is ! Verse 7, '⁷ The Lord God formed the man from the soil of the ground and breathed into his nostrils the breath of life, and the man became a living being.'"

"Just Adam," I comment. "No Eve as yet."

"Yes, that is, yes, no Adam and yes, no Eve."

"What's next?"

"Well…" says Faith scrolling further down the screen, "there's a description of the Garden of Eden." She reads:

⁸ The Lord God planted an orchard in the east, in Eden; and there he placed the man he had formed. ⁹ The Lord God made all kinds of trees grow from the soil, every tree that was pleasing to look at and good for food. (Now the tree of life and the tree of the knowledge of good and evil were in the middle of the orchard.)[12]

"There are those two trees, and there are a few verses about the rivers and the gold and other jewels around one of them." Faith looks up. "This is different from the order of the Genesis 1 creation!"

"Yes, told you there were two accounts of creation. One starts with the rivers in place, the other starts with nothing."

"Hmm! Or unruly female things!" Faith grins at me and continues.

"Then God puts the man in Eden and tells him about what tree he can eat from and which he should not eat from."

¹⁵ The Lord God took the man and placed him in the orchard in Eden to care for it and to maintain it. ¹⁶ Then the Lord God commanded the man, "You may freely eat fruit from every tree of the orchard, ¹⁷ but you must not eat from the tree of the knowledge of good and evil, for when you eat from it you will surely die."[13]

"So… then the animals are created as companions for the man, but they don't do the trick. Ah, here's where woman arrives on the scene." She continues reading:

[18] The Lord God said, "It is not good for the man to be alone. I will make a companion for him who corresponds to him." [19] The Lord God formed out of the ground every living animal of the field and every bird of the air. He brought them to the man to see what he would name them, and whatever the man called each living creature, that was its name. [20] So the man named all the animals, the birds of the air, and the living creatures of the field, but for Adam no companion who corresponded to him was found. [21] So the Lord God caused the man to fall into a deep sleep, and while he was asleep, he took part of the man's side and closed up the place with flesh. [22] Then the Lord God made a woman from the part he had taken out of the man, and he brought her to the man. [23] Then the man said,

"This one at last is bone of my bones and flesh of my flesh; this one will be called 'woman,' for she was taken out of man."

[24] That is why a man leaves his father and mother and unites with his wife, and they become one family. [25] The man and his wife were both naked, but they were not ashamed."[14]

"Huh," says Faith reflectively, "that's the passage I remember, where Eve is created from Adam's rib. She's taken out of man, and it's then quickly linked with marriage. I didn't see that connection being made here before. It seems a little strange that something like marriage is being written in so early in the creation story. Also, it doesn't say here that woman is inferior to man as she was created second or from his side meaning she should not be in headship over him. But we were always reminded of that so often, I thought it was in the Bible."

"What impression do you get reading it all together now, coupled with the various preaching of this passage that you have heard over the years?" I ask.

"It mostly fits together the way I was taught, but not totally. Man is first. Woman coming from man is here, but her being less than man is not."

"And putting marriage right in there suggests that wives are less than their husbands in marriage too. At least that's how I was taught marriage should be. The man was the head of the two of them, and that was always linked to men being created first."

"Yep, that's pretty standard interpretation for fundamentalist churches where the Bible is read literally."

"You said there was another version?"

"Well, it's the same version, but interpreted differently. Look again at Genesis 2:7, ⁷Then the Lord God formed a man from the dust of the ground and breathed into his nostrils the breath of life, and the man became a living being.'"

"Now add Genesis 2:20ff."

> But for Adam no suitable helper was found. ²¹ So the Lord God caused the man to fall into a deep sleep; and while he was sleeping, he took one of the man's ribs and then closed up the place with flesh. ²² Then the Lord God made a woman from the rib he had taken out of the man, and he brought her to the man.[15]

"Phyllis Trible is a feminist professor who looked carefully at this section. There's an article by her about this passage. I'll send you the link. Phyllis does what is called a close reading of the text where she looks at the structure and the language very carefully. It's called rhetorical criticism. Listen to this paragraph of hers. Notice how she writes about the word we have translated here as 'Adam' like the male name 'Adam.' In the Hebrew it is 'adham." I go to the article which I have bookmarked and read the paragraph from the Trible article I've been thinking of.

> Ambiguity characterizes the meaning of 'adham in Genesis 2-3. On the one hand, man is the first creature formed (2:7). The Lord God puts him in the garden "to till it and keep it," a job identified with the male (cf. 3:17-19). On the other hand, 'adham is a generic term for humankind. In commanding 'adham not to eat of the tree of knowledge of good and evil, the Deity is speaking to both the man and the woman (2:16-17). Until the differentiation of female and male (2:21-23), 'adham is basically androgynous: one creature incorporating two sexes.[16]

"There is a footnote in the New English Translation pointing out that the word we have translated as Adam is very like the word for ground. So, the first creature 'adham created here is a kind of nongendered 'earth creature', neither a man nor a woman."

"Oh," breathes Faith.

" Uhuh. That makes a difference in two ways. One is what we are talking about here. That males weren't created first, but the androgynous earth creature was."

"The second point which will become more important later, is that the prohibition instruction is given to this earth creature (which later will become the man and the woman), so *both* the man and the woman are told not to eat the fruit of the tree of the knowledge of good and evil."

"So, how does Phyllis Trible see the creation of the woman?" asks Faith who is obviously fascinated by this turn of events.

"Remember," I said "Trible does a close reading. Her article is therefore quite finely focused on the words, grammar and the structure of the writing. She picks up on the usual meaning which is applied to the rib in this part here." I scroll down the article on my tablet:

> The rib means solidarity and equality. 'Adham recognizes this meaning in a poem: This at last is bone of my bones and flesh of my flesh. She shall be called 'ishshah (woman) Because she was taken out of 'ish (man). (2:23)

> The pun proclaims both the similarity and the differentiation of female and male. Before this episode the Yahwist [the writer of this section who is recognisable by always calling God Yahweh] has used only the generic term 'adham. No exclusively male reference has appeared. Only with the specific creation of woman ('ishshah) occurs the first specific term for man as male ('ish). In other words, sexuality is simultaneous for woman and man. The sexes are interrelated and interdependent. Man as male does not precede woman as female but happens concurrently with her. Hence, the first act in Genesis 2 is the creation of androgyny (2:7) and the last is the creation of sexuality (2:23). Male embodies female, and female embodies male. The two are neither dichotomies nor duplicates. The birth of woman corresponds to the birth of man but does not copy it. Only in responding to the female does the man discover himself as male. No longer a passive creature, 'ish comes alive in meeting 'ishshah.[17]

"So," Faith breaks in. "Let me see if I have got this right. First, there is created a non-gendered earth creature *'adham*. Then, in a single act, a new creature is formed and the two new creatures which are the result, are *ish* the male, and *ishshah,* the female. According to the way Trible reads the text, both man and woman are created in the same act."

"Well done!" I exclaim. "This is complicated textual criticism and obviously has escaped many a scholar before Trible did this in the early 1970s. That was early even for feminist theology."

Faith had been bending over the tablet intently. She now slumps back in her chair. "This makes such a difference," she says. "You have no idea how often the man-was-created-first argument has been used in my hearing. If that's not true, that makes a real change to how men and women have been presented in the Bible. It's there in the original languages, but they've been mistranslated and misinterpreted."

"Yes, and since many of us don't read the Bible in the original languages, we don't realise that the original languages may have different and more specific meanings than our equivalent words." I reply.

"You said that the instructions about the tree of the knowledge of good and evil were also affected by this understanding of creation?"

"Yes, Trible makes the point that the instruction not to eat the fruit was made to the earth creature. Therefore, both the man and the woman have received this instruction. It is not only Eve. Trible goes on to list various scholars who have described the woman as weak and easily succumbing to temptation, but she rebuts this:

> But the narrative does not say any of these things. It does not sustain the judgment that woman is weaker or more cunning or more sexual than man. Both have the same Creator, who explicitly uses the word "good" to introduce the creation of woman (2:18). Both are equal in birth. There is complete rapport, physical, psychological, sociological, and theological, between them: bone of bone and flesh of flesh. If there be moral frailty in one, it is moral frailty in two. Further, they are equal in responsibility and in judgment, in shame and in guilt, in redemption and in grace. What the narrative says about the nature of woman it also says about the nature of man.[18]

"Huh!" says Faith, "quite, quite different from what I've been told all these years. First, the man and the woman are created in the same moment, equally created by God, NOT the woman coming from the man at all or after the man was created first. Then we find it can be interpreted that both the man and the woman erred in the eating of the forbidden fruit. This isn't about man and woman acting differently. It's about human beings and how they react."

"Well put, Faith," I reply. " I don't think a lot of people realise that the Bible needs a lot of careful interpreting. After all, the first half of the Bible was written more than 2000 years ago and so it was written in a completely different world from ours. People were trying to work out how the world began, how people came into being and how women and men should relate to each other, all without the benefit of modern science or psychology. We shouldn't assume, however, that they were unintelligent or primitive peasants. At the time the early books of the Bible were written there was already sophisticated work being done in mathematics and astronomy so they weren't as ignorant and uninformed as we might think."

"It was however, a very symbolic world. Their stories were written in symbolic language. An online preacher I watch regularly calls it the difference between 'day language' (scientific factual and historical accounts) and 'night language' (symbolism and poetry). We can forget we westerners have been trained in scientific thinking since the middle of the 18th century. We are trained to look for proof and facts and empirical evidence. We divide the world strictly into fiction here and nonfiction over there. Unfortunately, this means deeply symbolic stories with profound meanings are written off as fairy-tale like fantasies and rated as unimportant for adult living. We couldn't be more wrong." I draw a quick breath.

"And there's more! We've made the mistake of reading the stories as if they were not using symbolism but are primitive tales of events which people then thought were real. We make the mistake of reading the symbolic literally. This renders the stories unbelievable to most post Enlightenment thinkers."

Faith is nodding thoughtfully as I speak.

"This story is a good example. To many it is obvious that God did not get a piece of earth, mould it like a clay sculpture and breathe life into it. But the symbolism is clear. We are creatures of the earth and we have the breath of God animating us and changing us from inanimate creatures into living human beings with a spark of divinity at our core."

"Yeah!" Faith breaks in. "I was talking to Hope the other day – you know, she and Charlie run Shalom? She was saying she'd enjoyed conversations with you. The biggest 'aha' moment for her, she said, had been learning the difference between pre-Enlightenment thinking and post-Enlightenment thinking. It was a real light bulb moment for her. She said the best quote for her was one from a guy… Cross.. something?"

"John Dominic Crossan is the guy. Yes, I think that is my own favourite quote in this area of how we read the Bible. He says"

> My point is not that those ancient people told literal stories and we are now smart enough to take them symbolically, but that they told them symbolically and we are now dumb enough to take them literally. They knew what they were doing: we don't.[19]

Faith joined in my laughter. It wasn't often that western university students were 'allowed' to think of their scholarly teachers as dumb. She speaks, leaning forward eagerly.

"This really makes a huge turn around for me. Firstly, I'm learning some assumptions about who wrote what biblical books and when they wrote them might be inaccurate. If I do a biblical studies paper next year that will be brought out more?"

"Yes. I'll tell you one day about my panic attack in a biblical studies paper on John's Gospel. The day I felt the Bible was falling apart like a jigsaw puzzle when you break it up on the table. It was a good experience in the end, however."

"That does sound alarming," smiles Faith. "I think the other thing I've learned these last two weeks is that the Bible is clear, when you take into account the original languages, about women being created equal with men. I feel good about that!"

"Yes. I remember the first time I heard that. A friend had a recording of Phyllis Trible lecturing about it and we were amazed at what she was saying. I remember too in the question time, three men asked questions and then either she or the female convenor said that if there were no questions from women, they would finish the session. That helped some women to speak up. I'd never heard that done before!"

"That must have been some time ago?"

"The 1980s. Though, I found in the late 1990s that in postgrad seminars at my university there were usually more men present and more men asking questions at the end. I trained myself to listen for something I could ask about and to ask the question."

I remembered my embarrassment when my initial questions had sounded trivial even to my ears. I also remembered the delight I had felt when my supervisor told another male lecturer that he thought my question on a particular day had been a very good one. I had asked a philosophy doctoral student why he hadn't given us definitions of the word 'faith' when his whole article was debunking faith. He avoided my question by not answering it directly.

"Even now in our classes it is still more guys than girls asking the questions but only slightly more," responds Faith. She hesitates…

"I'm interested in the different imagery for God – I got Mollenkott's *The Divine Feminine* and am part way through it. When I've finished it, I'd love to discuss it with you?"

"Sure. Where did you get it?"

"Like you suggested, in the Theological College library." Her eyes gleam. "There are heaps of books in there. I could spend the whole semester just reading their shelves from end to end!"

"What do you want to do next time we meet?" I ask.

Faith considers my question as she begins to put her notebook away in her backpack.

"I'm intrigued that the prohibition about the tree of the knowledge of good and evil was made to the earth creature and so to both the man and the woman. Women really come off badly with the so-called 'apple incident.' Are there any other interpretations of that?"

"Good question! I've read a good book on that, so I'll dig it out and refresh myself on the arguments. Got a busy time ahead?"

"Yeah. Two major assignments – one in Philosophy and one for Theology. I'll need to remember which lecturer believes in God and which one doesn't!"

"Yes, wouldn't be a good idea to mix that up! All the best then, see you in 2 weeks."

"Oh." Faith stops. "That reminds me, could it be same time on Friday instead? My assignments are due midnight Thursday!" She looks sheepish.

"You think you might need some last-minute space?" I tease.

"Definitely!" She laughs back at me.

"That would be fine."

"Thanks again, it's been great." She hefts her backpack and is out the door.

I sit back in my chair, amazed at her appetite for new ideas. She is quicker and more open than I thought she might be. It seems she is more than ready for this journey.

Dust to dust and breath to Breath

The biblical myth has it
that God fashioned humankind
out of the dust of the earth
and then breathed that clay figure
into life with God's own breath.

At the end of life, that figure of clay,
fashioned from the dust of the earth,
is no longer the person we knew,
and so, with respect,
we now send it on its mortal journey
to rejoin the earth from whence it came.

Departed from that clay body
is the essential breath of life,
which animated her and gave her vitality.

The great myth of life tells us
this one person's breath of life
sprang from that original breath of God.
Now, by the act of death,
it is freed to return home to its Source.
So we can let go.

Dust goes back to dust
and life's last breath
joins indivisibly
with the Breath of Life.

5 – A Fall or An Awakening?

Faith walks slowly into *The Cup* on Friday a fortnight later. She has dark shadows under her eyes and looks tired.

She looks around the coffeeshop and I wave, pointing to the two cups in front of me. With a sigh, she walks over and shrugs off her backpack.

"Long night last night?" I ask sympathetically, remembering my own undergraduate days.

"Wow, too right – two assignments due the same night. That's what happens when you take papers from different departments, the assignments aren't necessarily coordinated."

"Which papers were they?" I ask.

"Philosophy, where God does not exist, and Theology where God does. I hope I sent the right assignment to the right lecturer." We laugh together, indeed I hoped that was true.

"Maybe you don't want to plunge into the depths of theology today then?" I ask.

"If you don't mind talking to a very tired girl, I'm still up for it," replies Faith, pushing her sleeves up and getting the ubiquitous notebook and pen out of her bag. I notice she can find the pen very quickly. I must get her secret.

"Where were we?" I ask. I knew, but I wanted to make sure she did.

"We've looked at the creation and how the feminine principle is rated either a nothingness or unruly and needing to be controlled. That's a view both in the interpretation of scripture and also in philosophy around the turn of the 19th century."

"Right."

"Then we moved on to the creation of human beings and found that man and woman are created in the same moment from an andro… androg… androgynous earth creature. Sorry!" Faith smiles apologetically around the yawns which are interrupting her speech. "I was saying I was interested in the eating of the apple. I think you had said that Phyllis Trible clarifies that the instruction NOT to eat the fruit was made to the earth creature, so both the later man and woman would have known the fruit was forbidden."

"Yes. The conventional Christian teaching is that God's commands were disobeyed and the two human beings were banished from the paradisical Garden of Eden as a punishment. It then follows that our mortality and the struggles of life on earth as human beings are a result of that. In conventional theology, every human being born since then is automatically seen as a sinner, in a sense inheriting from this original couple sinfulness and disobedience to God as an essential part of our nature."

"That's what they call Original Sin, isn't it?"

"Yes."

"And that event with the serpent and the fruit and the banishment is what's called 'The Fall.' Every time someone says that you can virtually 'hear' the capital letters. 'The. Fall.'"

"That's right."

"But you said there was another interpretation?"

"Since just before World War II, when psychology developed through the work of people like Freud and Jung. The resulting Depth Psychology[20] would look at it another way. It would say that in the Garden of Eden the human beings were in an age of innocence. It was paradise in the sense that nothing would ever go wrong, no one would be selfish or evil. It was like a little baby's experience of the world. They are not responsible for anything. They might cry and dirty their nappies and not sleep when adults want them to, but everyone knows that's all a baby can do, they are simply following their animal instincts and urges."

"So you could think of Adam and Eve in their Garden of Eden phase as innocent babies?"

"Yes, like a child really doesn't properly separate from its mother for quite a while. The child for some time thinks of itself as part of the mother, not as a separate being. There comes a time when the child must develop as its own person, develop its own ego. That might be why they call the early years of life the terrible twos or threes. The child is defining itself over against parental authority but struggles to communicate this clearly, so does it through tantrums, and saying 'No!' or 'Why?' all the time."

"Adam and Eve stand symbolically for a kind of theological version of this. Will they remain in this paradise, innocent and trusting and giving in to God all the time, or will they develop as people with their own ego structure and functioning will?"

"Hmm. That gives a very different view of God than I've heard preached. In everything I've heard, God is always right and disobeying God is the worst thing you can do. The Fall is a terrible thing because it puts us against God. Women of course get the worst rap because it was thought that Eve ate the first fruit. But growing up and saying 'no' and 'why?' to your parents is just a natural part of growing up into an individual."

"Exactly. If we didn't grow up, we would all just be a bunch of helpless babies."

"I was reading a bit about this in between writing assignments this week and I was surprised to find that the serpent might not be all bad."

"Remember I was talking about reading the Bible symbolically? The serpent as a symbol signifies transformation. Serpents are a symbol for transformation because they shed their skin periodically and transform themselves that way."

"Isn't a serpent used as a symbol of healing too – like on the symbol for the medical profession?"

"Yes, that endorses the idea that the serpent turning up symbolically in a story means some change from one state to another is possible here – from illness to healing perhaps or in this case from innocence to maturity."

"But … the man and the woman do disobey God?"

"Yes, but Depth Psychology would interpret that 'disobedience' as being a necessary step to bring awareness. It would see Adam and Eve as beginning their life as conscious human beings rather than as innocent unknowing babies, as not fallen in a bad way, but awakened." I pause, wondering how best to put this.

"It is a difficult thing to do. They become aware, for instance, of being naked and we know that sexuality all through human history has been a tricky theme for humans to handle. It's not easy growing up. The protective boundaries put there by God or put there by our parents or put there by the church are firmly fixed in our thinking. Crossing those boundaries, even though we have a strong urge to do it and more than an inkling this will pay off in the end, takes a lot of courage."

"Sometimes the eating of the fruit is portrayed as greed and unthinking disobedience but all the people who have followed Adam and Eve in this kind of transformation can tell you it is not easy nor easily done. YOU know that, this is exactly what you are thinking through at the moment."

"What? Who? Me?" Faith choked on the mouthful she had just sipped.

"Yes, you. You are asking me all these questions because you are working out whether or not you will stay inside the boundaries which have been drawn for you apparently by God, definitely by your parents and the Assembly, or whether you will cross them and begin your own journey towards being your own person."

"Hmmm," is Faith's only response, but I can see that brow wrinkling again. I let the silence grow as she thinks through what I had been saying. Finally, she speaks.

"My exploring this stuff. It's more important than I thought it was, isn't it?"

She looks up at me, unconscious of the hot chocolate moustache on her upper lip, talking slowly as she thinks things through.

"This is a 'growing up' challenge. It's a life lesson moment, a pivot, an... an...." she gropes for the word, "... an intersection in my life. Will I remain an innocent and good Brethren woman, or will I find my own truth? If I do the second thing, I won't be in paradise anymore. I will have to grow up in all sorts of ways and there will be consequences."

"You're right. One writer I like, Edward Edinger, puts it like this." I scroll to the part of the phone where I keep my favourite quotes:

> Eating the forbidden fruit marks the transition from the eternal state of unconscious oneness with the Self (the mindless, animal state) to a real, conscious life in space and time. In short, the myth symbolizes the birth of the ego. The effect of this birth process is to alienate the ego from its origins. It now moves into

a world of suffering, conflict and uncertainty. No wonder we are reluctant to take the step to great consciousness.[21]

"So the question is, did Adam and Eve 'fall', or were they enlightened or awakened in the moment they ate the forbidden fruit? You could say both, because in a way they fell out of an inflated way of being in which they thought they were innocent and able to simply enjoy paradise for eternity. But also this 'fall' actually awakened them to the good and evil in the world. That is the significance of the tree, it is the tree of the knowledge of good and evil. Once you know about good and evil you cannot be innocent or unknowing ever again. Innocence is sweet and cute in a baby or a puppy or a kitten, but in grown adults it is inappropriate and disingenuous."

"So we kind of 'get real' about the world in this process you are talking about, this transformation which is begun by the serpent talking to the woman?"

"Yes, and it is significant that it is the woman. Rather than blaming her for bringing sin into the world, we can thank her for helping to bring us to consciousness. The psyche, of which Depth Psychology speaks, is essentially feminine and we need the feminine to help us navigate this kind of transition."

"Wow!" Faith exclaims as she leans back from the intent listening position she had been holding. "Wow!"

"I can see," she continues after a moment, "that strict churches and parents would still see this as sin, because it involves you not complying with their rules and boundaries anymore."

"Yes, but to another person who knows about consciousness and unconsciousness, being aware and being unaware, this step is seen as courageous and necessary for your development as a person. The depth psychologists have a word for it: individuation."

Faith scribbles in her notebook. "Can you tell me the reference for that Edinger book?"

"I can, though I have to confess I don't know that I understand everything in it. I've read and re-read it and things come clearer each time."

"He points out, by the way, that the story of The Fall gives us a pattern and process which we follow each time we make another step forward in consciousness. I am afraid that if you make a step now, it will only take you so far. Sooner or later another boundary will need to be crossed. We grow incrementally. Look at this comment from Edinger." I scroll down further in my phone.

> I believe… that it is onesided to depict Adam and Eve just as shameful orchard thieves. Their action could equally be described as an heroic one. They sacrifice the passive comfort of obedience for greater consciousness. The serpent does indeed prove to be a benefactor in the long run if we grant consciousness a greater value than comfort.[22]

"He also comments that people may dream about serpents or about committing crimes when they are going through a transition in consciousness. Look, this is another thing he says."

> …one cannot reach a new stage of psychological development without daring to challenge the code of the old stage. Hence every new step is experienced as a crime and is accompanied by guilt because the old standards, the old way of being have not yet been transcended. So the first step carries the feeling of being a criminal.[23]

Faith sits up straight half way through the quote.

"Yes!" She exclaims. "Yes! That is exactly how I feel! I do feel like I'm committing a crime – against my parents, against the Assembly, for even thinking differently and seeking out more information. That is exactly how it feels."

"Depth Psychologists would say it is a necessary crime. It is as if you were trying to rescue someone or even yourself and you had to trespass across someone's land. If you didn't break that rule, you both would die. It is necessary to break the trespass rule to save a life."

"It's like the end of Mary Oliver's 'The Journey'!" exclaims Faith. She flips to the front cover of her journal and reads the end of the newly pasted-in poem.

But little by little,
as you left their voices behind,
the stars began to burn
through the sheets of clouds,
and there was a new voice
which you slowly
recognized as your own,
that kept you company
as you strode deeper and deeper
into the world,
determined to do
the only thing you could do–
determined to save
the only life you could save.[24]

"That's it. I think you've got it. Maybe being tired made it easier to pick up on the symbolism with the lateral thinking side of your brain today!" I suggest with a smile.

"Mmm," replies Faith stifling a yawn. "Oh, sorry! It's not this stuff putting me to sleep, just not having got much sleep last night. After I'd got the essays in, I was too wired to settle to sleep very quickly, so I've only got a couple of hours behind me. Perhaps I'd better go and catch up! Thanks for today. It was a real eye opener. I need to think about that idea of it seeming like a crime when we make a transition to the next stage. That's ringing lots of bells."

She sends me a tired smile and wave as, still yawning, she goes out the door.

I watch her go. She's right to catch up on her sleep. I get myself a fresh vanilla latte and carry on thinking about the significance of the alternate reading of the Garden of Eden story. If Faith had the energy, we could have moved on to the consequences of knowing about good and evil. That introduces us to a dualistic world where opposites conflict all the time. As we grow more conscious, we are less likely to be fooled by the way others might use those dualisms against them. I remember my conversation with Hope about dualisms. They lie at the base of a lot of questions people have about how the world works and how they work in the world.

Dualisms aren't just opposites. In our western world they have been assigned value – making them what are called ethical dualisms. One list of items is labelled 'good' and the other list 'bad' or 'evil.' Hence 'the tree of the knowledge of good and evil.'

One of the problems for women's being in the world is that they are named 'bad' because of their opposition on the lists to 'male.' I'd always wondered when misogyny came into being. Was the answer 'from the beginning of the world.'?

Maybe not, because in earlier times, the division of labour between female roles of homemaking and childbearing and male roles of farming, hunting and gathering may have meant that the value placed on the two lists of dualisms might have been just about difference and not about value.

For example, I mused, in a primitive society these lists might provide a complementary pairing which is vital for survival.

Woman	Man
Private (home)	Public (hunting)
Body (child bearing)	Mind (strategising for food gathering or defence/protection)
Emotions	Logic

Perhaps later as societies grew and infrastructure and collective organisation was required, the power balance may have shifted.

Woman	Man
Private (domestic, mothering)	Public (government, governance)
Body (child bearing)	Mind (logic, rationality

In this case the women were seen as most useful when 'barefoot and pregnant in the kitchen', while men were the organisers and rulers of society.

Two key changes in the 20th century have been as significant as the change from small clans hunting and gathering to urbanised villages, town and cities which required governance. There were first, the increasingly higher levels of education reached by women in sophisticated societies and secondly separation of sex from childbearing with the advent of the contraceptive pill and the safe, public availability of abortion.

This changed the dualisms.

Women	**Man**
Private	Public
Body	Mind
(*not necessarily bearing children or bearing fewer children*)	(*logic, rationality now taught also to women and girls*)

It was still however evident that the basic list of dualisms were buried deep in the western psyche. Patriarchal societies thrived on the relegation of women to the private sphere. It was noticeable during World War II that women entering the workforce to both replace men in their regular occupations and also to produce armaments for the war effort changed the balance of private and public within society. Not, however, as a planned and welcome move, but as an enforced move in a situation created by war. When men returned from war, women were urged to go back home to free up jobs for returned soldiers, but also, perhaps, to reduce their increasing independence and public participation.

Women who are given or who gain public office are critiqued in a particularly personal way different from the critique made of male leaders. I mused on, thinking of social media comments I had seen criticising and vilifying our female prime minister. There was also that comment a friend had heard recently from a right wing relative: "And oh, for a male prime minister again!"

One of the dangers of the ethical dualisms is that they render women inferior. When someone is thought to be generically inferior, it is easier to critique them, bully them, victimise them, rape and kill them. Organisations which work to help rape victims or to reduce the number of rapes in our society talk about 'rape culture.'

As the term 'rape culture' came into my mind, I wondered if I really knew what it was. I checked with Wikipedia for a quick summary and found the term was coined by second wave feminists.

The term "rape culture" was first coined in the 1970s in the United States by second-wave feminists and applied to contemporary American culture as a whole. During the 1970s, second-wave feminists had begun to engage in consciousness-raising efforts designed to educate the public about the prevalence of rape. Previously, according to Canadian psychology professor Alexandra Rutherford,[25] most Americans assumed that rape, incest, and wife-beating were rare.[26]

That was interesting – I remember in the 1950s and 60s as a little girl not knowing much at all about rape. There wasn't much evidence of it in the TV news we watched as a family. This was quite different from now when rape, especially those committed by high profile celebrities, was given lots of air time. I read on:

The concept of rape culture posited that rape was common and normal in American culture and that it was an extreme manifestation of pervasive societal misogyny and sexism. Rape was redefined as a violent crime rather than a sex crime and its motive redefined from desire for sexual pleasure to male domination, intimidation and a sense of control over gender norms.[27]

There was that term again – misogyny. I checked an online dictionary. Here it was: '

Misogyny: hatred, dislike, or mistrust of women, manifested in various forms such as physical intimidation and abuse, sexual harassment and rape, social shunning and ostracism, etc.:'[28]

I also had noticed in the Wikipedia description of rape culture that it argued it arose from 'male domination, intimidation and a sense of control over gender norms' that sprang from the dualism lists. Dualisms provided the 'gender norms.' Women inside, men out in the world; women inferior, men superior; women as passive receivers, men as active actors; women taking it, men giving it, so it went on.

I could feel a familiar tide of depression starting to sweep over me as it always did when I probed into the underlying causes of the way women did not feel entitled or safe or valued in the world. I recalled the many times in the church when I had felt I was a second-class member of the church, even after I had been ordained as a minister. The occasion when a senior minister leading a brainstorm had ignored my suggestions until another senior male minister repeated them.

The same man had dismissed a question I had and yet I heard him checking my query out with another male staff member at the break which followed.

I had never been at threat of rape, though drunken university 'hops' or dances had frightened me a lot. I could not imagine the pain and horror which rape, and the threat of rape, caused in women. I had, however, encountered more subtle forms of misogyny from male church goers, male elders and ministers and male administrators. The power within the church, even one with a co-ed clergy these days was not in women's hands, despite women forming the majority within the church membership.[29]

After over 150 years of church-based ministry training the women employed in substantial teaching positions by my church didn't need two hands to count them.[30] The handful of other women who had worked there were only ever adjunct faculty.[31] It was difficult to believe there were no adequately qualified women for the many teaching positions which had come available in a century and a half. Also, this is analysing the teaching staff by gender only. How many non Pākehā/Pālagi teachers had there been in the same time? How many gay or lesbian teachers had there been? How many disabled teachers? Only one hand to count with would be needed for most of those questions.

In 162 years of my church being organised in New Zealand, there have been 4 national women leaders, with a 5th in the wings for the next changeover. Women were admitted to the eldership in 1955 and to the ministry in 1965, but even adjusting these figures from 1955, it is only 5 women leaders in 68 years. The message to women is clear.

Just as well Faith had gone home to rest. Stats such as these kept one awake at night.

When did I fall asleep?

When did I fall asleep?
Was it my first Barbie doll?
Or that princess outfit?

Was it when impressing and enticing a lover
became all important?

Thinking mother was right?
If I was bossy, no one would marry me?

At some point
I settled
settled in
settled down
to what everyone expected of me.

Now alarm bells are ringing;
it sounds like a wake-up call
urgent
demanding
"Wake up!"

Paradise and innocence
are traps for the unwary.

Stop sleepwalking and
reach for knowledge.

Eat that fruit and
acquaint yourself
with good and with evil
so you know.

6 – Can girls do anything?

Faith looks thoughtful as she enters *The Cup* for our next session. I wave to her from the queue at the counter and she comes across.

"Time I bought the drinks," she says. "What would you like? You get a seat and I'll join you when I've ordered."

"Thank you," I reply. "I think I'll have a tea. You know my favourite." I'd had three back-to-back meetings that day and the caffeine levels were getting silly.

I found our usual space was free and slid into the booth at the back of the shop. I watched Faith as she ordered. She was still looking serious, and I wondered if the email I had sent summarising my musings after our session last week had been a downer. She was absorbing quite a lot of new ideas in a short space of time . In my experience, negative reaction was inevitable.

"Hi!" I say when she arrives at the booth and deposits her backpack. It looks heavy as usual.

"Hi," Faith replies somewhat absentmindedly. "Hey, I've been thinking about your email…."

"Uhuh," I thought. "I knew that stuff was pretty heavy." Faith surprises me however, as she continues.

"I'm wondering how misogyny started. I mean is it recent, kind of like a backlash against feminism or has it been there forever? I mean that apparent editing in Genesis 1 where verse 2 is kind of left as an unimportant remnant of another idea of creation suggests it's been around for thousands of years. And the other thing, why does misogyny exist? What is the motivation for it?"

"Wow!" I say, laughing a little. "Let's move into the conversation with a little small talk first!"

Faith laughs, her expression clearing for the first time.

"Yeah. Thinking about it has been preoccupying me for a day or two now and… and I suppose it's been getting me down. I mean, I tend to work quite hard, you know, to get people to like me. But, if I am disliked just because I'm female, there's nothing I can do about that. I am a girl, a woman, and if that's not OK, then I'm not OK and I can't fix that!"

Tears well up and she scrambles in her backpack for the pack of tissues she always carries.

"I know what you mean," I empathise. "I find this quite depressing, and, you know, I've wondered the same thing about how long and why and where about the origins of misogyny. Last week got me thinking again and just last night I looked up a few references. When I was in academia, I would not have used Wikipedia as a reliable reference but it is good for an initial overview. Don't do as I do for your essays! This is what I found."

I go to the bookmarked page and paraphrase out loud what is there.

"We know misogyny is hatred, contempt and/or prejudice against women. Wikipedia links it with sexism and credits it with keeping women in a lower social status compared with men. That enables patriarchy to be the working structure of society. It says here that misogyny has been around for thousands of years and is in almost everything. Look at the list 'art, literature, human societal structure, historical events, mythology, philosophy, and religion worldwide.'"[32]

"That pretty much covers the field!" mutters Faith. "Oh, thank you."

The server places our drinks on the table. I inhale the lovely aroma of my Earl Grey tea and open my eyes wide at Faith's cup.

"Coffee? Yours?"

Faith grins sheepishly. "Yes, I had a flat white last week and really loved it. I thought I might need something more substantial than a hot chocolate for this topic!"

I perform the familiar ritual of pouring my tea and turn back to the screen.

"OK. So, this article connects misogyny with violence against women, with sexual harassment and also, listen to this..."

> ... psychological techniques aimed at controlling women, and by legally or socially excluding women from full citizenship. In some cases, misogyny rewards women for accepting an inferior status. Misogyny can be understood both as an attitude held by individuals, primarily by men, and as a widespread cultural custom or system.[33]

"I wonder what kind of rewards that refers to? The ones for accepting an inferior status," asks Faith.

"Sometimes they are quite subtle, like societal approval for woman who do not work outside the home and so do not claim working equality with men." I reply.

"Oh, right."

"This next piece is interesting in how misogyny also affects men. It says here that misogyny also rejects feminine qualities and therefore anything associated with women (institutions, hobbies, habits) and rejects any so-called feminine qualities which men show. That's where misogyny can be the base motivation underneath homophobia. See here: 'Misogyny may or may not include hate towards LGBT people, in the forms of homophobia and transmisogyny. Racism and other prejudices may reinforce and overlap with misogyny.'"[34]

"Why is that?"

"Well straight men can think that one of the gay men in a couple would be taking a female role in intercourse. And a misogynistic man would think that was the worst thing you could do."

"Oh, my gosh," gasps Faith.

"You should read my second book in the trilogy. I go over all that there in my conversations with Charity. Have you met Charity?"[35]

"Yes, she runs the Younger Group at church."

Faith scribbles something in her notebook. "I'll look for that book. So how long has misogyny been around?"

"There's an interesting piece here in the introduction. Apparently, the Oxford English Dictionary places the actual word in the 17th century, using two Greek words, for hatred and women. It wasn't used much until it was picked up by the second wave of feminism in the 1970s."

"So if the word is relatively new, and its widespread use is even newer, is the attitude new too?

"When you get into the article, their opinion is that misogyny probably started with patriarchy; and that is placed at the beginning of the Bronze Age, about 3200 to 5200 years ago.

"Why?"

You won't like this. It's matched here to the rise of monotheism, the belief in one God and guess what sex that God is?"

"Male?"

"Right. Listen 'The three main monotheistic religions of Judaism, Christianity and Islam promoted patriarchal societal structures, and used misogyny to keep women at a lower status. Misogyny gained strength in the Middle Ages, especially in Christian societies.'"[36]

"Christianity!" Faith's disappointed expression is poignant.

"Misogyny is pretty widespread, not just in Christianity or the other monotheistic religions. Almost every society apparently has some degree of misogynistic attitudes."

"So that is how it started and when approximately. What about why?"

"I have my own theory and I was interested to see a quote here from a male anthropologist who partly echoes what I think. He is David Gilmore, who's written a book called *Misogyny: The Male Malady.* This is what a reviewer says about it."

> …Gilmore argues that misogyny is rooted in men's conflicting feelings: men's existential dependence on women for procreation, and men's fear of women's power over them in their times of male weakness, contrasted against the deep-seated needs of men for the love, care and comfort of women—a need that makes the men feel vulnerable.[37]

"I found the Amazon blurb for the book quite detailed and interesting too: It begins with a quote which I assume is from the book. 'Yes, women are the greatest evil Zeus has made, and men are bound to them hand and foot with impossible knots by God.' – Semonides, 7th century B.C.'"[38]

"That's early in history – 7th century!" exclaims Faith. "The 'greatest evil'! Huh!" She looks offended on behalf of the women of the world.

"Here's the rest of it." I push my tablet across to Faith. "I'll get us another drink. I think we need it."

Faith bends over the tablet and reads more of the Amazon description of Gilmore's book.

> Men put women on a pedestal to worship them from afar – and to take better aim at them for the purpose of derision. Why is this paradoxical response to women so widespread, so far-reaching,

so all-pervasive? Misogyny, David D. Gilmore suggests, is best described as a male malady, as it has always been a characteristic shared by human societies throughout the world.

Misogyny: The Male Malady is a comprehensive historical and anthropological survey of woman-hating that casts new light on this age-old bias. The turmoil of masculinity and the ugliness of misogyny have been well documented in different cultures, but Gilmore's synoptic approach identifies misogyny in a variety of human experiences outside of sex and marriage and makes a fresh and enlightening contribution toward understanding this phenomenon. Gilmore maintains that misogyny is so widespread and so pervasive among men that it must be at least partly psychogenic in origin, a result of identical experiences in the male developmental cycle, rather than caused by the environment alone.

Presenting a wealth of compelling examples – from the jungles of New Guinea to the boardrooms of corporate America – Gilmore shows that misogynistic practices occur in hauntingly identical forms. He asserts that these deep and abiding male anxieties stem from unresolved conflicts between men's intense need for and dependence upon women and their equally intense fear of that dependence.[39]

Faith looks up as I return from the counter.

"The reviewer makes a couple of interesting points. One is that the basic misogynistic attitude springs from men being conflicted over needing women and yet not wanting to be dependent on them."

"Yes. That ties in with my theory which isn't so much anthropological but developmental. I think for boys, their developmental task is to separate from their mothers upon whom they start out being completely dependent. Their task is to become a different gender. From being 'at one' with their mother in the womb and as babies, they need to become the 'other' kind of person – a man. I wonder then, in later life when any woman is put in authority over a man, whether it unconsciously brings up the image of something they need to separate from and no longer depend on."

"Hmm, interesting. When we talk about an adult man being a 'Mummy's Boy' then we are saying that process of separation hasn't happened quite right."

"Yes."

Faith turns back to the tablet. "The other thing I noticed here is that not only might men feel this way – have this dependence/interdependence conflict, but there are societal structures which back up that feeling." She points to the screen. "See here."

> However, misogyny, according to Gilmore, is also often supported and intensified by certain cultural realities, such as patrilineal social organization; kinship ideologies that favor fraternal solidarity over conjugal unity; chronic warfare, feuding, or other forms of intergroup violence; and religious orthodoxy or asceticism. Gilmore is in the end able to offer steps toward the discovery of antidotes to this irrational but global prejudice, providing an opportunity for a lasting cure to misogyny and its manifestations.[40]

"There's religion again." She continues, "I suppose fraternal solidarity is men's sheds and gentlemen's clubs and male service organisations and things like that. Perhaps you could include the elders of a Brethren Assembly too. No wonder there's resistance to allowing women into formerly male-only domains. And gangs are largely male organised aren't they, though I was surprised to see a female PR person speaking for a gang on the news recently. What kind of reviews did Gilmore's book get?"

"I found an interesting one by Sander L Gilman who teaches at the University of Chicago, Illinois.[41] Gilman basically agrees with Gilmore's presentation of the widespread nature of misogyny but suggests there are two more areas which need some study. One is that not only men imagine women as a certain image or type, cultures do."

> What is quite possible is that the images of the female are regularly linked to broader fields of images, including taboos about blood, reproduction, and incest that focus on the woman. It is probably better to speak of misogyny as a cultural malady, rather than as solely a male one.[42]

"Gilman goes on to say that since the need for reproduction necessitates men cooperating with women, then men too are 'defined by this role.'"

Faith nods. "I think I see what you mean. There do seem to be implications for what men are like and how they work in society alongside this misogyny. It feels really, really complex, about men and about women but also about culture too."

I nod in my turn. "That's what often happens with a prejudice. It seeks to resolve a complex situation into a simple one. In this case into 'women are not to be trusted, they are bad, deviant etc. etc.'"

Faith is thinking hard, brow wrinkled.

"So is that why there have to be slogans like 'Girls can do anything' – because it's not clear that girls and women are human beings just like you and me are, and everyone in that sense is equal? I mean, traditionally men were stronger than women but there are a lot of sportswomen and females in other formerly traditionally male occupations that put that to the lie. And, once education of girls and women got under way, it has been clear that some women have brains as precise and logical as some men do. It is not that a whole gender is automatically fluffy headed. Nor is it that the other gender are all muscle bound. Can't people see there are variations in each group? Some blondes are dumb, but other blondes are not!" Faith's voice is rising as she gets more and more heated in her argument.

"What you are describing, Faith, is the kind of blindness that one group often takes in regard to another, unknown group. White skinned people can assume all dark skinned people are primitive and backward. People of one language group can assume all those who speak their language as a second language are uneducated because their grammar and accent are not perfect. Older people can assume all younger generations are heedless and careless because they have met one or two who are."

"So girls can do anything?" asks Faith.

"I think it would be truer to say some girls can do some things, other girls can do other things while some boys can't do everything but can do some things, etc. etc."

"There are still those stereotypes, aren't there. That a girl should be helpless and clingy, not brainy and self-sufficient."

"Yes, and that a boy should be muscular and sporty. Brainy, tech-loving boys must dread the word 'geek' since that stereotypically means a boy is a loser on the sports field."

"I think since the technology revolution geeks have proven they might be on the right side of history – certainly they are on the right side of the pay packet!" retorts Faith.

I chuckle along with her.

"One of the difficulties girls and women face is that though they may be able to do things which formerly were reserved for men to do, those pesky dualisms still operate. Particularly the public/private one. Some men and some women seem to not have adjusted to women being in charge – like prime ministers, as CEOs, or medical superintendents, or ministers of religion. New Zealand did have a dizzy moment there for a while when we had a female chief justice, a woman prime minister and a female governor general."

"But then, we have had men in all three positions at once more often than that and no one thought that was unusual!" Faith retorts.

"Because it wasn't!" I quipped back. We laughed. One of those moments when if you didn't laugh, you'd cry. I think for a moment, then add:

"One of the dilemmas for women comes through religion. Are women mothers or virgins, who have a 'respectable' place in society or are they whores – wanton, sexual beings, as Eve has been painted in the orthodox version of the Garden of Eden narrative? It's called the virgin/whore dichotomy."

"Does this relate to misogyny being connected to men needing women at different parts of their development and hating that feeling of being vulnerable?"

"Yes. In a way the veneration of Jesus' mother Mary in the Catholic Church was a good thing because it introduced a symbol of the feminine into what was regarded as holy. Unfortunately, when they assigned her virgin status in perpetuity, that made her the impossible ideal for women – both mother and virgin at the same time. Mere mortal women cannot reach that contradictory status."

"Sheltered as I have been all my life, even I know that something sexy has to happen to get a woman from virgin to mother," says Faith, blushing slightly.

"Yes, dealing with women in public roles and in any kind of authority must be a dilemma for men. Is this woman my sister? Is she my mother?

Is she a potential lover? The virgin-mother stereotype may be useful to put women into a no-go zone for the purposes of business and commerce and education, whatever field the woman is involved with. In a way during the 2020 global pandemic, our female Prime Minister was seen as a kind of a mother to the nation, and that soured as people began to get tired of instructions and mandates. The female PM became to be seen as a bossy, nagging mother."

"Interesting how women seem to still be women when they take on a role in public whereas men are regarded as sort of neuter. I never have heard of a male prime minister being vilified for telling people what to do in the same way our female Prime Minister has been." Faith comments.

I add, "I think that might be the Hegelian influence still coming through – men are regarded as minds, as embodying logic and rationality whereas women are still, deep down, regarded as bodies, embodying, well, bodily functions, like menstruation, seduction, childbearing, child-birthing and breast feeding."

"Hmm. Makes sense," muses Faith, "makes sense of all the secrecy around periods at our house. With four brothers, it was like being in a secret society with only my Mum and me as members. 'This isn't boy's stuff,' she would say."

I nod, recalling the same attitude in my family of origin. "Remember that quote from Sander Gilman's review of Gilmore's book?"

> What is quite possible is that the images of the female are regularly linked to broader fields of images, including taboos about blood, reproduction, and incest that focus on the woman. It is probably better to speak of misogyny as a cultural malady, rather than as solely a male one.[43]

After reading the quote on my tablet again, Faith asks, "so did Gilman mean that not only men participate in this exclusion of women? That it's a culture-wide kind of agreement that we would avoid or keep secret things to do with blood and reproduction and incest?"

"If you mean by keeping it secret, making them a taboo, yes," I reply.

"Hmm. What do you think of that new ad on TV selling those all-in-one period pants? They show a girl wearing them, then hands washing them showing blood in the rinse water, then they're shown drying, obviously for re-use. What're the words they use? 'Wear', 'Bleed',

'Wash', 'Repeat'? I was really shocked when I saw that on national television." Even now Faith is blushing slightly at the memory.

"That's because in making the bleeding part of menstruation so visible they are either breaking a taboo or almost breaking the taboo. When I was just starting puberty the only thing available was disposable sanitary towels and they were placed on the shelves of the supermarket already wrapped in anonymous brown paper. A friend who's five years older than I am, said she had to go to the chemist to get supplies before there were supermarkets and that at that stage all the chemists were men. She found it very embarrassing. We've come a long way!"

"Yes! I was proud of a pasifika schoolgirl who was interviewed about the supply of period materials in schools. She said to the camera that it wasn't girl's fault they had periods, so they should be helped with the solution. I could never do that!" Faith exclaims.

"The whole provision of free period materials in schools so girls don't miss school during their periods because of lack of money to buy the gear is pushing hard at the taboo too. It used to be something girls just struggled with on their own. I remember it used to be called 'the curse'!" I reply.

"Where does that come from?" asks Faith curiously

"Unfortunately, maybe from the Bible. When Adam and Eve are expelled from the Garden of Eden, childbirth and the pain associated with it are translated as the punishment for eating the forbidden fruit. I would say that experiencing pain and having to toil in the fields was more a consequence of knowing the truth about good and evil rather than a punishment or curse. Nowhere in the Bible does it say God gave menstruation as a curse to women, but it has become that kind of folk legend information passed down from mother to daughter and woman to woman."

"It does give the whole menstrual cycle deal a bad name, doesn't it," adds Faith.

"Yes. The many blood taboos in the Hebrew Bible certainly associated menstrual bleeding and the bleeding during childbirth with ritual uncleanliness. There are several passages specifying the times a woman was to be considered unclean around her period and around childbirth. Mary and Joseph attending the temple with the baby Jesus was for them to perform the ritual which ended Mary's period of uncleanliness after giving birth, for example."

"Is that right? I didn't know that! Not something included in the sermons at the local Brethren Assembly!" Faith laughed.

"There's a book a friend of mine's been reading called *The Red Tent*.[44] It's written around the story of a biblical woman. In the novel, the women of their little tribe used a menstrual tent when they are ritually 'unclean.' I didn't know, but I found out through living in a university hostel that women living together find after a while that their cycles start to align."

Faith, a hostel resident herself, nods. "It's true! So, in a small clan, all the women would end up menstruating together and would be in the tent together."

"I googled the idea of a menstrual tent and apparently there isn't any evidence that Jewish women used a menstrual tent, though some other cultures did," I add. "Women did need to eat separately during their period of uncleanliness so their husbands would not be made unclean by association. Seems a bit draconian to me but a Jewish friend told me that she regards that period of time (if you'll excuse the pun) when she was menstruating as a bit of 'me' time, a quieter, more peaceful time."

"I guess it can be seen all different ways," responds Faith. "Did women have to go to the temple every month to perform a cleanliness ritual?"

"No, but there was a bathing ritual and sometimes women's public baths were used for that. Bathsheba was performing her monthly purification ritual when King David saw her bathing on the roof of her house as he looked down from the palace."

"Really! Another part of a story we never heard at the Assembly!"

We smile ruefully at each other. "Stands to reason a male elder at a Brethren Assembly would find it difficult to include such intimate feminine details, even if he knew them."

Faith catches sight of the time. "Oh, need to go. There's a special dinner at the hostel and our floor is meeting first for appetisers."

She gets up to go, pushing her notebook into the back pocket of her pack. "Same time and day in two weeks?"

I check my calendar. "Yep, should be right. See you then."

Misogyny/Philogyny

The dictionary says the word is specific.
Misogyny specifically references a hatred of women.

Not a woman
not her over there, or her indoors, or that other girl.
No, all of us. It is quite specific.

The word originates from two Greek words
Misein – to hate, *Gyne* – woman.
Both roots can be found in other words,
some common, some obscure.

Misogyny is common, but not obscure.
It is specific.
I am woman. I am hated.

Let's make a new word.

Let's take the root for love – *phil*,
Make a new word:- philogyny.
Let's make that common and not obscure.
It can be specific too.
I am woman. I am loved.

Biblical women

7 – Brave and Prophetic Women

A month later, I sit in *The Cup* wondering about today's session with Faith. She had emailed two weeks ago after our last session asking for a break. She said she'd been finding the work we were doing quite depressing and unsettling. Perhaps concentrating on other stuff for a while would be a good idea. She hoped I understood that she needed to take some time out. She would get back to me when she was ready to re-start if I was still prepared to talk with her.

I certainly understood. The work we had been doing was depressing. I felt it myself. I had been wondering when Faith's apparent acceptance of many new ideas was going to result in a meltdown of some sort.

I had replied with some ideas of how to lighten up and look after herself. I knew I was associated in her mind with the 'depressing stuff.' I wasn't the one to help her, but I gave her Aunt Hazel a call and suggested Faith might need some contact from a warm and sympathetic living being who's 'been there, done that.'

It had seemed a long month to me. I had kept Faith in my thoughts during my meditative ritual and was hoping she was OK.

Then during this last week, she had emailed, asking if there were other bible passages which held details about women and their lives that she might not have heard about in her home church. Indeed, there were. I smiled to myself as I read her words. Faith was back, and on point as usual.

Even in less male orientated churches, it was only since the second wave of feminism that feminist theology had come to life. It was then Phyllis Trible and Virginia Ramey Mollenkott had spent time combing the texts for women's stories and feminine images. Carol Newsom and Sharon Ringe had co-edited the *Women's Bible Commentary*[45] giving a new perspective on well-known stories which previously had often been interpreted with an overly pious or judgemental bent. In my own training, I'd enjoyed a paper on Women in Biblical Texts taught by a feminist professor of Hebrew and Old Testament.[46] It had been a real eye opener. There was plenty of material of the type Faith was requesting.

"Hi! Lost in thought?" Faith's voice breaks into my reverie. "What will you have today?"

"Oh! hello Faith! Good to see you again! I was lost in the past, actually. Um… I think I'll have a hazelnut latte please. Sure I can't get it?"

"No, I'm good. That sounds yummy. I think I'll have one too." Faith disappears to the counter.

By the time she returns, I've looked up the list of biblical women I'd prepared the previous night. It is a lot longer than Faith would be expecting, I thought.

When Faith returns to the table, I look up and smile at her headgear. Today her turquoise scarf has sparkles and a big fringe which lies down her back. It gives her a very gypsy-like look with her extra curly dark hair and she'd complemented it with golden hoops for earrings. …. Wait a minute!

"Earrings?" I ask quizzically.

Faith smiles and blushes, flicking the hoops gently. "Yes! Must be my rebellious side coming out. You know, I felt like a scarlet woman getting it done. My parents are quite disdainful of girls with pierced ears." She flicks the ends of her scarf over her shoulder and sits down.

"I can't tell you how much I appreciate your giving me that break without any comment or criticism. I needed to breathe a bit," Faith started.

"What did you do with yourself?"

"I sat a lot. Tried meditating – at which I am going to need heaps of practice! Went to the beach for a few walks. You know, chilling out. Letting it all settle. Went to the movies a couple of times with Hazel. That was fun."

She smiles. I smile back, keeping it casual. If I had started to tell her how relieved I was, I'd have burst into tears. "That's great," was all I can trust myself to say.

"Now," she carries on briskly, "have you got some 'hidden women' stories for me?"

"Well, I thought you might be able to tell me first how many women in the Bible you can remember off the top of your head," I say, pushing the blank side of my paper across to her. "Try just the Hebrew Bible, the First Testament. You might know it better as the Old Testament."

"Hmm," said Faith, digging a pen out of the back pocket of her pack. "Let me see. Eve. Yep. Sarah. Yep. Rachel. She was... Isaac's wife? No? Jacob's? Right." She scribbles furiously.

"You mentioned Bathsheba last time. Oh." She moves her pen back to Sarah and writes in '& Hagar.' Let me see...." Faith bites the end of her pen, thinking hard. "Oh yes, Ruth and Naomi, and there was another woman in that story, but I can never remember her name. I think that's about all I can remember, off the top of my head," she says after a moment's more thinking.

"Turn the paper over then," I reply.

"Wow," breathes Faith. "That's heaps more than I thought."

"This list is not exhaustive either. I've just included women relevant to the main arc of the Judeo-Christian narrative. And this list doesn't have unnamed women, like Lot's daughters, Jepthah's daughter, the unnamed concubine, and lots more. Phyllis Trible includes Lot's daughters, Jepthah's daughter and the concubine in her book *Texts of Terror*[47] alongside Hagar. Notice each entry comes with the biblical books in which they appear in italics at the end of their description."

Faith bends over the list and reads it through, commenting as she goes.

'Bilhah – Rachel's handmaid bore Jacob two sons, Dan and Naphtali, as his concubine. *Genesis.*' I didn't know Jacob had concubines!"

I nod. "He did. There's another concubine further down – the handmaiden of Jacob's other wife Leah. Here she is," I run my finger down to near the end of the list. "Zilpah – Leah's handmaid. She bore Jacob two sons, Gad and Asher. *Genesis.*"

"Hmm," replies Faith, "would like to hear more about that story!"

She carries on down the list. "Deborah – oh! She was a prophetess and it says here she was 'the fourth, and the only female, Judge of pre–monarchic Israel in the Old Testament. *Judges.*' Wow. I didn't know there were any women judges in ancient Israel. How about that!" Faith looks up at me with a delighted grin. I nod, smiling back. Deborah is one of the few women in the Bible who were 'successful' in what was usually a male's role.

Faith carries on down the list. "Oh yes, 'Delilah – The "woman in the valley of Sorek" who Samson loved. *Judges*.' We know all about her! One of those wicked women."

"Oh, who's this? Dinah? It says here she is a daughter of Jacob. I didn't know he had any daughters. I thought he only had sons, the 12 sons who fathered the 12 tribes of Israel? Haven't heard much about her."

"Mmm, she was a rape victim required to marry her rapist. Probably not a good story to use in church I suppose." I reply, sighing inside at how often stories including women weren't rated 'good enough' or 'interesting enough' for church.

Faith looks as pained as I feel. "Mmm," she says, "too many of those. Oh, I know this one, 'Esther – Queen of the Persian Empire in the Hebrew Bible, the queen of Ahasuerus.' She was brave, and look," she continues running her finger down to list to find the name, "here's Vashti – queen, and former wife of King Ahasuerus. She was brave too. I remember their story now."

"And…" she continues, going back to her former place in the list. "Hagar?– it says here 'Egyptian handmaiden of Sarah, wife of Abraham. Hagar became the mother of one of Abraham's sons, Ishmael. *Genesis*.' Abraham had another son besides Isaac? I've heard the name Ishmael, but there must be a story behind this."

"There is!" I reply, a little grimly. "Sheds light on Sarah which isn't too flattering either. And there's another story behind the next woman, Jael – see she's listed as a 'heroine who killed Sisera to deliver Israel from the troops of king Jabin. She was the wife of Heber the Kenite. *Judges*.'

"She killed someone? A woman? Another story you say? I should think so!"

Faith is obviously very intrigued by the glimpses she is getting into the community of women in the Hebrew Bible.

She continues. "Here's another baddie. Jezebel #1 – Queen of ancient Israel. *I Kings, II Kings*. I remember learning about her giving Elijah a hard time…. And, look, 'Jochebed – Mother of Moses, Aaron, and Miriam. *Exodus, Numbers*.' You know, I never really knew Moses' mother had a name? Though of course we had the story of Moses in the bulrushes when I was in Sunday School."

"Were you ever told the story of how Jacob came to have two wives? Here's the first one, 'Leah – First wife of Jacob who was given to him in place of Rachel whom he loved. *Genesis, Ruth.*' That rather sounds like the plot for a romantic novel, doesn't it!"

Faith nods as she keeps scanning the list.

"I heard something about how he was tricked by his father-in-law, but not much detail after that. Here's another woman I know little about. Lo–Ruhamah – Daughter of Hosea and Gomer. *Hosea.*' Sounds like there's a story there."

Yes," I replied, "there is, though not what you might expect. She and her mother are kind of part of a metaphor. The nation of Israel is unfaithful to God and Hosea uses his apparently unfaithful wife as a metaphor for that."

Faith thinks for a moment. "So Gomer the wife is seen as solely responsible for the marriage not working?"

"Yes, in a feminist biblical studies course I did we read an article questioning that. I wrote a poem about it."

"As you do," says Faith, teasing me just a little.

I do the usual tap and scroll and show her the screen.

Gomer

Gomer.
Why is it always us, we women
who take, no, rephrase that, who are assigned
the role of temptress, of sexy one
(the sinful kind of sexy).

Why not men?
Why could it not have been wife-God
yearning after wayward, whoring husband?
Why is it never that way round?

I asked that question in the exam, you know.
Asked why not faithful wife and promiscuous husband?
My pen faltered on 'promiscuous.'
I haven't seen 'promiscuous' and 'husband'
written together before.

Why are women bodies while men are persons?
Why are we 'promiscuous' and men 'experienced'?

Metaphors are fine, helpful, useful and compelling even,

God married to wayward Israel
opens depths of intimacy the covenant never reached before,
but why male God and wayward wife,
not female God and wayward husband?

We need more metaphors.

Metaphors to redress the balance
deconstruct assumptions,
freeing men and women
to be more completely themselves,
giving each the chance to be sinful
each the chance to be made in the image of God.

Faith looks up at me as she finishes reading. "Hmmm. I'll have to think about that giving each the chance to be sinful part!"

I have the impression the poem has hit a difficult spot inside. I debate about probing, but I figure she will tell me when she is ready. I sit quietly, creating the space if she wants to use it, but it seems this is not the moment.

Faith looks down at the list and keeps on talking.

"Here are a bunch of M's from different parts of the Bible. Michal who's connected to two famous men. She's King Saul's daughter and married King David. Then here's Miriam. I know her, Moses' sister. I know her from the bulrushes story."

"Here's another one I don't know – the mother of King Lemuel. It says here that she gave him a 'prophetic instruction that became Proverbs 31.' Proverbs 31…. Oh, I know, that's the 'above rubies' chapter. Huh, is that a Mum's advice to her son? I have never heard that explained!"

"No, you probably haven't," I reply. "Look," I continue, "here's Naomi – mother–in–law to Ruth and Ruth's sister-in-law. You were wondering about her name – it's Orpah. Also Ruth herself of course. See this? 'Boaz and Ruth get married and have a son named Obed. Obed is the descendant of Perez the son of Judah, and the grandfather of (King) David. *Ruth, Matthew.*'" "Oh," exclaims Faith, "I hadn't realised Ruth's story was so close in the generations to King David! And here's a flashback to the Moses story. 'Puah – one of two midwives who saved the Hebrew boys. *Exodus.*' I don't know if I know that part of the story."

"It might not have been thought suitable for Sunday School, but it's a great story of two brave women. The other midwife was Shiphrah. Together they defied Pharaoh, a very risky thing to do." I wonder briefly if I would have had such courage. "Look at the next few, they are a bunch of wives."

"Let me see…." Faith returns to the list. "Sarah. Yep. 'Wife of Abraham and mother of Isaac. Her name was originally "Sarai." According to Genesis 17:15 God changed her name to Sarah as part of a covenant with Yahweh after Hagar bore Abraham a son Ishmael. *Genesis, Isaiah, Romans, Galatians, Hebrews, I Peter.*' Right, she gets a lot of press!! Then here's 'Rebekah – wife of Isaac and the mother of Jacob and Esau. *Genesis, Romans*' and 'Rachel – second wife of Jacob, and sister of Leah. Mother of Joseph and Benjamin. *Genesis, I Samuel, Jeremiah, Matthew.'* Rachel was Leah's sister? Didn't know that!"

"Looks like you have a lot to catch up on! You'd enjoy the set of books on biblical women by Miriam Therese Winter.[48] Here's one you also may not have heard about. 'Rahab – of Jericho. *Joshua, Matthew, Hebrews, James.'*"

"And look," exclaims Faith. "There are no less than three Tamars! I don't know if I've heard of any of them. Let me see…. 'Tamar #1 – daughter-in-law of Judah, as well as the mother of two of his children, the twins Zerah and Perez. *Genesis.'* What? How can you be a man's daughter in law and mother his children? You've got to tell me that story."

"Don't worry, I will. The other two Tamars belong in the David story. 'Tamar #2 – daughter of King David, and sister of Absalom. Her mother was Maacah, daughter of Talmai, king of Geshur. *II Samuel.* She's in one of Trible's texts of terror. Tamar #3 – daughter of David's son Absalom. *II Samuel.'*"

Faith ends the list with an air of triumph. "Finally, 'Zipporah – wife of Moses, daughter of Jethro. *Exodus.* I didn't know Moses had a wife! Though come to think of it he was tending his father-in-law's flocks when he saw the burning bush, wasn't he? It stands to reason there was a wife."

Faith sits very still for a moment, then looks up at me, mixed emotions flitting across her face. "I don't know whether to be glad or angry. I'm glad to find all these women, and you say this isn't the end of the list. But I'm angry that it's taken till now for me to know they existed or to know they have names, not just relationships to men – like so-and-so's daughter or that man's wife."

"In a patriarchal society," I reply, "it suggests you were a pretty important woman in the community's history if you make it into the final versions of the oral legends complete with a name. So, if a woman is named, she's worth looking into. Also, however, the unnamed women are interesting too – even without a name their story stuck. I like to think because it was compelling and didn't drop out of the community's memory. Feminist theology has done a lot for biblical women, not only finding them, but also reinterpreting their stories in a less judgmental way. Sometimes the Victorian moralism which still pervades church can mean a woman who simply acts boldly or courageously without a man's direction can be harshly judged."

Faith nods a little absently because she is looking through the list again. "There's something here which caught my eye as we went through this list," she says. "All these women are from the Hebrew Bible aren't they? Well why do a few of them get mentioned in Matthew?"

"Look, here's Tamar who was that daughter in law of Judah." Her pen jumps around the page. "And Bathsheba. And Rahab. And Ruth. Where are they mentioned in Matthew?"

"Good spotting. You'll find them all in Matthew chapter 1." I wait to see if the penny will drop. She's a Brethren girl, so knows her Bible well.

"Matthew 1?" Faith thinks that brow wrinkling again. "Matthew 1? But isn't that that long genealogy of Jesus? Women didn't get included in genealogies in those times."

"Exactly. They don't usually but have a look." I push my tablet over to her, opened at Matthew chapter 1 in an online bible.

Faith scrolls down through the long list. "Yes, here she is, Tamar! Verse 3. 'Judah the father of Perez and Zerah, whose mother was Tamar'"[49]

She carries on scrolling. "And here are Rahab and Ruth right next to each other in verse 6. 'Salmon the father of Boaz, whose mother was Rahab, Boaz the father of Obed, whose mother was Ruth.'"[50] Eagerly, she runs a finger on down the list.

"You'll need to be imaginative to find Bathsheba, she's been hidden a little. Not too far from Ruth, don't go too far down."

"Oh yes! Here she is. I see what you mean about being hidden. Verse 6 'David was the father of Solomon, whose mother had been Uriah's wife.'[51] Why would they do that when the others have their personal names?"

"It might be because of what David did to Uriah," I reply. At Faith's puzzled face, I say, "we'll go into that later. Can you find any more?"

Faith's finger runs down to the end of the chapter. "Oh yes, see here. Verse 16 'and Jacob the father of Joseph, the husband of Mary, and Mary was the mother of Jesus who is called the Messiah.'[52] So that's a complete handful of women, Tamar, Rahab, Ruth, Bathsheba and

Mary," states Faith holding up one hand in a jazz hand spread, with a grin. Her pun is not entirely unintentional.

"I think you could say they are a handful," I reply, the same glint in my eye.

"Tell me," demands Faith. "Oh wait, do we need another drink for this? I think so. Iced chocolate all round?"

She disappears to the counter. I reach in my bag for an anthology of poetry relevant to our discussion, then sit back for a moment, trying to relax, taking some deep breaths.

I get the same mixed reaction as Faith admitted to earlier when having this kind of talk about the hidden women in scripture. Why have these brave, patient and faithful women been side-lined in favour of the male heroes? Why are their stories deemed not worthy of sermons, reflections and study groups?

Imagine, I think, if in our country a woman was the only female in a long line of judges. She would be celebrated, and histories written about her. She definitely would be preached about. Deborah was revered and respected in her time, admitted to the councils of men at the city gates where judgments were sought and made. Yet, we hear little of her today as a role model for women of faith. I send up a silent apology to the universe and women everywhere.

Faith bounces back to our seats, bearing two plates. "I thought we'd go for death by chocolate!" she exclaims, "I bought us some brownies too."

I thought about the scales I'd stood on this morning and decided afternoon tea could be followed by a simple evening meal tonight just once this week.

"Lovely! Thank you! Are you sure you can afford all this?"

"Yep. Mum sent me some money the other day for a treat when she sensed I was down a bit."

"Right! Tamar? What's her story?" Faith asks when the ordering and other preliminaries had been sorted. We were in the central courtyard of *The Cup* today since the weather was surprisingly warm. Faith was shrugging herself out of her brightly-coloured long cardigan. She had knitted it herself before coming to uni. "One of the wifely arts, knitting," she'd said with a wry grimace when I'd first admired it.

"Tamar's story is in Genesis 38. Look it up so you can refer to it as we talk. Bring up the New English Translation. They've good footnotes."

Faith gets the chapter found on her phone just as our iced chocolates arrive at our table and we pause for a moment, enjoying the cool beverage.

"So," I said around a particularly delicious pink marshmallow. "The chapter starts with Judah finding a Canaanite wife and her bearing him three sons. He finds a wife for the first and this is where Tamar enters the story. Sadly, her husband, Judah's first-born, dies. This triggers what we could call the Ancient Israelite Social Welfare System of levirate marriage. Judah gives Tamar to his second son as wife. Look up that footnote on verse 8."

Faith takes another sip as she scrolls and clicks. "Here it is:

> The purpose of this custom, called the levirate system, was to ensure that no line of the family would become extinct. The name of the deceased was to be maintained through this custom of having a child by the nearest relative. See M. Burrows, "Levirate Marriage in Israel," *JBL* 59 (1940): 23-33"[53]

"That's right. That levirate system was a kind of social welfare protection for a widow because she was then still under a man's protection which was pretty vital at the time. So Tamar is married to the next son, Onan. But as footnote p says in verse 9…"

Faith clicks and reads, "'under the levirate system the child would be legally considered the child of his deceased brother.'[54] Oh, so Onan is not happy to have a child who is not legally his?"

"No. Onan 'spills his seed on the ground' to avoid impregnating Tamar. He then dies. Rather dramatically, this is attributed to God, but remember this writing is symbolic rather than factual."

"Coitus interruptus," says Faith blushing brightly.

"Yes," I reply, trying not to look surprised. I wonder if Faith learned this at home or whether it is part of her newly acquired knowledge since becoming a university student. "Usually not a reliable method of contraception," I add hastily so there will be no misunderstanding.

"I know," replies Faith her blush subsiding a little, "my cousin got caught out by an overconfident boyfriend who thought he could do that successfully only to find he couldn't. Caused a lot of hassle in the family!"

"I can imagine! I hope nevertheless that the boyfriend hasn't been in fear of God striking him dead."

We smile but tacitly agree to not pursue the subject.

After a pause for a mouthful of brownie, I continue.

"So Tamar is sent home to her father because although he has another son, Judah does not want to lose him too. It must have been a disgrace to be sent back home and possibly Tamar's father wasn't too happy to have another mouth to feed. Tamar is told the younger son is too young to marry. But look down the story and tell me what Tamar does."

Faith scrolls through chapter 38 and finds the place. "Here we are…"

> [12] After some time Judah's wife, the daughter of Shua, died. After Judah was consoled, he left for Timnah to visit his sheepshearers, along with his friend Hirah the Adullamite. [13] Tamar was told, "Look, your father-in-law is going up to Timnah to shear his sheep." [14] So she removed her widow's clothes and covered herself with a veil. She wrapped herself and sat at the entrance to Enaim which is on the way to Timnah. (She did this because she saw that she had not been given to Shelah as a wife, even though he had now grown up.) [15] When Judah saw her, he thought she was a prostitute because she had covered her face.[55]

"Oh my gosh! Covering herself with a veil is a euphemism for dressing up as a prostitute! So Tamar sees that the third son is old enough to be married but she hasn't been sent for! And it looks like Judah's going to fall for it because his wife has died and… well… you know… men…"

"You've got it. Read on."

Faith bends over the phone, her lips moving as she reads silently to herself. I think I hear "clever girl!" and "silly man!" and "of course she wasn't there!"

Faith raises her head. "So does she use the pledge he gives her?"

"Read on," I reply, with a grin.

"Oh my! When Judah hears she's pregnant, he's going to have her burned for being promiscuous!… She shows them the ring and staff!… Oh, look what he says when he sees them: Verse 26. 'Judah recognized them and said, "She is more upright than I am, because I wouldn't give her to Shelah my son.'"[56] And there's a big footnote here." Faith skims through the reference. "Listen to the end of it."

> Though deceptive, it was a desperate and courageous act. For Tamar it was within her rights; she did nothing that the law did not entitle her to do. But for Judah it was wrong because he thought he was going to a prostitute. See also Susan Niditch, "The Wronged Woman Righted: An Analysis of Genesis 38, " *HTR* 72 (1979): 143-48.[57]

Faith slumps back in her seat. "Wow. No wonder they include her in the genealogy. That is an amazing story. And you wrote a poem about it?"

"Yes, this page here," I say handing over the anthology open at the poem. "It's a collection that's unpublished, but I hope to bring it out next year."[58]

Faith reads silently. I watch the fleeting expression on her face as I sip my chocolate drink and finish the gooey brownie. Tamar had been way more courageous than I would ever have been. She deserved her place in history. I was glad Faith was understanding that, not writing Tamar off for the rather scandalous way in which she had claimed her rights in a patriarchal world.

"I'll send you all the five poems by email[59] and you can read the bible narrative and then the poem which goes with it. Rahab is in the second chapter of the book of Joshua. Ruth, of course, is in the book of Ruth – it's interesting to read the whole book right through, there are little touches which aren't always brought out in sermons. Bathsheba is in 2 Samuel. I guess you know the Mary story after nativity plays each year!"

Faith looks up, tears in her eyes. I can see her searching for the words and not finding them. I reach over and touch her hand. "I know," I say. We sit silently for a moment, revering Tamar, this foremother of ours, grateful for the role she and many other women played in our common history, grateful that even in such heart-stopping texts we could find resource for our own journey as women in the world.

Tamar

Tamar, Canaanite woman,
yet chosen by Judah for his son
a son who so displeased Yahweh that you were widowed soon.

To us it seems too much like Pass the Parcel,
to you it was survival.
A man needs sons whether he be alive or dead.
A widow woman needs another man to be protector.
Ancient law demanded it be the brother.

But Onan deprived you of the children owed
his brother's name,
spilling his seed upon the ground,
and so he died too, the second son of Judah.

Maybe with two husbands to mourn
you were glad to suffer the indignity
of return to your father's house,
to await the third son's coming of marriageable age,
according to Judah.

Time passed,
a widowed daughter still unmarried is a burden on a father.
You went waiting where Judah must pass,
you saw with your own eyes the slight done to you;
the boy was of marriageable age already,
yet you had not been sent for
by Judah.

How many advances did you repel while waiting,
waiting on the roadside
dressed as a woman of the world
for Judah?

He came at last, asked, it was agreed, a pledge was given,
a pledge which would be later recognisable as Judah's.
What was it like to be used as whore by your husbands' father
the man who had insulted you; to be used for
the pleasure of Judah?

Of course you were not there when Judah's man returned
with the kid goat, the promised payment!

How quickly had you changed your clothes,
washed your body, now strangely dirty
and returned to your widow's life,
hoping, wishing, praying as the month took its course
that you would be given the only bargaining power
you could have
sons of Judah?

What was it like as neighbours sniggered and family recoiled,
as morning sickness and thickening waist told their tale
and you were branded whore again?

As word spread far and wide,
how quickly Judah moved now!
'Burn this wicked daughter-in-law!' cried Judah.
Would you get word to him in time?
Would he acknowledge the pledge?
Would he admit you were in the right?

You won your lawful right, but at what cost?
Your body had played you true,
your courage, screwed to the sticking point,
had seen you through.

You, widow-whore, daughter-in-law of Judah,
known now as one who stood for right,
for justice and for truth,
fighting Judah with the weapon he gave to your hand,
his lust for a female body.

And so, Tamar, Canaanite woman,
by daring and by courage
begat the twin successors
to the line of Judah.

8 – Me Too

"Right," said Faith settling back into the booth. "I've read up on Rahab and Ruth. I found I already knew their stories quite well, and I've also read up on them at home alongside your poems. They were brave women – both of them foreign to the tribe of Israel so it's doubly unusual that they would be named in a genealogy of Jesus."

She continues, "you hinted at more to Bathsheba's story – something to do with Uriah? I don't think I ever heard about Uriah – just Bathsheba herself, and David of course. I only ever heard about her as the woman who seduced King David. I suspect there might be more to that than I was ever told."

"Indeed, there is," I reply, wondering if the women of the bible would ever get their rightful stories out there in the public domain. "Her story is in 2 Samuel 11. Can you find it?"

Faith is now quite adept at getting the bible passages on her bible search engine. "Yup. Here it is. Oh. Look at that heading. 'David commits adultery with Bathsheba.' That doesn't sound like all the guilt falls on Bathsheba."

I nod, "think for a moment about David and Bathsheba's relative positions in their society. She's a woman and commoner. Her husband is a soldier, an employee, if you like, of the king. Who is David?"

"Well… he's the king obviously and definitely superior to her husband – what was his name…" she scrolls through the pages, "… Uriah."

"That's right. Can you think of similar contemporary pairs of women and men. Such as …. Harvey Weinstein and aspiring actresses?[60] Jeffrey Epstein and aspiring models?[61] President Clinton and Monica Lewinsky?[62] Would you say even if the sex might seem to be consensual that there is a power imbalance between those pairs of people? David, particularly in that day and that time, could call all the shots – as we will see. Perhaps if there had been 'Me Too' marches in Bathsheba's time, she would have joined in. There might be a whole section of this story you weren't told. How does the story start?"

Faith turns back to her tablet. "Let me see. It says, first of all, that it was spring and usually kings went to war then, but for some reason David hasn't that year."

"That's true. And David is restless, gets up, looks out and sees?"

"A woman bathing. An attractive woman," reads Faith. "Oh. He asks who she is and is told her name and who her father and husband are. I suppose that was your major claim to fame in that kind of time."

"Yes. Your connections with men were what gave you status and protection in ancient societies. By definition, in any patriarchal society it is your male connections which work best."

"So is that a protection for her in this case?" Faith asks.

"Well…," I reply.

Faith looks at me, rather puzzled, but bends her head again over the tablet to raise it with a jerk a moment later.

"No! He sends for her and 'goes to bed with her.'" Faith's fingers do air quotes over the tablet. "I suppose, if he's the king, she can hardly say no."

"Exactly. You said she's been portrayed to you as a seductress, by bathing on the roof in full view of the palace? Why was she doing that?"

Faith looks down again "It says here she was 'purifying herself from her menstrual uncleanness.' That's the blood taboo you were talking about before. She's doing what she does every month, her purification rituals."

"That's right. It's the age-old thing about girls and women being told not to walk certain streets or wear certain clothes or perform certain acts in public. As if going about their daily business needs to be done with an eye to how men will interpret it. What happens next?"

"She goes home and, oops, she's pregnant, so she sends word to David."

"Awkward! And no doubt it would not have been private that Bathsheba had gone to the palace. Plenty of servants around, including the one whom David asked about her. So, what does David do? Read the next paragraph or two."

"Let's see, David sends a message to his military commander Joab and asks for Uriah to be sent home. He then tells Uriah to go home and relax and he sends a gift too. But Uriah stays with the servants of the palace that night. David gets told this and asks him why not."

"See what I mean about everyone knowing all about this?"

Faith nods thoughtfully and asks, "what does Uriah reply? Let me see… he tells David that he can't go and be with his wife when the rest of the army are camping out in the field. This is amazing!" Faith looks up, her face flushed.

"It is. Read on," I say.

"Well, David gets him to stay a couple more days, then David gets him drunk, but Uriah still doesn't go to his house." She looks up. "Presumably David's idea is to get Uriah to sleep with Bathsheba so that the baby can be passed off Uriah's child! How sneaky is that!"

"Read on," I said, gritting my teeth. I hate this part most.

Faith is silent as she reads the next couple of paragraphs, then slumps back in her seat, looking shell shocked.

"The rat! He gets Uriah put in the 'thick of the battle' so he'll get killed. The great King David. The cute little shepherd boy who killed Goliath. The brave warrior who survived King Saul's anger. The one whom God anointed through Samuel. Huh!" Faith's hands are waving agitatedly. I move her cup out of danger.

"The great King David." I nod, giving her time to absorb the implications of this act of treachery from the one with all the power.

"What happens to Bathsheba now?" she asks.

"Read on," I say. I don't like this part either. "Read it all, but notice particularly verses 26 and 27."

Faith silently reads through the messages sent by Joab and the report of Uriah's death and then reads out loud:

> 26 When Uriah's wife heard that her husband Uriah was dead, she mourned for him. 27 When the time of mourning passed, David had her brought to his palace. She became his wife and she bore him a son. But what David had done upset the Lord.[63]

She looks up at me, lost for words. I put it out there as starkly as I can.

"Bathsheba has to marry her rapist. For many reasons. Protection for herself and her child. Because David is the king. For her own reputation. Because she had nowhere else and no one else to turn to."

"Aah!" Faith is shocked and saddened, I think, studying her closely, but also angry.

"How dare they preach her as the seducer!" I realise the anger is directed not only at David but also at the misrepresentation of this woman over years of Christian preaching. I understand her rage and talk of my own, similar, experience.

"Shortly after I learned this version of the story, I walked out of a sermon when the minister was preaching the usual line about Bathsheba. He spoke to me later. I said I saw it as institutional rape. He just said 'I've never heard that point of view.' That was the end of our conversation. He was a temporary minister. I never knew whether he changed the way he preached about Bathsheba or not."

"So, is this child Solomon?"

"No, there is more to this sorry tale. You saw that it says God was not pleased with David?" Faith nods "The prophet Nathan is sent to talk with David, and he tells him a story. Have a look in the next chapter."

Faith scrolls down. "It's a story about two men. One rich, one poor. The rich man has huge flocks…. The poor man has one lamb to which he is very attached. There's quite a lot of detail about how the lamb is part of the family….. Oh!" she looks up at me, "that's Uriah! And the lamb is Bathsheba!"

I nod. She's quick. "What happens next?"

"Well….oh! The rich man takes the poor man's lamb."

"And David's reaction?"

"Um… let me see…. He's angry and says 'the man who did this deserves to die'[64] and Nathan says…. 'You are that man!' Wohoo! Gotcha King David!" She looks up and stabbing the air with and accusing forefinger, repeats. "You. Are. That. Man."

There's a moment.

Faith reads on. "Oh my, the punishment hits David right where it hurts – in his desire for women. But, oh, he's forgiven, says Nathan, and so David won't die ….., but…. his child will?" She looks up at me, unshed tears sparkling in her brown eyes.

I nod sadly. "Yes, that first child dies. I imagine Bathsheba might have felt a lot of pain over that, though the next few verses are all about David trying to atone by fasting and praying; a lot of dramatic stuff which worried even his own servants. But in verse 24, see, he does comfort Bathsheba. At last, you might say after all that. They then seem to have what would be called today 'makeup sex' and Solomon is born."

"Solomon, David's successor?"

"Yes, though that wasn't simple either. There was fighting among David's sons once they had grown. Bathsheba advocated for Solomon and got David's endorsement while he was on his death bed. You can find that in the first chapter of First Kings."

"Another brave woman!"

"Yep, they're all there, hidden behind the patriarch's stories and often misrepresented in sermons over the years, or not mentioned at all."

With a glance at her phone, Faith starts packing up to go. "I wish I could say I'd enjoyed today's session. Endured might be a better word, but I need to know these things. Two weeks time, OK?"

I nod and she walks out the door without the usual spring in her step. Oh, that we could all remain innocent and ignorant of these terrifying stories.

Bathsheba

Bathsheba,
for us your name conjures images
of sultry Easter nights
half-veiling draperies, seduction and beauty;
by winks and nods, and the odd raised eyebrow
we suggest we know the kind of woman you were.

But your story
read without innuendo
or western ideals of romantic love
shows a different woman.

Married to Uriah,
you were a respectable Jewish matron, albeit, beautiful.

Was it an arranged married where love was not spoken,
or did you love each other, Bathsheba?
Was he kind? Considerate?
We know he was an honourable man.

And David, a restless king,
unaccustomedly home from war that spring
life so slow he napped in the afternoon,
stretching lazily with bored eyes,
saw you
as you performed your monthly rite of purification.

What was it like to be sent for by royal messengers?
What was it like when he made love to you,
your protector-king?

A royal rape.

Some would say his right,
but rape it was.
He looked,
he saw,
he took.
Exercising his rights of kingship,
forgetting his responsibility to protect.

How many messengers, servants, neighbours knew?
How many whispered behind their hands?
And after the one-night stand, when you went back home
how did you feel?
Did you feel you needed to bathe again
to seek the purity you had once had?

When you discovered you were with child
and sent your message to the King, how did you feel?
When you heard Uriah was in town
but he did not come and sleep with you, how did you feel?
When you heard the king had supped with him and made
him drunk
and still he did not come, how did you feel?

What thoughts were in your mind
about men and war, kings and subjects, love and lust
about power and honour, being a woman,
and the child in your womb?

When you heard of Uriah's death, you mourned for him.
Did you mourn also for yourself and the child
and maybe even the king?
Did you mourn for the man who for all his kingly state
had lost his integrity while a simple soldier kept his;
a sovereign caught up in a web of deceit and desire
of his own making?

Sent for again after just a few months grieving
and brought to the palace, you married your rapist,
for what else could a widow woman do
when her king commanded, and you bore his son within you?

Did David tell you of Nathan's prophecy?
Did you have that hanging over you when the child grew ill?
And when he died, what was that like?
All your grief rolled into one great bundle of pain.
Everything you had lost coalescing together
into one river of tears.

Loss of trust in a protector-king
of reputation
of husband
and now your son.

We read of David's grief.
We have the psalm they think might have been sung by him.
full of remorse and penitential phrase.

What psalm did you sing, Bathsheba?
What lament left your lips?
What cries filled your heart while you dwelt in Sheol?

We do not have the psalm you might have sung.
Was it the one women have sung out through the centuries
as they cry out to their God from the hell they live
because of violence, rape and lust?

We read that David comforted you
now he saw what he had done.
Was it different? New? Loving?
Can we rely on the words 'he had intercourse with her',
so different from 'he made love with her.'

Were you finally able to come together,
so that it was from a loving union
that Jedidiah, the beloved Solomon, was born?

We know David made his peace with God
and found forgiveness for his deeds.

Bathsheba (beautiful one),
how did you find peace,
did you find forgiveness in your soul,
for what had been done to you?

• • •

Content and Trigger warning

Chapter 9 may trigger flashbacks for anyone with experience
of domestic violence.

9 – Terrible texts

During the week, Faith emailed me asking about the Phyllis Trible book which I had mentioned – *Texts of Terror*. She was wondering if we could talk about it at our next session. I took my copy down from the bookcase in my office with a feeling of dread. These too were stories I did not enjoy discussing. Terror indeed.

The story of the unnamed concubine is graphic and brutal. She is dragged out to be gang raped. We do not know when exactly it is that she dies as she is voiceless. We can only hope it's before she is cut up and distributed as a lesson to the unruly tribes of Israel.

The male student who presented an article about this passage to the class of biblical studies students obviously did not get the serious, violent, uncaring, nature of this incident. I will not forget that grin. I had been shaken by the article when I read it at home and to have a man grin about it turned my stomach.

Raped by the Pen

"R-r-r-raped by the pen." He rolled the words off his tongue
"R-r-r-raped by the pen,"
and grinned

The writer of this provocatively titled piece
points out that rape by the pen is different from
rape by other means
but in effect,
literary rape still degrades and silences women
so it's no grinning matter.

Rape is not a word to roll off a male tongue,
nor any other for that matter.

Not only you, Bathsheba,
were (in literary fashion) raped,
but also the concubine who never speaks,
who is so silenced,
we do not even know when exactly she dies.

In life she is given no voice,
so we do not know when it was voiceless death took over.
We do not even know whether she was dead
before being dismembered
to be distributed among the tribes.

What world is it
when women can be raped
their voices cut off
their stories told by men
while other men grin?

I remembered too my reaction when I was introduced to Jepthah's daughter's story from her point of view. As a child I had been told the story and had thought of it as just another fairy tale like the story of King Midas with his wish to have more and more. Granted a wish that everything he touched would turn to gold, he forgot he might want to embrace his daughter.[65] Jepthah's story in the book of Judges, chapters 11-12 seem to show him having a similar 'lapse of memory' when he vows to sacrifice the first person he met on return home if only he could be victorious in battle.

After hearing the feminist critique of the story, I'd been haunted by wondering whether Jepthah was always met by his daughter, or whether it was unusual she came out to greet him that day. Even if I found an acceptable answer to why killing his own daughter was a mistake, the story still meant any person who came to the gate would have been sacrificed all for his vanity. Even the life of a servant or slave was precious, though maybe not then seen as much. The loss of innocence I felt on hearing a more critical reading of the incident than my Sunday school version haunted me.[66] I turned the page and a paper fell out. It was a poem I had written about Jepthah's daughter when we had studied her story.

Bat Jepthah

Daughter of Jepthah? Your only name merely a relationship
not you yourself, but to whom you are daughter.

Feminist writers have named you to redress the balance
but 'Bat' still means 'daughter of.'
Well, Bat, they have all speculated, if only you could speak.

Had you heard of your father's vow?
Were you protecting someone else?
Did you set him up deliberately? Or
did you always come out singing and dancing
for a victory so we are forced
to the conclusion that your father either didn't expect victory
or had forgotten you did that or
had set you up deliberately so he need not give you
to another man?
What were the dynamics that made you victim?

Even we who have striven to find you
in the patriarchal discourse
must guess, an educated guess maybe,
but still a guess.

And having found you,
having guessed what might-have-been,
I ask 'So what?' Where was God for you?
Did God demand your sacrifice
or foolish/conniving/forgetful father?
Was it God made sure your story stuck by being told and told
and told again acted out by wailing virgins until it made it to
the holy of holies – Canon of Holy Scripture?

Even then, so what?
What good does it do me, twentieth century woman
to read this shadowy story of women
kept nameless, ambiguously voiceless, and then sacrificed?

What does this tell me of how God and woman
can deal together?

You bewailed the childhood left behind as have
generations of women since.

So I too cry for innocence lost.

Now I am too aware.
I cannot go back to childish trust
now I know what sacrifices women may be made.

I also had found hard to swallow the actions of Abraham's nephew Lot on that dark night in Sodom when strangers demanded the handing over of angelic messengers.[67] To prevent a crime against morality and hospitality he offers his virgin daughters to the demanding mob. What father does that? Offers up his daughters to be raped? Somehow when I was younger, I hadn't thought of the girls' point of view. Probably that was because stories of abuse and rape were downplayed in the fundamentalist culture in which I grew up. The girls were not handed over in the end, but perhaps it would matter just as much to them that he would have handed them over, that he had made the scandalous offer.

It turned out, when Faith arrived, she had worked out that the story of Tamar in Trible's *Texts of Terror* was a different Tamar from the daughter in law of Judah and she was intrigued to know more.

"We've looked at Tamar who was Judah's daughter-in-law and yet bore his children," she said, "what about this other Tamar here on the list – a daughter of King David? Why is she in Trible's *Texts of Terror*? What criteria does Trible use for including these four women in her book?"

I was glad I'd refreshed myself with Trible's introduction last night. "She says they're all stories where women are the victims. As to why she chose these four women, she says that was by 'choice and chance.' See, this is what she says here about the experiences she had which led to her working with these stories."

> Hearing a black woman describe herself as a daughter of Hagar outside the covenant; seeing an abused woman on the streets of New York with a sign, "My name is Tamar"; reading news reports of the dismembered body of a woman found in a trash can; attending worship services in memory of nameless women; and wrestling with the silences, absence, and opposition of God.[68]

"So it was contemporary experiences which led her to these stories. The biblical stories resonated with the experiences she was having in the real world?" asks Faith.

"Indeed," I reply, "and she adds this warning about this territory. 'All these experiences and others have led me to a land of terror from whose bourn no traveler [sic] returns unscarred. The journey is solitary and intense. In joining this venture, the reader assumes its risks.'"[69]

I look at Faith. She has gone a little pale, but she squares her shoulders and takes a deep breath. "Well, let's take that journey."

I nod, admiring her courage. It is less than a year since she was at home in her sheltered Brethren family. The Bible she learned about there is very different from the stories which have been unearthed and exposed by feminist and critical scholarship.

"You asked to look at David's daughter Tamar. You might find that enough for one day. You're welcome, of course, to borrow the book if you want to follow up on the others – Hagar, Jepthah's daughter and the unnamed concubine. Or we can discuss them together if you feel company would be welcome!" I grin sympathetically.

"Yes, I might need company," Faith replies with a tentative smile. "I'll look up the passage," says Faith. "Where is her story – Samuel? Kings?"

"This Tamar is in the second book of Samuel chapter 13." I watch Faith clicking and scrolling to get to the chapter. She knows where to find it. Taking a deep breath, I begin.

"Perhaps first we should establish the characters. David married Micah, daughter of King Saul and we know he later married Bathsheba, but he also had many other wives and concubines. Nice for the king perhaps, though I am not sure it would have been great for his partners with their various status differences."

"How many wives did he have?"

"David had 8 wives in total, though his marriage to Michal was interrupted by her father. The other seven wives are listed here, see? 'Ahinoam of Jezreel, Abigail the Carmel, Maachah the daughter of King Talmai of Geshur, Haggith, Abital, Eglah, Bath-shua (Bathsheba) the daughter of Ammiel.'[70]

"He must have had a few children then!"

"Yes, Wikipedia says that David had 19 sons and 2 others died in infancy. One of them probably Bathsheba's child. Only one of his daughters is named and that's Tamar. Here's the list of the sons in the same article. You can see by the descriptions that having many sons proved a political risk on more than one occasion!"

The named sons are as follows. First those born in Hebron:

- Amnon, David's firstborn, born in Hebron to Ahinoam of Jezreel…

- Kileab (or Daniel), second son, whose mother was Abigail from Carmel. It is not known what happened to this Daniel.

- Absalom, the third son, born to Maacah, the daughter of Talmai, king of Geshur. He was killed by Joab (1 Chronicles 3:1-2) after he mounted a rebellion against his aging father David.

- Adonijah, the fourth son of King David from Haggith (2 Samuel 3:4). He attempted to usurp the throne during the life of David (1 Kings 1:11ff). Solomon had him executed after being warned to remember his place in the line of succession per King David's instruction regarding the crown. 1 Kings 1:32–35; 1:50–53; 2:13–25.

- Shephatiah, whose mother was Abital.

- Ithream, whose mother was Eglah, "David's wife."

- The sons born to David in Jerusalem included the sons of Bathsheba:

  - The infant who died without being named.

  - Shimea, or Shammua, probably the first surviving child of Bathsheba.

  - Shobab, from Bathsheba.

  - Nathan, from Bathsheba, the ancestor of Jesus according to the Genealogy of Jesus in Luke 3:31, considered by some to be the maternal line via Heli, possible father of Mary.

  - Solomon, also called Jedidiah whose mother was Bathsheba.

Nine other sons were born of other wives:

- Ibhar, Elishua, Elpelet, Nogah, Nepheg, Japhia, Elishama, Eliada, and Eliphelet, and one further unnamed son, who would also have died in infancy.[71]

"Wow, that's quite a list. I see what you mean about political risk – all those sons wanting the kingdom to be theirs. So, who do we meet in this story?"

"First, Absalom."

Faith runs her finger down the list of sons. "Absalom is the third son and he is the child of Maacah."

I continue, "…and he has a beautiful sister called Tamar… We know from the other list of biblical women that she was also the daughter of Maacah, daughter of Talmai, King of Geshur.

"So Absalom and Tamar are full brother and sister."

"Yes, and then there's Amnon…"

"Let me see," says Faith as she consults the list. "He was the son of Ahinoam of Jezreel. It says he was the heir apparent."

"Yes, he was David's first born. David and Michal did not have any children, it seems – that story's quite complicated. So Amnon is Absalom and Tamar's …."

"…half-brother!" exclaims Faith triumphantly, quite pleased with herself for making her way through the beginnings of the labyrinth of the line of the royal house of David. "Something must happen to him because it was Solomon who succeeded."

"Yes. Keep Alert! There's a passage in 2 Samuel 14:25 which describes Absalom as the most handsome man in the kingdom. He was a favourite with David."

"Right, I think I have the family relationships sussed. Now to the action." Faith turns to her tablet and the 13th chapter of the second book of Samuel in the Hebrew Bible.

"Huh. If Absalom was handsome, Tamar is beautiful and …. her half-brother Amnon falls in love with her. He gets frustrated because he is – aha – 'lovesick.' We're told Tamar is a virgin and Amnon didn't think he should follow up on his feelings." Faith lifts her head. "Well, he's right, isn't he! On more than one count!"

She drops her head and keeps scrolling and reading. "Hmm. Amnon's friend doesn't sound like a good man. He's got this scheme to lure Tamar into Amnon's bedroom by getting Amnon to ask David to send her in to cook for him."

"Does he do it?" I ask.

Faith reads on in silence for a moment then looks up, startled. "Yes! He does. Amnon fools David and so it is David who orders Tamar to go into Amnon's house and cook cakes – sounds like a kind of oatcake. Then… Oh my gosh. Amnon tells everyone to leave … and they do."

"I guess we need to remember Amnon is the ancient Israeli equivalent of the Prince of Wales. He is the second top royal of the kingdom. People will follow his orders," I add.

Faith reads on, gasping now and then. She looks up, face flushed and eyes flashing. "He gets her to come into the bedroom, saying he will eat there, but when they get there he grabs her. She makes quite a speech and it seems that what she's objecting to is being taken by force. She actually says that if Amnon speaks to the king he would give his permission and that would be OK. Then she wouldn't be humiliated. Eww! What a choice! Look here in verse 14. So sad."

> But he refused to listen to her, He overpowered her and humiliated her by raping her. Then Amnon greatly despised her. His disdain toward her surpassed the love he had previously felt toward her. Amnon says to her, 'Get up and leave.'[72]

"Oh, the poor girl. She pleads to be able to stay because being kicked out now would be worse than the rape even. Oh!" Faith grinds her teeth, her hands fisted on the side of the table till her knuckles showed white. "What does Trible say about this?"

I pick up *Texts of Terror* and open to the section on Tamar. "First she points out that this story comes after David's seduction of Bathsheba, the birth of Solomon and victory over the Ammonites. David in this story is only a supporting actor, however. She also points out how Tamar is introduced in a kind of sandwich between Absalom her brother and Amnon her half-brother. She then notes that Tamar is later brought into the story now encircled by Amnon's lust for her. Look at verse 2."

"Yeah, that's right. Fascinating," murmurs Faith scrolling back to the beginning of the story.

Trible points out that though Tamar is introduced as Absalom's sister, when Amnon talks with David he requests the aid of his (Amnon's) sister. Emphasising the familiar relationship diverts suspicion David might have held. She is ordered by the king to go to Amnon's house and so is trapped into being too close to a man who is lusting after her. Trible says that from verses 9 to 16, events lead up to the central act of rape and other events lead away from it – that's the part we just read. Interestingly enough, Trible writes that at the height of the events when her plight is most desperate, Tamar is not named. This makes her seem even more powerless as a character in this drama. Look what she says about Amnon's dismissal of Tamar after the rape. "She has become for him solely a disposable object....She is trash. The one he desired before his eyes, his hatred waits outside, with the door bolted after her."[73]

"That's fascinating. Trible's doing a literary criticism, like we are learning in Medieval Literature, paying attention to the nuances of how the story is told. What does she conclude about Tamar and Amnon once she is thrown out?"

"She writes that Amnon is indeed a fool and by locking Tamar out, he actually locks himself in and leaves her free to tell her story to others.[74] After the rape, Trible writes this haunting passage"

> In the house of her brother Absalom (2 Samuel 13:20c) she is a desolate sister. When used of people elsewhere in scripture, the verb be desolate (šmm) connotes being destroyed by an enemy (Lamentations 1:16) or being torn to pieces by an animal (Lamentations 3:11) Raped, despised, and rejected by a man, Tamar is a woman of sorrows and acquainted by grief. She is cut off from the land of the living, stricken for the sins of her brother, yet she herself has done no violence and there is no deceit in her mouth. No matter what Absalom may plan for the future, the narrator understands the endless suffering of her present.[75]

"Mmm," murmurs Faith. "Mmm." She reaches out for my tablet and reads the words again silently to herself. "Mmm. Those are the words written about the Messiah in Isaiah."

"They are indeed," I reply, again surprised by the depth of Faith's biblical knowledge. "Isaiah 53 in fact. I looked it up to compare the two. I noticed too that Trible highlights that at the beginning of the story Tamar was named as a beautiful virgin princess but now is simply an isolated, raped sister."

"Is her rape avenged at all?" Faith asks, unshed tears clinging to her eyelashes.

"Yes. It takes Absalom two years to achieve it, but he has Amnon killed, then flees for three years. It is said that David mourned but it is not clear whether it was for Amnon or Absalom. Trible is quite sure he would not have been mourning over Tamar being raped."

"What happens further down the line?"

"Absalom names his daughter Tamar and she grows up to be a beautiful woman too. Later Absalom is killed in another incident. You might have heard that story because David cries out 'O Absalom, Absalom my son.' Funny that we don't hear David cry out 'O Tamar, Tamar my daughter' at the time of her rape."

"I have heard that story of Absalom's death. It reminds me of the death of Thomas Becket in the 12th century when he was killed by a soldier thinking he was doing the King a favour. That's what happened in that story too."

I raise my eyebrows at the connection Faith is making.

Faith catches my expression and smiles "Med. Lit.," she says. "What does Trible say in conclusion?"

"Well, first she connects wisdom with sisters and makes an ironic play on words about how Tamar is wise, but that Amnon ignores his sister's wisdom in this story. She calls Amnon's embrace of Tamar as his sister 'a royal rape of wisdom.' Then she writes this at the end,

> Moreover, compassion for Tamar requires a new vision. If sister wisdom can protect a young man from the loose woman, who will protect sister wisdom from the loose man, symbolised not by a foreigner but by her very own brother? Who will preserve sister wisdom from the adventurer, the rapist with his smooth words, lecherous eyes, and grasping hands? In answering the question, Israel is found wanting – *and so are we.*[76]

"If Bathsheba's story connects with the Me Too movement, then Tamar's connects with the white ribbon movement against domestic violence. I looked up the statistics for sexual abuse in New Zealand and this is what I found on one website." I click and scroll and show Faith the website page:

- **1 out of 3 girls** may be sexually abused before she turns 16 years old. Most of this abuse (90%) will be done by someone she knows and 70% will involve genital contact
- **1 in 7 boys** may be sexually abused by adulthood
- Approximately **1 in 5 New Zealand women** experience a serious sexual assault. For some women, this happens more than once

- **Young people** are statistically at the highest risk of being sexually assaulted; **the 16-24 year old** age group is **four times more likely** to be sexually assaulted than any other age group…

- **More then 23% of women** who participated in a recent Auckland study reported that they had been sexually abused as children. Most of the abuse was perpetrated by male family members with an estimated median age of 30 years. For **50%** of the women, the abuse had occurred on multiple occasions. The study also found that victims of childhood sexual abuse are **twice as likely** as non-victims to experience later personal violence.[77]

"That's pretty sobering reading," says Faith quietly, raising her head from the tablet. "I suppose Tamar might fit several of these statements, like she could have been younger than 16. We're not told how old she was. Or, look, being older 16-24 is almost as bad. And here it says that assault as a child is mostly perpetrated by male members of the family. Wow." She falls silent, thinking of the young Tamar.

"The police in New Zealand have a list of what they call myths about rape on their website.[78] That's an interesting read. Look at the first one '**Myth:** Sexual assaults are only committed by strangers. **Fact:** The majority of people who commit sexual assaults know their victims and in some cases are relations, friends or work colleagues. Partners and spouses can also commit sexual assaults.'"

"And half-brothers!" retorts Faith. "I think you need to write a poem about this Tamar too. And Hagar. I notice you've written about Bat Jepthah and the unnamed concubine – but not these two."

"I do have a hymn published which includes Hagar, though I don't know how often it will get used. Here it is. Read while I get us another drink. I think we need it."

Faith bends over the book I had been using to prepare a service before she arrived.

"It's sung to Cwm Rhondda, you know, the hymn usually known as 'Guide me O thou Great Jehovah.'"

'To the wilderness so hostile'

1. To the wilderness so hostile,
   Hagar went with Abram's son.
   Sent in shame, her mistress cursing,
   suffered they under hot sun.
   She seemed destined for oblivion,
   but she wasn't there alone,
   but she wasn't there alone.

2. For a long time Israel wandered,
   through the Sinai's desert paths.
   Egypt's bonds were looking better,
   every aching step they passed.
   But they made their destination,
   living, loving there anew,
   living, loving there anew.

3. To the desert, hot and thirsty,
   Jesus was compelled to go.
   Still warmed by the water's blessing,
   there he found he faced a foe.
   He rejected fame and glory,
   for his goal was only truth,
   for his goal was only truth.

4. Solo mother, ancient people,
   novice teacher, looked for help.
   Spirit of the wilderness and desert,
   help us find our inner Self.
   In the dust and thirst and hunger,
   may we hear that inner voice,
   may we hear that inner voice. [79]

Faith looks up as I return from ordering. "That's good, but I still think she needs a poem all to herself, as does this Tamar!"

"Challenge heard," I respond with a grin. "Look here's the hot chocolate. Let's relax and talk of other things. How is Med. Lit going? I was interested to hear you'd done the story of Thomas Beckett. What was the context of that?"

"We were looking at Chaucer's *Canterbury Tales*....."[80] replied Faith.

We settled back into our seats and plunged into the fascinating world of 12th century pilgrims.

We hadn't forgotten Tamar, woman of sorrows, just emerged from the nightmare of her story for a moment. We would always now be acquainted with her grief, but right now we needed normality for a moment. We needed to catch our breath before we continued with the rest of this difficult journey about discovering how it truly was to be woman in this world.

Tamar

Tamar, what do we know?
You were beautiful,
well connected,
yet this did not help you at all.

Daughter of a powerful king,
sister to a handsome princely brother,
princess of the land yourself,
half-sister to an older brother,
whose lust for you
crossed the acceptable line
acknowledged even in those brutal days.

Three men,
all responsible to protect you
yet your father fooled into placing you in danger
your half-brother able then to seduce you
in his own house.

Absalom gets the credit for sheltering you
after the act.
He avenged you in the end,
named his daughter for you
yet told you not to make too much of the incident.

How often have we heard those words, we women?
How often will we hear them again?

O Tamar! O Tamar!
Our sister! Our sister!

0 – Women disciples followed too

In a couple of weeks Faith and I were organised to meet in *The Cup* again. Her other two papers had assignments scheduled and she'd had her head down getting them done. I wondered if she'd welcomed the break after the stories of Bathsheba and Tamar. I didn't know if she had been doing more reading in Trible's terror texts. If so, she had a lot to digest.

I thought I might talk with her about the difference between a story being in the Bible and it being a command from God or even blessed by God. I wasn't sure whether, with her background, she was clear on the difference.

Sometimes it was obvious the biblical writers thought God disapproved of what human beings were doing in the world. God is often portrayed by them as being the reason behind calamities and defeats which the nation suffered. These were invariably linked back to misdeeds and disobedience of divine decrees. I had wondered, as a teenager, once I started thinking more critically about the Bible, whether the real explanation was that the calamity happened, then leaders looked back for a reason why Almighty God'd 'sent' this famine or defeat or natural disaster.

Even today when people do something they suspect a powerful God would object to, they joke about waiting to see if they would be struck by lightning – something they see as an act of God in retaliation. There's even a love song in the iconic movie *Sound of Music* where the hero sings that he must have done something good in his childhood to earn the love of Maria, the nun-become-nanny.

So much of our view of God's dealings with human beings is transactional. If we are good, we seem to believe, deep down, we will be rewarded. If we do something bad, deep down we believe we will be punished. Yet life so often is not that fair. I am always baffled when people complain about the unfairness of life – healthy joggers dropping dead with a heart attack, good living people getting terminal cancer, a child dying inexplicably. Who ever said life would be fair? It seems there is a deeply buried belief in a justice of life which doesn't always work out. Belief that if you are good, God will reward you buys into that instinctive feeling we should be treated fairly, and always get justice in the world.

"Mmm," says Faith when I had spilled all this out. She was dressed brightly in shades of orange today; bright road-cone-neon-orange pants with a tangerine and peach striped top, a scarf of burnt umber on her dark curly hair. Her gold hoop earrings swung as she talked. It seems that her usual up-beat mood had returned.

"I think our local Assembly assumed that fairness thing. If you didn't do well in business, it wasn't said, but there was an undercurrent of feeling that you mustn't be being spiritual or moral enough."

"In other settings it's called the prosperity doctrine – wealth as a sign of God's favour," I interpolate.

"But tell me more about that idea of if it's in the Bible it's not always a command of God. I think that was always the case back home."

"Take the treatment of women in the Bible which we have been looking at, for example," I reply, breaking off to thank the server who'd brought our drinks, hazelnut latte for me and a flat white for Faith.

"We hear in some of the stories that this was a bad act or that both humans in the story and apparently God too were angry with what had happened. But in the story of Hagar and the story of the unnamed concubine there is no disapproval mentioned. Hagar, on the contrary, is singled out for divine favour when the angel of the Lord speaks to her and makes a promise to her which is almost identical to the one given to Abraham – that she will have many descendants."

"Add the silence which we often 'hear' in the Bible to the lack of praise given to these women who risked their lives approaching powerful men in unconventional ways, like Tamar seducing Judah and Ruth creeping under Boaz' blanket after the harvest. Those stories are often tacitly condemned as tainted or risqué or not proper when they are left out of the commonly preached stories from the Bible. Also, sometimes the victims have been turned into perpetrators in the popular perception – like Bathsheba has been for years."

"Just because our sacred book was written during a period of unrelieved patriarchy does not mean that 'God ordains' – it was my turn to use air quotes – that patriarchy is the only way to be a society. We see a push against patriarchy already in the way Jesus treats women in the Second Testament." I pause to sip my hazelnut latte. Oh, it was good.

Faith stirs sugar into her flat white.

"What," she says in answer to my look. "It's Thursday remember? Does-God-exist, does-God-not and then God-exists-forever day? My blood sugar needs help." She grins and continues questioning as she stirs.

"So, tell me about the places where you think Jesus shows us another way?"

"First of all, we know that Matthew's Gospel starts with women in his genealogy of the Christ. That's not Jesus doing that, but it suggests a different approach. Remember Matthew's gospel was written decades after Jesus' death, probably between the years 80 and 90, or maybe within a range from 70 to 110. That means words and concepts in the Gospel don't so much reflect the first few years of the new calendar, CE [81] (or AD) immediately after Jesus' death. Rather they reflect experiences of the early Jesus followers and the ongoing formation of what would come to be called the early church. What?"

Faith has made that funny squeak again. "I didn't know it was that long before Matthew's Gospel was written? What about the others?"

"Scholars think Mark was written first, probably around the years 66–70, then Matthew and Luke about the same time, the years 85–90, and John was a lot later, around the years 90–110."

Faith makes that shocked, squeaky sound again. I nod.

"Yep, John's Gospel is more than half a century after Jesus' death. The other shocker which follows on from those dates is that given the lower life expectancy of the time, it's unlikely the Gospels were written by the original disciples of Jesus who are named as the writers. Especially with the Gospel of John coming that many years later. Though, it's not impossible it might have been the original John. It depends how old John was when Jesus died. There is that little comment when Peter and John run to the Jesus' tomb on Easter Sunday morning, that John is younger and can run faster." I smile. I have always loved that little comment. I continue.

"The later date of authorship for John's Gospel does account for how reflective that Gospel is – there's been time for a lot of theologising to have gone on about the significance of Jesus in relation to what they already knew about God through their Jewish faith."

Faith is gulping a few mouthfuls of coffee as I speak. This has shocked her. I mutter to myself. I'd forgotten what a surprising revelation this information had been to me when I first heard it. Perhaps I should have been more careful. It constantly surprised me what basic information had not been passed on to congregations from preachers who might have learned this in their training.

"Sorry, I didn't prepare you for that very well."

"Mmm, it's a bit of a surprise to say the least! I had no idea. I suppose it's a bit like how it will be when they write histories of Queen Elizabeth II in 70 years' time, isn't it? They'll write very different things then from what they've written up till now. And even later, in a century's time, about the time distance in which John's Gospel was written, there'll be different incidents reported and reflected on."

I nod, thinking she had done a good connection with what was going on in our contemporary world with the death of Queen Elizabeth II. "I was thinking the other day, there are parts of the new king's proclamation which seem like gobbledegook to us because we are at such a distance from the 17th century. Yet when they were first written it was for reasons which were very important politically in that century. We need them explaining, just like we need to explain and interpret carefully what's written in scripture. It's been written in a completely different world from ours. I've been reflecting on that quite a lot while I have been watching the TV news and feature programmes around the Queen's death."

"Do the Gospels have different backgrounds then, if they were written at different times?" asks Faith.

"Clever girl to think of that," I reply. "Yes. Luke's Gospel seems to address more gentile communities of believers. Matthew's Gospel, though, seems to be addressed to a Jewish audience, hence the genealogy in chapter 1. Throughout Matthew there are plenty of Hebrew Bible quotes to link Jesus with the line of prophetic sayings that all good Jews would know. It seems the writer's intention is to legitimise Jesus as one who is in the same line and the one sent by God."

"That's handy to know," replies Faith. "Or, like you were saying before about defeats and punishments, maybe convinced about Jesus, they looked back into the Hebrew Bible for quotes to connect with him to validate their convictions about him."

"That's a good piece of critical thinking, Faith!" I exclaim, a little surprised at her clarity of thought considering the shock she has just had.

"Well, in Chaucer's *Tales,* they are on a pilgrimage to St Thomas's shrine. It's a wee bit the same. Did St Thomas come first or did the idea of a pilgrimage come first and then St Thomas was brought in as a worthy object of devotion?"

"Still clever of you to make the connection," I respond.

Faith blushes slightly and then a whole lot of questions pour out. "What was the world like for Jesus' followers by the time the Gospels were being written? Did the early church form quickly? Where did they base themselves? There are all those letters to the churches at Ephesus and Corinth and Galatia in the Bible. What did the word 'church' mean then? Oh, and when did all that persecution start? We got told about some of this in preachings at the Assembly but no one ever linked it all together with dates or a timeline."

"There's a brand-new book out about this from the Christianity Seminar which followed on from the Jesus Seminar writers.[82] It's called *After Jesus Before Christianity* and subtitled *A Historical Exploration of the First Two Centuries of Jesus Movements.*" I get the book out of my bag. "It's been my reading for the month."

Faith takes the book from me, turning it over in her hands, like the seasoned student she is becoming. "Huh, Sue Monk Kidd and John Dominic Crossan have endorsed it." She flicks to the fly leaf and skims down it to three bullet points in bold print and says again. "Aah. Listen to this.

'...new insights and discoveries that provide a paradigm-shifting picture, including:

- That there was no religion called Christianity before the third century
- That there were multiple Jesus movements
- That there was much more flexibility and diversity within the Jesus movements including understandings of gender, sexuality and morality
- And much more.'"

"There's a summary in the first chapter of what this group found when they began to research these early years. Look." I point out the page and Faith bends her head over it, reading aloud.

> What happened surprised us. Within our first several years, it became clear that the missing two hundred years between Jesus and Christianity was not just a holding pattern. Those two centuries after Jesus were not full of implicit Christianness, so to speak. That period had lots of new – not Christian – innovative peoples, groups, and movements inspired by Jesus but going in many different directions.[83]

She looks up. "So The Early Church took a long time to come together?"

"It seems so," I reply.

Faith eyes narrow as she continues to look at me. "That sounds interesting. Again, completely different from how I expected it to be. That's becoming so common, I just brace myself now for what other long held belief I have is going to be challenged! I guess this book gels with the Second Testament women we were going to talk about today."

"I think it does, " I reply. "I was going to start with a small section in Luke 8 which indicates that in the band of followers who travelled round with Jesus there were women present. It seems like they provided for the group. That might seem like a stereotypical female role, but they also seem to have been financial sponsors too. I also wouldn't have thought travelling with a bunch of men was quite the thing a respectable Jewish women would be expected to do. It's in Luke 8, the first 3 verses."

Faith turns it up and reads aloud:

> 8 After this, Jesus traveled about from one town and village to another, proclaiming the good news of the kingdom of God. The Twelve were with him, [2] and also some women who had been cured of evil spirits and diseases: Mary (called Magdalene) from whom seven demons had come out; [3] Joanna the wife of Chuza, the manager of Herod's household; Susanna; and many others. These women were helping to support them out of their own means.[84]

Faith continues, "I've heard of Mary Magdalene of course, but not of Johanna and Susanna. Johanna's husband sounds like an important public servant." She looks at me enquiringly and I respond.

"Notice they are providing for them 'out of their own means.' It sounds like, unusually, these were well-off women in their own right. I was quite captivated by this little section, which I only heard about after a couple of years of study for the ministry. I remember writing a poem about it because I wondered how their families had felt about them leaving to go on the road with Jesus and a bunch of men. I had to make up some background, because we're not given much in the Bible, but I could well imagine their families thought they were a little unhinged!

Women of the Way

How did you gather the courage to go?
leaving home, husband, father and mother?

Did your father ever speak to you again, Susanna?
Or, were you as one dead
to them, throwing the family's reputation never mind about
yours, to the wind by going on the road with a bunch of men?
What did your mother say, Joanna?
Or did she say nothing, lips pursed in a tight mouth in that
familiar way you knew meant she was deeply disapproving
but would not speak.

Maybe you had the easiest part, Mary
for your demons had given you labels: mad, eccentric.
Maybe you no longer had a family who called you theirs
or did they wish now you were healed, sane and whole that
you would stay
to finally be the daughter you could never be before?

But the three of you left home and went with him
you had each other and the other, nameless women too.

Can you tell us what the men thought? Mark and Matthew,
Judas, Thaddeus Bartholomew and the rest
(we know their names).

How did they cope with Jesus' easy manner with you?
The way he welcomed your presence as he said the things
rabbis entrust only to their chosen disciples.

Did they expect it was an infatuation
only lasting for a week or two?
That the rigours of the road would prove too much
for women?
As you stayed with them, and days turned into weeks,
then months,
did they finally accept you would continue
following, supporting, ministering?

Perhaps they did, for decades later,
as they wrote the stories down,
the Jesus communities remembered your names.

Disciples by decision – like them.
Disciples in deed – like them

Disciples to the death.[85]

"They must have had a lot of courage as well as Jesus being a compelling teacher. What other ways are women shown in the Second Testament?" asks Faith.

"Let's do the same as we did last time with the First Testament women. How many women do you remember in the Gospels?"

"Let me see – there is Jesus' mother Mary of course." Faith is scribbling down the names as they come to her. "Then there's the widow's mite story... Mary Magdalene's got pretty famous especially after the Dan Brown book[86].... Umm... I'm running out, I think ..... oh! The woman caught in adultery.... Oh yes, Martha and Mary..." She frowns at her list for a few minutes. "I think I'm done! Remembering last time, I'm sure I am well short."

"I'm afraid so. Here's a list of the women in the Gospels alone." I tap and scroll and turn the tablet towards Faith who gasps as she scrolls to the end of it. I had added numbers to the internet listing to show her quickly how many there were. Some had bigger stories attached to them, others were just bit part actors in the biblical drama.

"42! I would never have thought that many." She goes back to the top and scrolls through, muttering "Of course!" and, "Why didn't I remember her?" and, "I didn't know about that one!"

1. Mary (Matthew 1:16, 18-25; 2-11, 13-14, 20-21; Matthew 12:46-50; Matthew 13:55; Mark 3:31-35; Mark 6:3; Luke 1:26-56; 2:5-8, 16, 19, 22, 27, 34-35, 43-51; Luke 8:19-20; John 2:1-5, 12; 6:42; John 19:25-27; Acts 1:14; Galatians 4:4)

2. Peter's Mother-in-law (Matthew 8:14-15; Mark 1:30-31; Luke 4:38-39)

3. Daughter of Jarius (Matthew 9: 18-19, 23-26; Mark 5:22-24, 35-43; Luke 8:41, 49-56)

4. Wife of Jarius (Mark 5:40-43; Luke 8:51-56)

5. Woman with Issue of Blood (Matthew 9:20-22; Mark 5:25-34; Luke 8:43-48)

6. Christ's Sisters (Matthew 13:56; Mark 6:3)

7. Herodias (Matthew 14:1-11; Mark 6:17-28; Luke 3:19-20)

8. Herodias' daughter (Matthew 14:6-11; Mark: 6:22-29; Luke 3:19-20)

9. Women and children among the 5,000 (Matthew 14:21)

10. Women and children among the 4,000 (Matthew 15:38)

11. Syrophenician woman (also called the Woman of Canaan) (Matthew 15:21-28, Mark 7:24-30)

12. Young daughter of the Syrophenician woman (Matthew 15:21-28, Mark 7:24-30)

13. The Mother of Zebedee's Children (Matthew 20:20-23; Matthew 27:56)

14. Woman who Anointed Jesus (Matthew 26:6-13; Mark 14:3-9; John 12:1-8)

15. Damsel to whom Peter denied Christ (Matthew 26:69; Mark 14:66- 68; John 18:17)

16. Maid to whom Peter denied Christ (Matthew 26:71: Mark 14:69-70; Luke 22:56-57)

17. Wife of Pontius Pilate (Matthew 27:19)

18. Many women beholding from afar (Matthew 27:55-56; Mark 15: 40-41)

19. Mary Magdalene (Matthew 27:57, 61; Matthew 28:1-10; Mark 15:40-41, 47; 16: 1-8, 9-11; Luke 8:2-3; 24:1-11, 22-24; John 19:25; 20: 1-3, 11-18)

20. Mary, the mother of James and Joses (also called "The other Mary") (Matthew 27:56, 61; 28:1-10; Mark 15: 40-41,47; 16: 1-8; Luke 24:1-11, 22-24)

21. The Widow who Gave Two Mites (Mark 12:41-44; Luke 21:1-4)

22. Salome (Mark 15: 40-41; Mark 16:1-8)

23. Many other women who came up with Jesus from Galilee (Mark 15:40-41)

24. Elisabeth (Luke 1:5-80)

25. Anna (Luke 2:36-38)

26. Widow of Nain (Luke 7:11-17)

27. Sinner who washed Jesus' Feet with her hair (Luke 7:36-50)

28. Certain women who had been healed (Luke 8:2-3)

29. Joanna, the wife of Chuza (Luke 8:2-3; Luke 24:1-11, 22-24)

30. Susana (Luke 8:2-3)

31. Martha (Luke 10:37-42; John 11:1-6, 17-27, 34-45; 12:2)

32. Mary of Bethany (Luke 10:37-42; John 11:1-5, 17-20, 28-34, 39-45; 12:3-9)

33. Certain woman of the company (Luke 11:27-28)

34. Woman with a Spirit of Infirmity (Luke 13:11-16)

35. Women who bewailed and lamented (Luke 23:27-29)

36. Women who followed Jesus (Luke 23:49, 55-56)

37. Other women at the empty tomb (Luke 24:1-11, 22-24)

38. Samaritan Woman at the Well (John 4:7-42)

39. Woman Taken in Adultery (John 8:1-11)

40. The mother of the Man Born Blind (John 9:2-3, 18-23)

41. Mary, the wife of Cleophas (John 19:25)

42. His Mother's sister (John 19:25)[87]

"I see Luke mentions a lot of women and yet it was Matthew who put the women into the genealogy. Are there differences between the Gospels?" Faith looks enquiringly at me.

"Funny you should ask that, I was wondering whether to say or not. I once was shown an article that comments on how differently Luke treats or portrays women in that Gospel. This is what I wrote about that at the time."

"When was that?"

"Early 1990s."

"Ah, the old days!" Faith grins at me cheekily.

Whose Authority?

We all thought it,
some more than others
"It'll get better when Jesus comes.
These Old Testament stories
hide, gag, kill and maim women
but when Jesus comes,
so will the light."
And it seems he treated women well,
included, talked theology with, defended supported, healed.

But only a few years later
male disciples
showed their bias
as they wrote down The Story.
Paul, frankly, is confusing on the topic,
or just confused?

Luke, I read,
mentioned women most of all the Gospels
but what women!
Meek, submissive, quiet and obedient
A "dangerous Gospel" indeed.
Would no women be better
than role models as consistently quiet as these?

What does it mean for us
that women have to be rescued from the text
in order to appear at all
with any substance?
Can we appear at all?
Who will rescue us?
From what? For what?
Does "women treated thus and so in Bible times"
demand " women treated thus and so in modern times?"

Whose authority decides?

• • •

"Interesting," comments Faith. "Can you send me a copy of this? I'd like to think about it more."

"Sure can," I reply.

"Have you written poems specifically about any of these New Testament women too?" asks Faith.

"Yes. Mary, (Jesus' mother, as you know), about the woman caught in adultery, the widow of the widow's mite story, about Mary Magdalene – there are a couple about her. Martha and Mary, too – one poem each.[88] I've also written a hymn about Martha and Mary[89] and published one about the Samaritan woman at the well. I can send them to you if you like. Let me know what ones interest you most."

I pause, "there's a woman who's not here, the housewife who sweeps out her house to find the missing coin. I suppose she's not a real woman but rather a metaphor. I find it interestingly disappointing though, that she is often not thought of and yet the good shepherd who looks for the missing lamb and the father who runs out to greet the prodigal son have been made much of in the preaching of Luke 15. We know all about them!" I know my tone has turned sarcastic, so I carry on hastily with another thought.

"I've often reflected on what I call the Women of the Passion Narrative when I've been preparing Lent and Easter services. First, there's the incident which is placed in Holy Week by the lectionary. Oh, sorry," I interrupted myself, looking at Faith's puzzled frown.

"Holy Week?" she asks.

"I forgot. Open Brethren might not observe the seasons of the church year. Holy Week is the week before Easter, Monday to Good Friday. The lectionary is a list of readings for each Sunday of the year, (usually a psalm, one from the Hebrew Bible, a Gospel reading and an epistle) divided up into a three-year cycle, A, B, and C. In one of those years at least, the story about the woman anointing the feet of Jesus is included. It's thought this might be Mary of Bethany, perhaps the sister of Martha and Lazarus, though there's interesting new scholarship which suggests Martha is a later addition.[90] If it is another woman, that makes two women before Jesus has got to Jerusalem."

I turn to the list again. "Look at the women listed 14 to 23; mostly women in events before, during and after Jesus death. Mark mentions 'Many other woman who came up with Jesus from Galilee.' There's the woman who anointed Jesus, that story is in 3 of the Gospels. The story of the widow with her two mites is also often included in Holy Week readings."

Faith nods, that concentrating look on her face again, so I carry on.

"They don't mention it here, but we can assume women prepared the Passover meal for what we now call the last Supper. This metaphor/ theme is used in an Australian-published book of essays called *A Place at the Table: Women at the Last Supper* which was important in the campaign for the ordination of women priests.[91] The book was published on the 100th anniversary of women's suffrage in New Zealand and has an arresting painting on the cover which shows women including one with a babe in arms at the table."[92] I show Faith the painting on my laptop. She looks interested, scribbling down details of both book and painting.

"Then," I continue, "when we move on to the trials of the Thursday night, here's the young woman outside the court on Thursday night to whom Peter denied Christ and the other young woman, a maid of the palace, to whom Peter denied Christ. Then we come to Good Friday. Do you remember the role Pontius Pilate's wife played?"

Faith nods "She had a dream didn't she, and sent word to Pilate."

"That's right. When it gets to the crucifixion itself it's recorded that there were 'many women beholding from afar.' Mentioned specifically are Mary Magdalene, 'Mary, the mother of James and Joses (also called "The other Mary")' with, of course, Jesus' own mother Mary. Can you find any more women associated with the events of that first Easter?"

Faith looks through the list carefully. "Here are 'Women who bewailed and lamented' and 'Other women at the empty tomb.' Then didn't women come to the tomb on the Sunday morning and find it empty? They were bringing spices and other gear to prepare Jesus' body, weren't they?"

"Yes, do you remember Mary Magdalene's role in that?"

Faith sits back with her eyes half closed, thinking. "Yes, she's one of the small group of women. They were worrying about getting the stone rolled away. So it was a relief, but also a shock, to find it already rolled away and no body in the tomb. The angels tell them Jesus is gone. Mary Magdalene wanders about the garden for a bit I think, when Jesus turns up in front of her. She thinks he is the gardener, doesn't she at first? That's right, she does, and she asks him where they have put Jesus' body. And then there's that bit I love where Jesus just says "Mary" and bing! Just like that, she knows who he is."

"You've got it pretty accurately. Then what does Jesus do?"

Faith thinks for a moment. "He tells her to go and tell the others the good news."

"Do you find that significant at all?"

Faith thinks again. "Umm... um…. I suppose women weren't given important messages like that very often."

"Indeed not. Mary is appointed an apostle by Jesus here – one who spreads good news, who tells people important information, who is an eyewitness to a supremely major event. She's sometimes called the apostle to the apostles. I'll send you my poem about that moment in the Garden of Gethsemane[93] because it is really significant for women and just like the story of Martha's confession of faith, it doesn't get as much airtime as stories about men confessing the Christ is being apostles."

"That's fascinating. And if Mary Magdalene is mentioned this many times by name, it suggests she's important in those early Jesus groupings?"

"Yes, we'll hear more about that."

"Well, it will have to be another day," says Faith getting her stuff together. "Time I went now. Thanks for today. Another little army of women I knew little about!" She tugs the backpack over her shoulder and leaves *The Cup*, golden hoops swinging.

Mary M

Mary M, we sift and sort
dissolve away centuries of tarnish with academic solvents
searching for the original beneath.

Legends of Black Madonna, whispers of scandal and rumours
taint of mental instability discredit you
turn you into an emotional, extravagant sinner.

Patient sifting and study and we find a different Mary M.

Saved from seven demons
(Oh, frustration, seven, that number again.
Did they mean exactly seven, or just a lot?
Such biblical codes confuse and obscure)

And what were demons? Our modern-day depression?
Manic states? The catch-all schizophrenia?
We do not know! We do not know!

We do know, however, you were invariably listed first,
(the leader of the band of women?)
you followed him from Galilee,
you were there at cross and tomb
(and Supper too?)

John tells us you were commissioned
(not Luke, who likes to keep women extras to the main plot)
The first 'christophany' they call it, was to you
to you he first appeared as risen Christ
because faithfully as ever you were there
right place, right time, as always.

"Mary M, Apostle" sounds good!
If you can be that, then we can be
Professor, Director, Minister, Priest, Moderator, Nominator,
who knows, even Principal one day!

Your story tells us we can experience 'christophany' too.

11 – Women mentioned in despatches[94]

When Faith arrived for our next session, she was agog. I'd emailed her not only the list of women named and unnamed in the Gospels, but also the list of women mentioned in the following books in the Second Testament. She waved a paper copy of it at me as she arrived at our booth having ordered at the counter.

"Just as many women in the rest of the Testament, after the Gospels!" she exclaims, plunking the list down on the table between us. We bend over it together.

All the Women in the Epistles

1. Apostles gathered in Prayer and Supplication with the Women (Acts 1:14)

2. Sapphira (Acts 5:1-11)

3. New Women Believers (Acts 5: 14)

4. Widows who were neglected (Acts 6:1)

5. Women committed to prison by Paul (Acts 8:3; Acts 22:4)

6. Samaritan women baptized by Philip (Acts 8:12)

7. Candace, queen of Ethiopians (Acts 8:27)

8. Women Persecuted by Paul who would bring them back as prisoners (Acts 9:2)

9. Tabitha/Dorcas (Acts 9:36-42)

10. Mary, the Mother of John Mark (Acts 12:12; Colossians 4:10)

11. Rhoda (Acts 12:13-15)

12. Devout and Honorable Jewish Women (Acts 13:50)

13. Eunice (2 Timothy 1:15; Acts 16:1 – the son of a certain woman)

14. Lois (2 Timothy 1:15)

15. Women at the Place of Prayer in Philippi (Acts 16:13)

16. Lydia (Acts 16: 11-15, 40)

17. Certain Damsel Possessed with a Spirit of Divination (Acts 16:16-19)

18. Chief and Honorable Women of the Greeks (Acts 17:4, 12)

19. Damaris (Acts 17:34)

20. Priscilla (Acts 18:2-3, 18-20, 24-26; Romans 16:3-5; 1 Corinthians 16:19; 2 Timothy 4:19)

21. Wives and children of Tyre (Acts 21:4-6)

22. Four Daughters of Philip (Acts 21:9)

23. Paul's sister (Acts 23:16)

24. Drusilla (Acts 24:24)

25. Bernice (Acts 25:13-14, 23; 26:30)

26. Phebe (Romans 16:1-2)

27. Mary of Rome (Romans 16:6)

28. Junia (Romans 16: 7)

29. Tryphena (Romans 16:12)

30. Tryphosa (Romans 16:12)

31. Persis (Romans 16:12)

32. Mother of Rufus (Romans 16: 13)

33. Sister of Nerus (Romans 16: 15)

34. Julia (Romans 16:15)

35. Chloe (1 Corinthians 1:11)

36. Euodia (Philippians 4:2-3) – she is called Euodias in the KJV (a male name) but it is possible she was female

37. Syntyche (Philippians 4:2-3)

38. Claudia (2 Timothy 4:21)

39. You adulterers and adulteresses (James 4:4)

40. Apphia (Philemon 1:2)

41. The Elect Lady (2 John)

42. The Elect Lady's Sister (2 John 1:13)

43. Nympha (Colossians 4:15) – called Nymphas in KJV but is possibly female.[95]

"I'm thinking about what you said about the significance of being named or being unnamed – either way there is some significance about the woman concerned," comments Faith. "Some of these women are named and some are not. What do you think that means about those Jesus movement groupings in those two centuries after Jesus's death?"

"I have always thought that if a woman is named, then the eyewitnesses and the people with whom they shared their eyewitness accounts included and named women who, in turn, were important in the following movements in those early years. As we commented last week, the strong story which is Mary Magdalene's is a good example. She seems to have been an important influence in at least one of those early groupings."

"How do we know that?"

"The Westar Institute points out that there's a fragmentary Gospel of Mary which has an interesting exchange in it. The woman in the Gospel is only named as Mary, (not with the additional Magdalene), but her position seems to suggest it is Mary Magdalene. She is described as comforting and encouraging the group, 'exhorting them not to doubt for the Saviour's "grace will be with you and shelter you." She then "turned their heart to the Good" and calming down, they begin to discuss the Savior's teaching (5:4-10).'" [96]

"A fascinating spat develops after Peter asks her to teach them, saying, "Sister we know that the Savior loved you more than the rest of the women. Tell us the words of the Savior which you remember, which you know and we do not, nor have we heard them." (6:1-2)." [97]

"That sounds good! Far more inclusive than I would have thought," comments Faith.

"Ah, but as Mary shares her information about Jesus, Andrew objects and Peter then turns on Mary saying, "Did he choose her over us?" [98]

"Green-eyed jealousy creeping in!" Faith exclaims.

"Aha. It's Levi (Matthew) who supports Mary, saying 'Surely the Savior's knowledge of her is trustworthy. That is why he loved her more than us.' [99] The point is made by the authors that this Mary, see here."

"...is obviously a leader. She is a teacher, revealing and relaying words of the Savior unheard by the other followers... She is an authority, exhorting the followers of the Savior to action when they would fear and despair, giving focus and stability to the group." [100]

"If they are saying that Jesus loved her more than the rest of the women, that suggests there were other women followers too in those early groups, and I suppose in Jesus' band of disciples. That fits with the section in Luke 8, doesn't it?" asks Faith.

"It does," I respond, "and there's an interesting couple of sentences here. 'Women and men have equal right to teach and to lead. This equal right derives from a shared focus beyond gender: a focus on the attainment of true, perfect human status.'[101] It's an interesting emphasis for times which we have painted in our minds as solely patriarchal."

"Tell me more about what kinds of groupings they found in their research," asks Faith.

"In the first chapter of *After Jesus*, the group lists six discoveries they made. The early movement groups first, resisted the Roman Empire, second, practiced 'gender bending', third, lived in chosen families, fourth, claimed belonging to Israel, fifth, had diverse organisational structures and sixth, had persisting oral traditions.[102] They say that at the end of the second century there was 'a wide range of possibilities and combinations of organisation and meaning making were on the table. There were, they write '...diverse experiments in identity, power, and belonging by those seeing to live in an Empire of God while negotiating the Empire of Rome.'" [103]

"Were these early Christians in the same kind of group in each place?"

"That's one of the surprising findings. There was no single name which they used for themselves. They had many names and sometimes no name. They rarely used the word 'Christian.'" [104]

I pause. "You might be interested to read their section on what the word Christian means. They note that the Greek word *christianos* occurs only 3 times in 138,015 words in the Second Testament, never in the Gospels or the letters of Paul. It was mostly used in the second century as describing those being persecuted, a word used by others about the emerging Jesus movements. The authors make a significant point here, see?"

> It (*christianos*) most probably was an imperial Roman bureaucratic term used to identify a subgroup of the larger groups of Israel, specially one that had the potential to cause trouble, like other groups from the region. This trouble-making affiliation made membership in this group a chargeable offense against the empire. Like many nicknames, the word was used against the group or party but then later was adopted as a badge of honour and symbol of resistance to dominant structures of power.[105]

"That wouldn't encourage you to call yourself *christianos!*" comments Faith. "Do we need another drink to help all this amazing stuff go down? What would you like?"

As Faith orders our lattes, vanilla for me, hazelnut for her, I flick through the next few pages of *After Jesus*, covering what the emerging Jesus groups called themselves. The comment is made that mainstream scholarship, while acknowledging 'Christian' isn't quite the right term, still uses it rather than the actual names used by the actual groups.

The Seminar writers did not come to a perfect answer themselves. General terms they employ are "Jesus peoples" or "Followers of the Anointed" – they feel these too are inadequate because they were not names used by the groups themselves. They also point out that the word 'disciple' as used then meant 'student', though in our present English usage of the word disciple, the meaning has developed a more specialist meaning.[106]

I read that when some groups referred to Jesus as the 'Anointed One', they were setting him up in opposition to the emperor. They used names like 'Believers of…, Confidants of … friends of …, Sister and brothers of… and Intimates of….. the Anointed.'[107] The Seminar has found 24 different names for Jesus peoples in the first two hundred years, though they suspect there were many more in actual use.[108]

Faith returns from the counter with her own question. "Apart from the Gospel of Mary are there any other references to women leaders in those groups?"

"There's a fascinating glimpse in some Roman documents. Pliny the Younger corresponded with the Emperor about the *christianos* early in the 100s. He tells him he has tortured two women who were named as officials of one of the Jesus groups. The Christianity Seminar highlights the fact that while the reference to torture has been noticed by scholars, scholars have not made much of the fact that these two women officials were enslaved."[109]

"Really!" says Faith, grasping the significance at once.

I nod. "That means these 'officials' deserve attention on two counts – they were women, and they were slaves. Even if women leaders were not unusual, that these two were enslaved is a surprise. In Roman society, slaves were not even given the status of full humanity and "were more often called 'bodies' than humans.""[110]

"If these two women were leaders, then it suggests other women were too – both free women and enslaved women," comments Faith. It is significant, don't you think, that Pliny in this letter does not express surprise that the groups should have female officials. That suggests they are used to that being so, within the Jesus movement groups."

I nod in agreement. "You might like to read the chapter where the book compares the Gospel of Mary passage with 1 Timothy which is much more draconian about women's role in the church. Or not. It's quite an unsettling book with its conclusion that in the first two centuries, there could have been many outcomes of the groups which were in existence. It wasn't inevitable then, they say, that it would turn into the Christianity we know, in the post-Constantine world."[111]

"Really! That is intriguing. But I think I'll stick with the woman theme. We haven't looked in detail at which women are included after the Gospels yet. Perhaps next time?" Faith drains her latte and packs up. "Same place, same time?"

"Sure thing. In two weeks…., that'll be fine," I say, quickly checking my phone calendar. "See you then, *christianos!*"

With a quick grin at the quip, Faith leaves *The Cup*. I sit back, reflecting on the origins of what we've come to think of as Christianity and the disturbing discoveries which the Seminar writers have revealed. It is evident it surprised them, and no doubt their findings will surprise others, men and women alike.

'Letters written to the churches'
The epistles from the point of view of the Reformation

1. Letters written to the churches
    give our earliest glimpses how
    Jesus seemed to his generation,
    who he was, both then and now;
    They debated his role and stature
    seeking how they should react;
    How to meet and how to worship,
    sorting anecdotes from the facts.

2. Paul with others travelled the circuit,
   calming, urging, making things plain;
   Nurt'ring those who followed Jesus
   linking all groups into the main;
   Creed and doctrine so developed,
   rites and rituals grew to be,
   customs, practice, all were fashioned
   through words penned by such as he.

3. Women too were following Jesus
   throughout danger, risk and strife.
   They saw loved ones taken and tortured,
   they, like men, also risked their life.
   Keeping faith and family together,
   their homes hosted believers too.
   They defied imperial edicts,
   they were leaders and followers true.

4. Writers then used ink and parchment,
   texting now is short and sharp;
   Twitter in the heat of the moment
   limits thought, can exclude heart;
   How will we in our generation,
   let our wisdom have good space,
   put our time to thinking through issues,
   deal with others in love and grace?

5. Thanks be giv'n to those before us
   who wrote words both living and true,
   spent hard time in prison and travel
   to ensure good news got through;
   Thanks to those who carried those letters
   for the danger and risks they took
   all combining to remind us
   Love shines forth from this sacred book.

Words: Susan Jones, Progressing the Journey 2022
Tune: Blaenwern WOV 165 (ii)
Verse 3 original to this book

12 – Who says women should keep silent?

When she made her way into *The Cup* for our next session, Faith's colour scheme was a little more subdued than previously. Her kilt had predominantly green and blue tones and she'd topped it with a navy-blue Guernsey style jersey. It was true that the weather was getting chillier. It had been some weeks now since we had sat in the courtyard, preferring the warmer atmosphere of the main café.

As usual questions burst out of her even before we got the orders sorted. "I want to know about Constantine and when he started to have influence on Christianity. I didn't know he had that much influence until I saw something on the History channel at home last weekend. Was he around in that first 200 years or not?"

"Good questions," I reply, "Let's order and get down to it." It turned out it was a hot chocolate day with a side of cheese rolls. Faith had missed lunch.

"Right," I said when we were settled, each stirring around the marshmallows with which *The Cup* were so generous.

"The first two centuries means the 'naughties' – 0 to 99 is the first century, then the second century is from 100 to 199. The third century begins with 200. That still leaves a gap between the work of the Christianity Seminar and the birth of Constantine. There were a lot of Roman emperors in these first few centuries."

I show Faith the list I had brought up in a Google search while she had been at the counter. Some of the names will ring bells for her, others won't.

I scroll and tap on my tablet. "See here, the first century CE has 12 emperors."

> Augustus (31 BCE–14 CE)
> Tiberius (14–37 CE)
> Caligula (37–41 CE)
> Claudius (41–54 CE)
> Nero (54–68 CE)
> Galba (68–69 CE)
> Otho (January–April 69 CE)
> Aulus Vitellius (July–December 69 CE)

Vespasian (69–79 CE)
Titus (79–81 CE)
Domitian (81–96 CE) and
Nerva (96–98 CE).[112]

"How many of those have you heard of?"

Faith bends over the tablet. "Hmmm. Augustus, Tiberius, Caligula, Claudius and Nero. Huh! I probably know about those because of the various stories about the emperors who persecuted the early Christians – or whatever they were called at the time. Haha, look at this one Aulus Vitellius. He only lasted from July to December. I wish I knew more Roman history to know that background!"

"Mmm, me too," I reply, "Domitian in this century was also known for his persecution of Jesus' followers."

I bring up the list for the next century. "Here's the next 100 years. Recognise anyone here?"

Trajan (98–117 CE)
Hadrian (117–138 CE)
Antoninus Pius (138–161 CE)
Marcus Aurelius (161–180 CE)
Lucius Verus (161–169 CE)
Commodus (177–192 CE)
Publius Helvius Pertinax (January–March 193 CE)
Marcus Didius Severus Julianus (March–June 193 CE)
Septimius Severus (193–211 CE).[113]

Faith bends over the tablet again. "Oh! Hadrian – that's the Hadrian's Wall man?" I nod. "And… Marcus Aurelius. Why do I know him… oh! The Gladiator thing. Oh look, another short lived one, Publius only made it from January to March and then next guy only from March to June – that was a big year for the Empire! Wonder what was going on?"

I bring up the third century emperors. "Here are the 200 to 299 group."

Caracalla (198–217 CE)
Publius Septimius Geta (209–211 CE)
Macrinus (217–218 CE)
Elagabalus (218–222 CE)
Severus Alexander (222–235 CE)
Maximinus (235–238 CE)
Gordian I (March–April 238 CE)

Gordian II (March–April 238 CE)
Pupienus Maximus (April 22–July 29, 238 CE)
Balbinus (April 22–July 29, 238 CE)
Gordian III (238–244 CE)
Philip (244–249 CE)
Decius (249–251 CE)
Hostilian (251 CE)
Gallus (251–253 CE)
Aemilian (253 CE)
Valerian (253–260 CE)
Gallienus (253–268 CE)
Claudius II Gothicus (268–270 CE)
Quintillus (270 CE)
Aurelian (270–275 CE)
Tacitus (275–276 CE)
Florian (June–September 276 CE)
Probus (276–282 CE)
Carus (282–283 CE)
Numerian (283–284 CE)
Carinus (283–285 CE)
Diocletian (east, 284–305 CE; divided the empire into east and west),
Maximian (west, 286–305 CE).

"Any you recognise here?"

"That's a long list. Maybe it suggests the empire is in a little trouble." Faith looks carefully. "I don't know much about them, but I've heard the names Valerian, Claudius – though this one is Claudius II so I am not sure whether I've heard of both or not, and I have heard of Diocletian. I see here he divided the empire into east and west so that might be why – that would be a big step. A couple more short timers, the first two Gordians. No Constantine yet?"

"Here he comes. Constantine was a 4th century emperor. He doesn't become emperor until 306 and he reigned till 337. Compared with some of the others quite a reign – 31 years. He'd been emperor for 7 years when he issued the Edict of Milan in 313 AD, granting religious tolerance to all views. It was much later when he converted to Christianity and people have always questioned whether that was sincere, or for political gain."

I continue. "Then in 325, 19 years after he became emperor, he called a Council together – in Nicaea – so known as the Nicene Council. It was an empire-wide summit of religious leaders to discuss doctrine – the first – and some of the differences between the various groups around the empire. While there was some discussion about the books of the Bible, the main talk was of the relationship of Jesus and God. If you read the Nicene creed which this Council wrote, you'll see a kind of 'bulge' in it about who how Jesus is defined. That's because that was the topic of the time."[114]

"Did Constantine have anything to do with what ended up in the Bible?" Faith asks. "I'm thinking of the Gospel of Mary which obviously didn't make the cut."

"Because the First Testament is the Hebrew Bible that was decided well before Jesus lived. It's just the Second Testament really, that you're asking about. The content of the Bible was pretty well set by the end of the first century, but it was discussed by the First Council of Constantinople in A.D. 381. Some criteria were established then for whether a book was worthy of being included. They thought it should be:

- Written by one of Jesus' disciples, someone who was a witness to Jesus' ministry, such as Peter, or someone who interviewed witnesses, such as Luke.

- Written in the first century A.D., meaning that books written long after the events of Jesus' life and the first decades of the church weren't included.

- Consistent with other portions of the Bible known to be valid, meaning the book couldn't contradict a trusted element of Scripture."[115]

"It took decades of debate to get it all settled apparently. It was a few years later that all the books were published by Jerome in a single volume – about 400.[116] That's a quick version of the story. You can see by the first criteria that they did not have the scientific means to discover which books were genuinely written by eyewitnesses."

"Wow! Another new thought. The Bible didn't really come together until the fourth … 5th century after Jesus died. So, if we began in 2022 to compile a history commemorating Queen Elizabeth II, it wouldn't all come together until 2422. Well beyond all our lifetimes! No one would be around to check the accuracy."

You can see the wheels churning in Faith's head about authenticity, reliability, accuracy and other aspects of scripture which she will never have questioned before.

"Perhaps you do need to take a course in biblical studies or church history to get all this down in detail," I suggest. "The problem with reading only one author is that scholars specialise a lot and can only speak knowledgeably about one aspect. Then if you use a summary article like the one I've used today you may not get the whole story – nor an up-to-date one. A lot of research is still ongoing on ancient documents, including the Dead Sea scrolls which were discovered as late as during WWII."

"Wow." Faith is a little bug-eyed. "So different from what I thought happened. And yet, did I ever think about how it would have all happened? Probably not. If you'd asked me how the Bible came together, I don't think I would have had any kind of process in mind."

"Perhaps another drink?" I suggest, needing one desperately myself. "I'm having tea, what do you want?"

"Oh… chocolate again I think," says Faith absently still mulling over the discoveries of the last few minutes.

I go to get the drinks and remember my experience of feeling the Bible was falling apart like a broken-up jigsaw during my first experience of biblical studies. What Faith was confronting was much the same. She was right that if she followed the woman-thread she would get other questions answered as well, sometimes questions for which she didn't even know she needed the answers. We had strayed away from women in the epistles somewhat.

Faith'd had the same idea. "We've wandered away from the biblical women," she said when I returned from ordering. "Are there standouts in this list you sent me last week?" She had taken it out and was reading and commenting at the same time.

"I know Sapphira. She and her husband kept some of their possessions back when they were meant to have everything in common, didn't they? And Rhoda was the one who opened the door to Peter when he got out of prison, but no one believed her at first. Eunice and Lois were Timothy's mother and grandmother weren't they? I can never remember which! Lydia? I know the name…."

"Lydia was a seller of purple cloth and met Paul by the riverbank in Thyatira. She's thought of as the first convert in Europe and she took Paul, Silas and Timothy to her home where they stayed for a while. Do you know who Priscilla was?"

Faith shakes her head. "Just know the name really."

"Priscilla and Aquila were a married couple who travelled as missionaries with Paul. They're thought to be quite important in keeping the little Jesus groups going and stable. Some even think that Priscilla could have been a kind of minister or pastor and might have been the unknown writer of Hebrews."[117]

"Really? I'm also intrigued," Faith adds, "that in the same chapter of Romans there is a Junia and a Julia, could they be the same person?"

"Definitely. It is thought that the word Julia (a female name) was changed to Junias (a male name) to disguise a woman's involvement. There's an author online who quotes two authoritative scholars, the first, Michael Bird,

> There is a tsunami of textual and patristic evidence for 'Junia' that proves overwhelming. Despite some naughty scribes, biased translators, lazy lexicographers and dogmatic commentators, the text speaks about a woman named 'Junia.' Jewett goes so far as to call the masculine 'Junias' a 'figment of chauvinistic imagination.'[118]

"The second author Mowezko cites is James D.G. Dunn.

> [The female name Junia] was taken for granted by the patristic commentators, and indeed up to the Middle Ages. The assumption that it must be male is a striking indictment of male presumption regarding the character and structure of earliest Christianity… We may firmly conclude, however, that one of the foundation apostles of Christianity was a woman and wife.[119]

"Fascinating," says Faith. "That's like the alteration of Mary's name in Papyrus 66 to create Martha. I read up about that after you'd given me the reference. Who's next? Chloe?"

"Chloe may have been a leader in the Jesus groups of the early church. You might enjoy Marg Mowezko's website which has a byline

'Exploring the biblical theology of Christian egalitarianism.'[120] She comes to this conclusion about Chloe."

> There is little information about Chloe in the New Testament, just one sentence that mentions her name. But one thing is certain, Chloe is known to the Corinthian church, otherwise Paul would not have mentioned her. And if she is the host of a house church that included her whole household, she would have been a woman of standing and one of the powerful. Considering the report that her people brought to the apostle Paul, it is likely Chloe is a prominent female minister like Priscilla and Phoebe who were also women ministers of standing connected with the church at Corinth (Acts 18:1ff; Romans 16:1-2).[121]

"Interesting. Yes, I think I will look that website woman up," replies Faith scribbling down the reference. "How do you spell her name?"

"Finally notice this comment about Euodia. It seems the same thing might have happened to her name as did with Junia/Julia. 'Euodia (Philippians 4: 2-3) — she is called Euodias in the King James Version (a male name) but it is possible she was female. And Syntyche (Philippians 4:2-3). I have always heard it assumed that these two women were having a conflict. But I saw an article the other day which suggests something different – this is the abstract. You might like to follow it up."

> In Philippians 4:2-3 Paul urges Euodia and Syntyche to unite with each other. He also addresses 'true yokefellow' and asks him to assist the two women. This paper disputes the almost universally held assumption that Paul was asking him to mediate a conflict between the two women. Rather, Paul is here calling the church leaders, Euodia and Syntyche, to have the mind of Christ and to foster unity among the Philippian churches, and the other church members to support them. The term 'true yokefellow' is a piece of 'idealized praise' and is Paul's way of diplomatically correcting one or more church members.[122]

Faith scribbles down some keywords.

"Huh, so I had heard of those women and was given the impression they were quarrelsome. There actually are quite a few leaders scattered around the place, aren't there? Women in charge of households some of them, so quite powerful in their society. What about women keeping silent then? Where does that fit in?"

"Well, hope you're feeling strong because I have news about the letters in the Second Testament which are attributed to Paul."

"Attributed!" exclaims Faith sitting up straight. "Is this Moses-not-writing-the-first-five-books-of-the-Bible all over again?"

"Kind of." I grin at her sympathetically as I continue with the news which still startles me when it comes up.

"Scholars have looked at the style of writing of all the epistles attributed to Paul and have decided there are probably three types of Paul. John Dominic Crossan is good on this topic. Altogether there are 13 so-called Pauline letters. Crossan and Marcus Borg argue that seven of these are probably by Paul whom they describe as radical: Romans, 1 & 2 Corinthians, (three long letters); 1 Thessalonians, Galatians, Philippians, Philemon, (four short letters). They then say that three of the 13 are not written by Paul: The Pastorals: 1 & 2 Timothy and Titus: They describe the person writing these letters as reactionary. Then there are another three letters whose authorship is questionable, and are probably also not by Paul: Ephesians, Colossians, and 2 Thessalonians. They describe this author as conservative."

"I'm gobsmacked!" exclaims Faith, looking indeed somewhat shell shocked. "Paul was preached all the time in our local Assembly. He was, really was, I often thought, presented to us as more important than Jesus. You're really telling me that scholars don't think he wrote all those 13 books?"

"That's what they are saying and Crossan and Borg are not the only ones."

"But it says 'by Paul' in several of those other books. I'm sure I'm right."

"You probably are. It was a known custom for people to write in the style of a leader or important teacher. Often the receivers of those letters knew they were not reading the words or hearing the voice of the original apostle. It's been less clear to us that is so."

"Why are you telling me this now?" asks Faith

"Because the passage about women keeping silent in churches is in 1 Timothy which is thought to come from the reactionary Paul, not the radical Paul. The radical Paul writes ' There is neither Jew nor Greek, there is neither..."

Faith nods and joins in, "…bond nor free, there is neither male nor female: for ye are all one in Christ Jesus. That's Galatians 3:28!"

"And who wrote Galatians?"

"The radical Paul?"

"Yes."

"So as time goes on, the mood for some in the church gets less radical and more reactionary?"

"Yes. The Christianity Seminar has something to say about this passage, comparing it to the piece in Mary's Gospel which we spoke about a couple of weeks ago. A few years ago, my own personal theory was that as the Jesus movement evolved and social acceptability seemed to be important, perhaps some groups thought women being less prominent in leadership would increase the acceptability of the Jesus movements in their patriarchal Roman society. It sometimes does happen that the radical view of an original leader or founder is too radical for their followers to continue, especially if the leader had been killed for those very views."

"What does the Christianity Seminar say?" asks Faith.

I dig in my bag for the book and turn to the chapter entitled 'Testing Gender, Testing Boundaries.' It contrasts the passage from the Gospel of Mary which Faith and I had discussed previously in the coffeeshop. It recognises that I Timothy was a more proscriptive passage than earlier writings, appealing to Genesis 2-3 and denying women the right to be active in the community.[123]

"They say that the Gospel of Mary and the 1 Timothy passage cannot be held as positions on a spectrum – cannot be 'held in common.' Also, that asking yes/no questions of these texts is too simple. Questions about the value in which early church women were held or whether Paul liked women can only be answered "Yes, no, and both."[124]

"So what is the early Christian position on women?" asks Faith, looking puzzled.

"The Christianity Seminar writers would say that these passages on women illustrate the reality of the Jesus grouping and movements in those first 200 years; the reality that they 'were incredibly diverse.'[125] The communities of the Gospel of Mary and the first letter to 1 Timothy likely had very different opinions on the role of women. This points, they argue, to a greater truth about Jesus followers in the first two centuries.

> ...it argues against the popular notion that "Christianity" was some kind of unified "whole" from the start and that fragmentation or disunity – diversity – came later. There was no such thing as "Christianity" in the first centuries of the Common Era.[126]

"That seems rather unsatisfactory," comments Faith. "There is no definitive ruling then about women in the church or in Christianity as a whole coming from the arrangements or organisation immediately after Jesus died."

"That might be true, but then there is also no universally negative view about the value of women in the growing movements, either. Also, if people are prepared to read the Bible in its context, they will take into account which 'Paul' is writing the passages under study. Is it the radical Paul who would be writing closest to eyewitness impressions of Jesus or the more reactionary 'Paul' or the conservative 'Paul', seeking to batten down the hatches as it were, turning towards institutionalizing behaviour for other ends like social respectability, perhaps, than simply following Jesus' ethos."

I pause and think for a moment. The Seminar's work is new to me too.

"Perhaps increasingly, the desire and perceived need to adapt back into the mores of Roman society begins to counteract the more revolutionary attitudes towards women which Jesus showed."

Faith breaks in, her face lighting up. "Perhaps then a group of Jesus followers operating in our contemporary world might decide whether their approach will be radical, reactionary or conservative and follow the teachings they prefer? I choose to be radical!" Her mischievous grin breaks out as she makes jazz hands to emphasise her commitment to radicality.

"At least you do not need feel bound to conservatism or to be reactionary just because it is in scripture, because apparently scripture offers you several ways to be. It's a paradox but also freedom at the same time," I reply.

We sit quietly for a moment. The day's conversation has covered a wide range of information, all of it with great significance to our lives.

Faith pushes her empty cup aside and gathers her things. "Thanks for this," she says. "Does this mean we've covered the biblical women now? What's next to do?"

"I think we should examine our ideas of God more closely," I reply. "We've talked about it a bit, but I think there's more to say."

"Cool," says Faith. "That would be God 'the supreme and ultimate reality.' One of our theology lecturers used that phrase and it's stuck in my mind. I'll look forward to it."

With a swing of her kilt, she was out the door into the crisp autumn air.

'For all the saints'

Hymn for Mothers' Day

1. For all the saints of every age and day
    who bravely seek to follow Jesus' way
    sharing Good News by what they do and say:
    Alleluia! Alleluia!

2. For hidden saints, who kept home fires alight
    nurturing faith through even darkest night
    that in our day Love's hope may still burn bright:
    Alleluia! Alleluia!

3. For those we know, whose given task was care
    who may have had to struggle to be fair
    and through their lives, faith, healing, love to share:
    Alleluia! Alleluia!

4. For sisters, wives, aunts, nieces, mothers too
    grandmothers, girlfriends, partners old and new
    midwives of faith, still bringing in the true:
    Alleluia, alleluia.

5. For women who work in the public place
    Dealing in law, in business, all at pace
    Drivers and builders, carving out new space:
    Alleluia, alleluia.

6. For women's work for justice and for peace
    for those who suffer and need Love's release
    for all our children, may war someday cease:
    Alleluia! Alleluia!

Words: Susan Jones, Progressing the Journey 2022
Tune Sine Nomine

13 – He or she or something else: who and what is God?

Faith and I didn't meet the following fortnight. She'd emailed to explain that the startling revelations about the early Jesus followers and the women amongst them had started a kind of chain reaction. She'd found herself really, really angry that she hadn't been told before about the presence and power of women in those early groupings. So, could she take another break, Faith asked. Same as last time, would I mind if she contacted me when she was ready to continue?

"I just think that if we kept on going, I would get even more angry and I need to deal with this lot of anger or I won't be able to 'hear' any more new stuff," she wrote. "In fact, at the moment, I'm not sure I want to hear anymore new stuff. But I'll decide that when I've taken some time out."

Again, I assured her that this was her journey, and she could take it as slowly or as quickly as she wanted to. I reminded her of the tools she'd used last time to work through her reactive depression, suggesting they might work again. I was always here to talk about anything at all – it didn't have to be our woman-thread theme. I suggested Hazel might be an understanding ear as she had gone through waves of depression and anger herself when she was working out her own stuff. I attached the poem 'Yes'[127] hoping it would be more helpful than hindering. I also simply held Faith in my heart, yearning for her to be able to face her anger constructively and powerfully.

This time it took 6 weeks before I heard from Faith again. Hazel had assured me she was OK, but my heart ached for her. I remembered the feelings of panic and anger and fear and guilt which had accompanied my own journey. I suspected Faith was experiencing some of the same. But, one Tuesday morning there was her email, suggesting we met that Thursday. What a relief!

Staring at the bookcase in my office, I wondered where I should start in my time with Faith in *The Cup* today. She'd already been introduced to the idea that God could be male or female when we discussed the gender of the Spirit at the beginning of Genesis. It would be good to see how that revelation had gone with her. We'd also talked about some feminine images of God used in the Bible.

More importantly perhaps, we had touched on the significance for women and for men whether the God they worshipped was male or female. Mary Daly's perceptive comment in the 1970s came into my mind again "If God is male then the male is god."[128] Any God being worshipped is, for the worshipper, the ultimate role model of goodness and greatness and authority. If that God is only thought of in terms of only one gender, then it is that gender which is primarily associated with goodness and greatness and authority. The other gender then automatically serves in the subordinate position.

The recent death of the longest serving monarch in the British constitutional monarchy had provided a fascinating picture of how that worked, I mused. One mother interviewed on television said she was sorry her daughter would now be missing a role model of a powerful woman. We had heard subjects and commentators alike speculate on how strange it will seem to them to have a king now, and what's more, to have three kings in a row if the line of succession turns out the way it is set up at the moment.[129] Contrary to the usual run of the British monarchy – a majority of kings rather than queens – many people in 2022 Britain have only ever known a queen on the throne. A king is unusual now to this population with few remembering the previous King George VI.

Watching a woman being a queen and a mother, grandmother and great grandmother and seeing her continue to reign, even though becoming increasingly frail, had given many women and many men an idea of how to wield authority when the human concerned was female.

Just the other day I'd heard a coloured woman speaking about the need to increase the percentage of ethnicities other than Pākehā as directors on Boards throughout New Zealand. While the proportion of women on Boards had crept up over 50%, an improvement from previously, the percentage of ethnicities other than European on New Zealand Boards of Directors was lower. The woman being interviewed commented that, "you can't be what you can't see."[130] The 2020 stocktake of Board memberships shows the numbers.

Ethnicity at a glance

Of the 98.6 percent of board members who have provided ethnicity information:

- 71.4 percent are European
- 22.3 percent are Māori
- 5.4 percent are Pacific peoples
- 4.0 percent are Asian
- 0.8 percent are Middle Eastern, Latin American or African.[131]

We accept the evidence of our eyes. When I was growing up it was 'obvious' that being a minister was a job for the boys while women could serve God mainly by becoming Sunday School teachers, Bible Class leaders or overseas missionaries. No one told me that, but as a child I made sense of the world through what I was seeing. In the same way I picked up the understanding that ministers and missionaries were the ones following God's will the 'best.' Other lay people were 'second class' in the Christian stakes. No one told me that, but I looked at the way ministers and missionaries were celebrated and ordinary people were not.

My thoughts returned to the 'Almighty One.' If God could not be anything else but male, then those who represented the divine, as in clergy, would 'need' to be male too. If this assumption was not pulled out and examined critically, it followed like night followed day.

I figured Faith would lean towards trusting most the biblical evidence of a possibly multigendered God, so from the bookcase I pulled out the Virginia Ramey Mollenkott book I'd already mentioned to her; *The Divine Feminine: the Biblical Imagery of God as Female*[132] and also Bridget Mary Meehan's *Delighting in the Feminine Divine*.[133] Rosemary Radford Reuther's *Sexism and God-talk* also had a relevant second chapter, 'Sexism and God-language,'[134] I remembered, and looked for that too. A New Zealand woman, Catherine Chrisp, had tackled the subject in 2002[135] and I added her book to the growing pile. Perhaps that was enough. I had to carry them all across the busy street to *The Cup*.

I load up with my laptop and the books and walk across the road, wondering what kind of Faith I would encounter in the shop. I open the door on to the coffee-laden atmosphere of the shop, drawing in an appreciative breath.

Faith is already there. She waves from the corner, easy to spot with her sparkly turquoise scarf and lime green top. I did like the way Faith's clothes reflected her increasingly confident presence in the world and am pleased to see her dressed in such an 'out-there' manner. It boded well. She beckons me over. "I've ordered lattes for both of us. Hope that's alright?"

"Mmm, lovely," I reply, stacking the books and laptop on the table. "Good to see you again Faith. I was so pleased to get your email."

"Looks like a lot of words in there," Faith comments, eyeing the pile. "Break's over then!"

"If you want it to be?" I noticed she hadn't responded to my comment about my getting her email. It seemed she didn't want ever to talk with me about her reactions. I was glad she had Hazel to bounce her ideas around with.

"Yes, I do. I'm ready to do some more," Faith replied with energy and an air of decision. Inwardly I note the greater intentionality in her voice. The anger has been productive then. Maybe one day she will let me in on her process.

"Well, God is today's topic and many words have been written on that theme," I reply. "These are just some I thought would be most helpful."

The lattes arrive and we sort the table so we can drink, read and talk. Sounds like the title of a movie, I muse.

Faith picks up the Mollenkott book. "This is the one you were telling me about earlier that I've now borrowed from the library. Is this your copy? It looks well worn," she comments as the first two pages break out of the old Sellotape holding them into the volume.

"Yes," I reply, reaching over to peer inside the front cover. "Judging from the address inside, I must have bought that book soon after it was published."

Faith is turning to the contents. "There's quite a list here. After the first and second chapters she just goes into the different images.... 'God as Nursing Mother'... 'God's Other Maternal Activities' – interesting chapter title!" She grins up at me. "'God as Midwife... 'The Shekinah' – need to check that out more. 'God as Female Pelican'.... and 'Mother Bear.' 'God of Naomi.' Huh. 'God as Female Homemaker'... 'Female

Beloved' ...'God our *Ezer*.' That was interesting. 'Bakerwoman God' ... 'God as Mother Eagle'... 'Mother Hen' ... 'Divine Wisdom' ... and the 'Divine Milieu.'" She looks up. "I remember thinking at the time this book was a real mix!"

"Sure is," I reply. "You can see this would have made quite a stir at the time. Mollenkott makes the point in her second chapter that while we can re-discover these feminine images, there is a greater problem to overcome. It's the different valuing of masculine and feminine roles. Charity and I talked a bit about this. The dualisms we've inherited remember as Christians, are ethical dualisms – there's a value put on one list of characteristics over the other and the feminine does not come out well from that typecasting."

"Women are praised when they join masculine pursuits, but men are not rewarded the same way when they pick up activities hitherto regarded as women's work," nods Faith. "I've been thinking a lot about that and watching to see how it works out in the world. I know mixed flats where the guys just make a mess all the time and the girls are expected to clean up after them, for example. A friend who's working as an intern in a law office says she is expected to get the coffee, never the male interns."

"True, it's still happening today in lots of places. At least we have a role model in the Prime Minister's husband who took the lead caring role when their daughter was little."

"Mmm. What are these Hebrew words she's used here? I presume they are Hebrew? *Shekinah* and *Ezer*? I think I've heard *Shekinah* before – isn't it about glory or something?"

"It's root means 'to dwell.' *Shekinah* was used to indicate God was present among the people of Israel and that presence was feminine. Mollenkott does say "*Shekinah* depicts the visible expression or residence of God's glory within the creation." She goes on to explain that in ancient Hebrew the feminine gender of a word was more obvious when that word was spoken. In Semitic languages, all "nouns, verbs and adjectives have male and female forms,"[136] so words used alongside *Shekinah* would have meant that the people knew Shekinah was a female concept. She cites an anthropologist writing before 1967 who says, "to say that God is either male or female is...completely impossible from the viewpoint of traditional Judaism.[137] This anthropologist, she writes, "…treats the concept of the *Shekinah*, God's feminine Presence in this world, as one development arising out of Jewish craving for the divine mother."[138]

"Where is *Shekinah* used? We don't have the original word in our translations," asks Faith.

"She mentions a few here. The thick cloud on Sinai in Exodus 24, the cloud descending on the tabernacle in Exodus 33, the cloud by day and the…"

"…fire by night. Is that *Shekinah*?" asks Faith eagerly. "I've always loved that idea of the cloud by day and the fire by night! Hmm. *Shekinah*." She rolls the word around her tongue.

"Yes. And whenever the phrase 'the glory of God' is used, it is probably *Shekinah* in the original language. Also, the Hebrew documents themselves associated *Shekinah* with God speaking through the burning bush, with Solomon's temple and with the synagogue."

"Fascinating. Whenever I've heard 'the glory of God' in English I have assumed that is a masculine term for a masculine Almighty Ruler."

Faith reaches for the book and reads ahead.

"Oh! Look! The *Shekinah* is present at the annunciation by Gabriel to Mary in Luke. '…the power of the most High will cover you with its shadow'… the shadow is *Shekinah*!" She is obviously gobsmacked by this discovery. She bends over the book again and reads on. I can see her lips moving as she forms the words. I sit quietly not wanting to disturb this epiphany moment for her. Finally, she looks up at me, then reads from the end of the chapter.

> As Tennyson notices, the *Shekinah* is both dark and light – dark cloud during bright day and bright fire during dark night. This image, derived from biblical narrative suggests that God's Presence is best discerned in that which is *other* from ourselves. And that in turn suggests that having been male dominated for centuries, the churches of Christendom and the synagogues of Judaism badly need more leadership and insight from the perspective of the majority "other" always in their midst: women. Perhaps when that happens, the *Shekinah* will reappear splendidly among us.[139]

"So we have excluded this really vital essence of God from our preaching and our imaginations," she adds. "I feel again that mix of real delight at finding this out and anger that we've missed out on this learning for so long."

I nod to show I understand her mixed feelings

"The same thing is true for the word *Ezer* too. It is used in Genesis to describe the person who will become Eve. It can be translated as helpmeet and has been used to suggest more something akin to handmaiden, a subordinate term. But it is used in the Bible for Eve and for God and mostly it is used for God rendering assistance to the people. A helpmeet is actually a colleague or a peer offering assistance. The whole chapter is very interesting but look at how she ends it." I reach over to find the place.

> Directly created by God who is our *ezer* both in huge public matters and in smaller internal crises, womenkind is a unique channel of God's power to the world. Julian of Norwich was blunt enough to identify motherhood with God in her book about divine love: "To the property of motherhood belong nature, wisdom and knowledge, and *this is God.*" I will follow Dame Julian's example by being blunt and unequivocal: because God is *ezer*like – because God is womanlike – women are Godlike.[140]

Faith is looking thoughtful. "So recovering these female images has several parts to it." She puts up a hand and counts her points off on her fingers.

"First to show that God has been referred to in feminine terms but this has been ignored, neglected or even suppressed."

"Second to understand the significance, symbolism and message of those metaphors and so to learn new things about the character of God through them."

"Then there is the difference this makes to the character of God as we speak and sing and pray, to the ways in which God can/should be portrayed in worship."

"Fourth, there is the connection between God and human beings. Up till this view of God starts to be talked about critically and radically from the 1960s and 1980s, we've had only male or neuter images of the Almighty One. With more balanced language, the character of worship changes."

"And, (fortunately I have a finger left) this has a profound significance for women. It underlines that idea that we all are made in the image of God. Now we also have some feminine images of God brought further into the light, we can believe that in a different way. And if the male could be god when God is male, then it follows that the female can be god when feminine images of God are used and valued."

Faith slumps back into her seat, bemused, I think, at what has just flowed so fluently from her.

"Preach it sister!" I offer a high five. "That is it exactly."

We grin foolishly at each other. I am glad too to be reminded of this seminal truth. Too often as a minister I am surrounded by conventional liturgies. I could frequently forget the importance of bringing these feminine images out into the light. My own internalised misogyny often prevented me delighting in the divine feminine. I think of a poem which had arisen out of that kind of epiphany for me years ago.

"You know, in *Sexism and God-talk*, Rosemary Radford Reuther writes about the Goddess religions which operated before monotheism arrived on the religious scene. It's in her chapter 2. Remember the definition of misogyny is linked to that 'arrival' of the one, male God?"

Faith nods.

"Here's a poem I wrote about that. Have a read while I get us another drink. What do you want?"

"Chocolate please," said Faith absently as she turned my laptop to her and began to read.

Was there once a light?

Was there once
long, long time ago
a time when women were revered
admired even
when once perhaps they ruled, even
(amazing thought).
Did they have a freedom
a feeling they belonged on earth
like men feel they do now
because
(is anyone listening, hush
come closer so I can whisper it)
because she was God
not only goddess
(an associate or assistant God)
but The Holy One?
Was there once that time?
when femininity was revered
treasured, worshipped as divine?

Do we women carry with us
some sort of genetic memory of that time
when our foremothers
lived in the light,
or has this long night
existed forever?

Whether there once was light
or only unrelieved blackness
now we can emerge
into a new dawn
weaving the morning
as Mother wove it once?[141]

Faith looks up as I finally return from the long queue with a large slice of carrot cake and two forks. "It's got vegetables in it, really healthy," I said with a wink. "What?"

Faith is looking sheepish.

"I clicked, and this other poem, came up too. I reckon this is what we've been talking about." She turns the screen towards me, and I read the poem which had spilled out of me on a retreat ages ago.

MotherGod

May I introduce God, my Mother?

As if after years of being adopted out,
my Real Mother, the One who gave me birth
has found me.

No simpering sixth century saint my Mother.
No, she's a twentieth century woman
tall and strong
proud of her femininity
unafraid of her gentleness
at terms with her sexuality
comfortable with the paradox
that she is both male and female,
both strong defender and gentle nurturer.

Pride in being her daughter warms my heart
like, mother, like daughter they say
for I am made in her image
and,
when all is revealed, I shall be like her.

Even now
incomplete as I am
I show some of her character.
Fitfully I share some of her great love to those I love
occasionally I am a fleeting likeness of Her.

And best of all,
when I am overwhelmed with being me
with the anger and the hurt
stemming from my fear
that being me is not enough,
then
she is near, closer than any other
there to love and mother me
to comfort, console, and yes
to challenge me to face the facts
pick myself up, dust myself down and try again.

I need my Mother.
She shows me how to be a woman
she models that paradox of gentle strength
and strong gentleness,
the true character of God.

She understands my adolescent gaucherie
and guides me through the twisting turns of spiritual puberty
reassuring me that awkwardness will fade
and confidence will come
and yes, that fat white larvae
encased in dull cocoons
are still potential butterflies.

She models for me confidence without arrogance
compassion without pity
weakness that is strength
and unyielding softness.

She is not jealous
of my developing womanhood
nor envies me my youth
but delights with me
in each new discovery
each fresh sensation.

She teaches me to stand tall
to love my body
to reverence its shape
to guard its strength
and delight in its humanity.

She brings new life
to ovum and ovary
uterus and tube.
In secret mystery
she tells me of my birth
within the womb
how even there she named me as her child.

And, as I am taught anew by her
the wonders of my womanhood
the little boys' snickers
the male embarrassment
the crudities, the rape, the chauvinism,
even female envy
pale into insignificance
beside the wonder of myself
a woman made in the image of her God
to be just like her.

May I introduce you to my Mother, God?[142]

"Oh!" I exclaim, a little embarrassed. The poem reveals quite a bit of my own angst at the time of writing. "Something I wrote last century!"

"I found it really special," says Faith. "It gives me a glimpse of how God being female might make a difference to me, a real woman living right now."

I nod. "It does seem to me that if I am able to think of God sometimes as feminine, then I have greater confidence that all the intricacies and idiosyncrasies of my life as female are understood, even the most intimate and private aspects of that."

"Yeah, the first poem kind of hints at that – those years when the goddess was the focus of religions."

"The feminist theologians that I have been re-reading for this session remind their readers that they are not seeking to replace a male God but to extend the vocabulary of the church, including alongside male images the female ones as well. As Catherine Chrisp says here," I open *Travelling with Sophia.*

> Sophia-God teaches that she is found in the 'both' and the 'and.' She is found where opposites meet. If the opposites are to meet they need to understand one another, or at least recognise the validity of the other and accept it. Where this happens is love. Another name for that place is God. It is a holy place.[143]

"Mmm," murmurs Faith, finishing off her carrot cake and draining the last of her flat white. "God is Love. That used to be on a poster on the wall of our Sunday school room. It's like we've come full circle, back to the beginning. There's a kind of quote about that isn't there?"

"There is. 'We shall not cease from exploration And the end of all our exploring Will be to arrive where we started And know the place for the first time.' It's from "Little Gidding" by T.S. Eliot."[144]

"'Know the place for the first time.' That just seems very, very true right now."

"Next time we'll look more closely at what women are doing in the contemporary world by way of leading or speaking in and around churches, if you like. That's kind of how we first got into conversation wasn't it – your Aunt Hazel and her being a woman who leads in church?"

"Yeah! That'd be good. Gosh this semester is almost over, isn't it? It's been a journey and a half. Two weeks' time, OK?"

"It is indeed. Go well."

Who is in charge?

14 – Women leading now

I scroll through my laptop as I wait for Faith in *The Cup*. I am looking for an e-book, first prepared in hard copy for New Zealand's women's suffrage centennial celebrations in 1993. *Women Together* is a book of essays on different types of women's organisations. For the 125th anniversary of women's suffrage in New Zealand, 2018, an updated online version had been produced: *Women together: a history of women's organisations in New Zealand / Ngā rōpu wāhine o te motu.*[145]

In the essay about women's religious organisations, Enid Bennet had begun her account back in 1822 with the advent of Christian missionaries to the country. This alone indicates a Pākehā bias, since women and religion presumably mixed within Māori tribes before European settlement. However, as she admits, "This essay is concerned mainly with Protestant and Catholic denominations and their associated women's organisations, with a largely Pākehā membership."[146]

Bennet describes women's initial involvement as filling traditional roles including significant work in fund raising. As the century progressed, pressure grew along with the rising feminist tide associated with women's suffrage and women began to ask for less traditional involvement. She covers the early missionary years and the later 19th century 'flowering' of women's organisations in churches which as time went on asked for speaking rights at official church gatherings. It was fascinating that the reply she quotes uses the word helpmeet as a term for an inferior rather than a peer like the word *ezer* (helpmeet) is used in scripture.

> Opposing this move, the editors of the *New Zealand Presbyterian* claimed in 1892 that the women's movement was placing women in opposition to men. They stated that for woman to be man's helpmeet and men to protect women 'is as clearly the order of nature as it is the ordination of heaven, and any movement which tends to frustrate it must be mischievous and end in failure.' Responding to a protest from the *New Zealand Methodist*, the editors referred to women meddling in matters 'for which they were practically incapacitated by their mental, moral and physical constitution.' [8] However, the women's organisations continued

to press for speaking rights within their respective churches, and by the late 1930s all had achieved this goal.[147]

Increasingly, women worked as missionaries in both Māori and Pākehā settings as well as overseas. Within New Zealand, deaconesses began working from the turn of the 19th century, often being key in building up a congregation in a new area which would then call a male minister.

Significant changes came to pass after WWII. "The significant changes which did take place in this post-war period involved three major elements: amalgamations within the women's organisations, women in ordained ministry, and the influence of feminist analysis."

"Aha," I thought, "feminism wave number two!"

Something makes me look up to see Faith entering the coffeeshop. She is all in black today, with a T shirt proclaiming "Keep Calm and Go Back to Sleep." I'd come to realise that the colour of Faith's clothing often relates to her mood, so I greet her cautiously.

"Hi." Indicating her T Shirt, I ask, "short of sleep?"

Faith flops down into her seat in our booth. "Too right. Two essays due in the same week only a day apart. I'm not sure I did the second one justice at all. Add the usual Thursday is-God-real-or-not rollercoaster and I'm done."

"Just as well I took a punt and ordered coffees for us then," I say as, right on cue two, flat whites appear at the table. "I ordered one single shot and one double. Can I guess which one you need?"

With a tired smile Faith reached for the double shot drink and added a generous spoonful of sugar. "Yep! Need all the aids to energetic living today!" she exclaims, stirring her coffee vigorously. "I hope you've got some good news today."

"Some, perhaps," I reply still cautious. "Some not so much." I think I might not bother her with the 19th century missionary work and pre-war traditional female work in the mainstream churches about which I had been reading.

I indicate the laptop and explain the origins of the material – the original 1993 book and the 2018 update.

"I've got to post WW II where there is some movement in women's roles. See these two paragraphs here:

Lay women now had a secure place in the voluntary organisations, and some voice in their churches as a whole; the work of deaconesses and missionaries was officially recognised. But the question of admitting women to full ordination remained unresolved in most denominations. It had been raised as early as 1928, when Congregationalist preacher Maude Royden visited New Zealand. Deaconesses with an evangelistic message could preach, but officially the ordained ministry was for men only. Even when there appeared to be no logical reason to exclude women, nor any theological objections, much of the traditional opposition remained.

In the 1930s and 1940s, several nonconformist women visited Britain and met women ministers. By 1950, both Presbyterians and Methodists had set up special committees to consider women's ordination. The women's voluntary organisations were represented in the debate; lay women clearly supported any extension of women's ministries, including ordination on equal terms with men. Between 1951 and 1977, the Congregational, Methodist, Presbyterian, Baptist and Anglican Churches and the Associated Churches of Christ all accepted women for training and ordination.[148]

"Mmm," says Faith. "Why am I not surprised at that opposition?"

"Bennet then moves on to Feminist Christianity. Some thought Christianity and feminism were incompatible, while those who were feminist could see how little substantive progress was being made in the acceptance of a non patriarchal approach." See, she cites Mary Daly about whom we've already talked. Then see this paragraph here..."

A change took place from the mid-1970s, as feminist theology and its challenges to patriarchy became more widely known. At the start of the United Nations Decade for Women, the Women's Committee of the NCC commissioned an enquiry into the status of women in the church. The report, published in 1976, concluded: 'the overwhelming impression was that many women are not satisfied with the present care-taking and fundraising roles they are expected to play.' Nola Ker referred to the paradox whereby Christianity advocated pursuing the highest values, including freedom, justice and equality: "Yet the church ... actually lags behind the progress towards equality for women which is being made in wider society. Within its own boundaries it perpetuates a restricting of freedom, an injustice, a lack of equality.[149]

"1976," muses Faith, "I wasn't born then."

"I was born," I reply, "but I wasn't married by then. I was only, in very small fits and starts, hearing some of this feminist talk. Bennet's got a couple of interesting paragraphs here which contrast the two basic reactions to feminism and how it might impact Christianity. Have a look." I turn the laptop around where Faith can see the screen and sit back, watching her face as she reads.

> Second-wave feminism brought forth strong protagonists and antagonists among Christian women of every denomination. Both sides believed God's design for the future contained a crucial role for women; it was the interpretation of this role which differed. Christian women who supported feminism believed God was calling them and their churches to be liberated from patriarchal theology and male domination, and to lead humanity into a true partnership of male and female based on a divinely ordained equality. This meant rejecting any biblical interpretation which supported women's subordination; it also implied recognising feminine as well as masculine attributes within the godhead, and seeing sexuality and spirituality as complementary, not separate or opposed.
>
> Anti-feminist Christian women espoused New Right doctrines which arose partly in reaction to feminism. They upheld traditional Christian teaching on divinely ordained subordination for women, whose 'liberation' was seen to come only through fulfilling both their nature and their vocation as women, and in particular as wives and mothers. The nuclear family and the nation were held up as the sole vehicles for righteousness, with women subordinate to men in both. Feminists were viewed as rebellious and disobedient to God's will. In particular, the extension of reproductive rights, especially the liberalisation of abortion laws, provision for sex education in schools, and the legal and social acceptance of homosexuality, were vigorously opposed as contrary to God's law.[150]

"That difference would be still true today," responds Faith when she had finished reading. "Perhaps the proportions of women and men in each of the two groups might be a little different – some more I would hope in the first group – but there are still a large number of people (I knew them in the Assembly back home) who are firmly of the view that the traditional women's place should not change much."

"Yes," I reply, thinking with a heavy heart that many women who held to traditional views had quite a lot of internalised misogyny of which they were generally unconscious. In our western society, there were many rewards, small and large, which served to keep them unconscious of it and complying with traditional roles and expectations.

"The next few paragraphs list briefly a lot of activity which happened in more than one denomination. I was involved in some of that. See she mentions *Vashti's Voice* here? I was a co-editor of that for a while. I also went to a women's conference in Christchurch – it was probably this one here. It was a wonderful experience."

"What?"

I sense Faith's attention has shifted and I look back at the screen. A large black and white photo shows a group of women greeting the first woman bishop in New Zealand, Penny Jamieson.

Faith is reading the caption. "1990? What does it mean 'first diocesan bishop'?"

"Penny was the first woman bishop in New Zealand but also the first one to be elected by a diocese or district in an Anglican church. You see Barbara Harris in the circle of bishops? She was the first woman in the world to be made a bishop, but she wasn't elected by a church district or diocese. She came over from America for Penny's consecration. It was heady stuff. I was up the back, watching."

"Were you? Wow. Fourteen years before I was born. In some ways 1990 seems like a long time ago, but in other ways it seems like only a short time ago, like, I mean, it seems like it had taken a long time, too long, for women to get there. When had women first been ordained in the Anglican church in New Zealand?"

"The first women priests in New Zealand were ordained in 1977. The first presbyterian woman minister had been ordained in 1965."

"So, it took 13 years from the first priest to the first bishop?"

"Yes, and Penny had only been ordained herself in 1985."

"What is the equivalent to a bishop in the Presbyterian church?"

I thought for a moment. "I suppose the strict equivalent is when the first woman minister was made a Moderator of a Presbytery which would be the equivalent to a diocese. In the 1990s, there was a lay woman in the south of the country who was made Moderator of the Synod of Otago and Southland which is a large regional body in the south end of the country. Another laywoman was Convenor of the Council of Assembly which does the business of the church between General Assemblies. We did a big thing of celebrating those appointments at the time because they were unusual, first, you know?"[151]

Faith nodded and I continued, "but perhaps a better equivalent would be the Moderator of the whole Church which was a one-year position but is now a two-year position. Since the New Zealand Church was formed in 1901, we have had only 4 female Moderators, in 1979,[152] 1987,[153] 1995[154] and 2006.[155] The first of those was a laywoman. A woman is due to become Moderator in 2023.[156] None of those women are Māori, but Millie te Kaawa was made Moderator of Te Aka Puaho, the Māori synod/Presbytery of the church.[157]

"Mmm," murmurs Faith, considering what she has heard. "Mmm. That statement, 'you can't be what you don't see,' applies here too, doesn't it? You can't be a Moderator if you don't see it happening, or a bishop. I noticed at the Queen's funeral the high predominance of men in the line-up of clergy – there was one woman bishop there, wasn't there, otherwise all the Anglican high ups were men."

"That was the Bishop of London. I looked her up in Wikipedia – this is what it says about her."

> Dame Sarah Elisabeth Mullally, DBE (née Bowser; born 26 March 1962) is a British Anglican bishop, Lord Spiritual and former nurse. She has been Bishop of London since 8 March 2018. She is the first woman to hold this position. From 1999 to 2004, she was England's Chief Nursing Officer and the National Health Service's director of patient experience for England; from July 2015 until 2018, she was Bishop of Crediton, a suffragan bishop in the Diocese of Exeter.[158]

"Wow! England's chief nursing officer! She was pretty special before getting ordained into the church!"

I nod. I too had been impressed by that former occupation. "You might like to look up that entry and read on further. Her route to being a bishop is very different from the kind of route a man would take. She was a non-stipendiary priest at first until she gave up the CNO position in 2004."

"I'll do that," says Faith as she looks at the laptop and scribbles down the bishop's name.

I continue, "there were other women from non-Anglican churches taking part in the prayers at the Queen's funeral, too. The two readers were women, but part way through I realised they were there because at the moment it happens that the CEO of the Commonwealth is female and so is the British Prime Minister. New Zealand is a bit freer than England and other denominations are a little less traditional than the Anglican church, but as you see from the Presbyterian track record of five women Moderators per 123 years, we're not doing that well either. They call it the stained-glass ceiling." I give a wry smile and Faith smiles back sympathetically sensing my disappointment.

"What did the 2018 update find?"

"It followed up on the Anglican bishops. I remember Bishop Penny saying she was disappointed all the time she was bishop – and it was 14 years – she was the only woman in the House of Bishops in New Zealand. She also commented on her retirement that there wasn't a female bishop to whom she could 'pass on the mantle' as it were. There's something very interesting here." I turned the laptop round and scrolled down into the updated section. "While you read it, I'll get more drinks – coffee again for you?"

"Chocolate please," says Faith absently as she moves to read the screen.

> ..., after 1993, women's ordained roles in the churches developed further, yet in most cases women continued to be poorly represented in elite church leadership. Anglican women bishops in New Zealand did score more remarkable firsts after Penny Jamieson was consecrated ... Victoria Matthews was the first woman bishop in the Anglican Church of Canada. Elected Bishop of Christchurch in 2008, she served through the devastating earthquakes of 2011 which partially destroyed ChristChurch Cathedral.... Helen-Ann Hartley, the first woman ordained priest in the Church of England to become a bishop, was elected Bishop of Waikato in 2014. In 2017, Eleanor Sanderson became assistant bishop in Wellington, the first woman bishop in that diocese. For 29 years, however, the New Zealand house of bishops

mostly included only one woman at a time, adding to the women bishops' isolation.

I return just as Faith raises her head from the laptop. "I see what you mean," she says.

"See Helen-Ann Hartley there? She was made Bishop of Ripon back in England in 2018 so she and Eleanor Sanderson didn't really overlap. Eleanor has just been made Bishop of Hull in Yorkshire so that has left no Pākehā women bishops in 2022, though a Māori woman was made bishop in 2019. I was shocked to read she was the first NZ born woman bishop – all the others had come from the UK or Canada."

"It's the old token woman thing, isn't it? Don't let women get any support from the power of numbers!" comments Faith, looking up to thank the server who's arrived with her chocolate and my hazelnut latte.

"On the other hand, a 95-year-old former parishioner of mine said when I left that parish that she hoped the next minister would be a woman as women knew how to do ministry best. So that's a vote of confidence."

"It is!" Faith is looking tired and, feeling the familiar tide of depression beginning to rise, I turn the conversation. "What did you think of the pageantry for the state funeral?" I ask.

Faith face lights up. "I couldn't believe all the work and time that must have gone into the preparation! So many people involved in so many details."

I nod, smiling at her enthusiasm. "Yes. I had wondered what was the difference between a state and ordinary funeral but it was obvious. Mainly lots and lots and lots of bands and soldiers, Air Force personnel and sailors marching."

"The job I'd have liked was where those guards kept on collecting the bearskins from the bearer party – off and then on again and then off again. Like an elaborate kind of coat check job." Faith grins.

"Won't see that again in our lifetime is what everyone's saying. It's true."

"We may see other things – just as amazing," says Faith, slurping the rest of her chocolate and packing up. "Hey in that update, there's mention of another Burning Bush report on how regular women ministers were finding their job. Can we look at those next time?"

I am amazed her tired brain had noticed that detail. "Sure thing. I'll look them out. I think I've got copies of both. See you next time then. Any assignments to negotiate? No? Great. You can catch up on that sleep your T shirt is recommending!" Faith laughs as she leaves the booth.

The dinner party – ended?

"It's been a lovely party." "Marvellous!"
"Such wonderful conversation."

    "I've found out so much from talking with you all."
    "I feel better about being a woman now."
    "I feel *proud* to be a woman." "Does it have to end?"

Judy Chicago gathered women about her triangular table
at her Dinner Party, thrilling and surprising us
with the number of women she discovered, resurrected,
uncovered.

At this more modest gathering
we too have recovered, named,
celebrated with and cried for women
who for generations have been reduced
to a few words or a sentence or two
women who, we could say, were 'raped by the pen.'

The conversation sparkled
as we sat about the table of biblical texts.
The heady wine of sisterhood flowed
as we moved from course to course,
the healthy food sustaining tired bodies,
sick of fighting the fight for human status
gratefully relaxing In the warm atmosphere of approval
in this room where it was safe to think and even to speak

This party is over, tugging on coats we call our goodbyes,
"Phone me."

    "You must come and see me soon."
        "I'll send you that address."
           "See you tomorrow."
                "What about lunch sometime?"

Yes, yes, we must phone
and call and see and lunch
write and talk, remind and support.
For as we continue the fight to be human
we need each other to remind each other
of the women we celebrated at this party around this table.

Let this not be the last supper
but the breaking of our fast
at the beginning of a new day.

15 – Women of The Burning Bush after 25 years

The next fortnight, however, did not find Faith and me in *The Cup* enjoying hazelnut lattes. Faith had texted to say sorry, but she'd forgotten it was the university's pre-exam break and she had said she would go home. She was studying and helping with her parents' 40th wedding anniversary celebration. Faith and her twin brother Mark were organising the party.

"It just went out of my mind about it being a clash," she explained when I phoned her as she'd asked. "There'll be time on Thursday to talk if you would like us to zoom," she adds. "I'm interested in that burning bush report and I'll be deep in exams when I get back the following week so I won't be able to take a break then."

So come Thursday here we are sitting at our laptops. Faith is sitting cross legged on her bed with her laptop in her lap. I can never work out how the generation younger than I can do that and not end up with pins and needles and worse! I have prudently been across the street and made sure I did not miss out on my hazelnut latte, beside now me in my eco cup.

"Hi!" I say as we see each other's faces appear on our respective screens. "Chrissie at *The Cup* asked me where Faith was today! You are officially missed."

"That's lovely," replies Faith. She sees my cup. "What are you drinking?"

"Hazelnut."

"That's not fair! We're not close enough to a coffeeshop here in the country. I had one yesterday in a shop in town, but I'm having tea today, since Mum and Dad's taste in coffee is economic rather than flavourful!" She grins a wry grin. I remember visits home myself. I particularly remembered clearing out my parent's kitchen cupboards when they downsized. All the various coffee-makers we children had bought over successive coffee fashions were there, looking mostly unused.

"I hear you, I hear you," I reply, smiling and wafting my cup under my nose just to make her more jealous.

"Stop that!" Faith was not amused. "Tell me about the burning bush. Does that refer in any way to the Moses incident?"

"Indirectly, yes. The burning bush is a symbol or logo of the Presbyterian denomination, I suppose to say the church will not be consumed. That's why this report on women ministers in the Presbyterian Church of New Zealand is called *Women of the Burning Bush*.[159] I'm not particularly pushing Presbyterianism, but their story is a good example of the way a mainstream church governed by tiers of councils and committees makes its decisions about letting a group in to the institution which they have previously excluded."

"The point of the Burning Bush metaphor is that it was not consumed in the fire. So, I think it could stand too for all those women who, though they went through fire of different sorts serving the church, yet were not entirely consumed. You know all the things women do besides official ministry: cake stalls, jumble sales, knitting, missionary support, fundraising, catering, looking out for those who are shut in, child teaching and minding. 'Ladies a plate please.' All that stuff which quietly keeps church communities going. Though if I'm honest, I think sometimes women did get close to being consumed by all the pressure." I shake my head to banish the memories.

"However, I digress. Churches like Church of Christ and Baptists can make their decisions a little more autonomously at the local level. Anglican and Catholic systems have the bishops, archbishops and/or the Pope in control of such decisions."

"I'm learning slowly how the different churches work their governance. It's all quite different from what I've been used to."

"In academic theology how the church works is called ecclesiology – maybe you'll come across that paper some time."

"How do you spell that?" Faith asks, scribbling quickly. "So who ordered this report for the pressies?"

"It was inspired by the 25th anniversary of women's ordination. Researcher Vivienne Adair was asked to survey women ministers in 1991." I looked up to see Faith counting on her fingers. "The rule was passed in 1964 and the first woman minister was Margaret Reid Martin who was already a deaconess."

"What was a deaconess and how were they trained?" Faith asks.

"Deaconesses were first used in Dunedin from 1901, when Irish-born Rev Rutherford Waddell asked for a deaconess to come from Melbourne, Australia.[160] I'll send you a link to the NZ Dictionary of Biography where there's a piece on him. This part is especially interesting. Listen."

> Waddell played a leading part in exposing sweated labour in Dunedin (he himself had worked long hours for nothing as a draper's apprentice in Banbridge). In September 1888 he delivered a sermon at St Andrew's Church on the 'sin of cheapness', arguing that a lust for bargains was forcing prices down to a point where wages fell below subsistence level. In November he took the matter to the Synod of the Presbyterian Church of Otago and Southland and a motion was passed deploring the existence of sweating in New Zealand. The press took up the matter and revealed cases of sweating in Dunedin. His blend of prophetic passion and skilful use of the press and public meetings led in 1890 to a royal commission on sweating on which he served. Its recommendations were an important part of the foundation for the social legislation of the 1890s. Waddell believed that trade unions were an essential part of reform: he became the first president of the Tailoresses' Union of New Zealand from 11 July 1889…

"Wow! He sounds quite a guy. I'll look him up." Faith scribbled in a reference.

"He was. Christabel Duncan whom he had brought over to New Zealand was the first deaconess in a NZ Presbyterian Church. Two more followed in other churches the next year, an Australian and a New Zealand woman. Adair notes here one minister said he was not worried about the deaconesses' training but, 'I want a person who can go into the homes of the richest and the poorest of my congregation and be equally at home in either.'"[161]

"In 1903, the Church opened a Training Institute in Dunedin. The report lists what they studied compared with the men training for ministry. Initially very practically based and taught by volunteers, by 1947 there was a General and an Advanced Course for university graduates. The advanced course could be with languages or not. It was generally thought the women would not be interested in studying the biblical languages."

"Really," said Faith dryly.

"While they studied some courses alongside the men, they were not eligible for prizes or scholarships.[162] Professor Ian Breward comments there was uneasiness in the church at the time seeing this expanding of women's role in the church as 'dangerous precedents.'"[163]

"Ha ha!" laughs Faith. "Little did they know they were completely right! When did the debate about women being ordained as ministers get going?"

"Overseas debate was happening by 1936. WWII changed women's participation in paid work but this was only seen as temporary because women's place was still seen to be the home."[164]

"Did the number of deaconesses keep on increasing?" Faith asks.

"Yes, by 1943, it says here there were 40 of them. Deaconesses weren't allowed to sit on parish Session even though they often did most of the pastoral work in the parishes. Yvette – you know that friend of mine – was doing some research on the deaconesses. She had steam coming out her ears the other day as she found out how some of them were treated." I grin at Faith. She knows my friend Yvette.

Faith is not smiling back as she responds, "Why does that not surprise me? Did the debate about elders and ministers keep going?"

"Debate about women being elders progresses in the 1950s. Interesting stats here: women communicant members were twice the number of men in 1953, (the year Queen Elizabeth was crowned), but women were not approved to be ordained as elders until 1955. The first three attended the 1957 General Assembly.[165] The thinking of the supporters of women ministers figured women would benefit from being able to serve as an elder first, getting to know how governance worked through Session before they had to lead one as minister."

"Of course, that makes sense," mused Faith, sipping her tea.

"There was quite the debate on women's ordination as ministers and some pretty silly arguments against it. Like the one that women wouldn't be able to understand the Westminster Confession."

"What's the Westminster Confession? "asks Faith, her brow wrinkling.

"It's a confession of faith. Actually, a small booklet with several chapters, written in 1646. The Scottish church (which was Presbyterian) hoped the English church (the Anglicans) would sign up to it so both

England and Scotland would be Presbyterian. The English rejected it while Scotland adopted it."

"Oh," muses Faith. "Is that why Church of England means Anglican but the Church of Scotland is Presbyterian?"

"How did you work that out?" I ask, surprised she knew that distinction.

Faith grins. "I wasn't sleeping while the accession ceremony was going on for Charles III! He had to sign a document saying he would preserve the Church of Scotland and the commentators were explaining the difference between the two Churches. He's the Defender of the Anglican Faith, but he has to preserve the Church of Scotland. It was a great big document! So, the pressies tried in 1647 to bring the Anglicans over, but didn't manage it?"

"No. The Westminster Confession is what we call in our church a subordinate standard of belief, that is, the Bible is the supreme "rule of life and faith" but the Westminster Confession comes next, but is subordinate to the Bible in importance. Ministers and elders sign up to it along with a newer expression of faith accepted only a few years ago."[166]

Faith laughs, "it's ironic that argument was used in the 1960s against women ministers because it seems to me that a lot of people would now find a 17th century theological document hard to understand!"

"You're right!" I reply. "It's a very Calvinist document, written by followers of Jean Calvin about a century after he lived, and you know what followers of a great person are. They sometimes say that Calvinists are more Calvinist than Calvin. Oh, I should check. You know about Calvin? Jean Calvin, French reformer, not Calvin Klein, American fashion designer." I add with a grin.

"Duh!" says Faith, grinning back.

"This Calvin was born early in the 16th century and died in 1564 just after the Church of Scotland was first inaugurated. He was a great influence on John Knox, the Scottish reformer and other protestant reformers."

"I've heard just a little about him. He's come up in Theology 101 when some of the theories about salvation were discussed. That's a long time for a church to be established, since the 1600s. The Brethren movement didn't really get going until the 19th century.[167] Looks like a side trip into the histories of both the Open Brethren and Gospel Halls and into Presbyterians and their confessions and churches might be a good thing to do some day when I've got nothing to do."

"Well, if you think you might ever want to jump ship in any future you might envisage, knowing what ship you're leaving and exactly which ship you're boarding would be a good idea."

"Mmmm," murmurs Faith, eyebrow raised. It is apparent the thought has crossed her mind.

"Just saying," I reply with my hands up in the air.

"Now, back to women ministers in the Presbyterian Church. Several deaconesses transferred to the ministry and were required to take different extra courses depending on previous qualifications and training. Then women began applying for training for the Ministry of Word and Sacrament (as it's called by Presbyterians) during the latter half of the 1960s. By 1970 the Deaconess College was being closed. Another five years later, the whole idea of deaconesses was 'terminated.' They list here the areas in which deaconesses had worked: "parishes, youth department, Māori mission, new housing areas, social service, Christian education and in various capacities in overseas mission."[168]

"That's a lot of different areas. How did the transition seem to the women who'd chosen originally to take the deaconess style of role?" asks Faith, thoughtfully.

"There's an interesting paragraph here in the report about that."

> For some then there was a reluctance to give up freedom to do "their own thing," there was a fear of loss of identity, and of being moulded to one parish "model" instead of the wide-ranging tasks which had been available to the Order of Deaconesses. Some of this reluctance is in recognition of both the dangers and the opportunities of not having many role models in the ministry to guide them in their use of power, and the struggle to be accepted as having the right to authority.[169]

"That's quite nuanced, isn't it," comments Faith. "There's a lot in that statement. What about the Church as a whole? Once the decision was made was everything OK, you know, full steam ahead?"

"In fits and starts. My mother-in-law remembers her local church looking for a new Session Clerk in the 1970s. The male elders couldn't see anyone suitable in the room. The minister turned to her, of the three women elders present, asking if she'd take on the job. There was someone suitable in the room! They'd obviously ordained women elders, but being Session Clerk was another adjustment."

"Adair writes here: "The church in general was (and still is) reluctant to accept women into leadership roles." She quotes a church report I remember reading when I was doing some research into this. It damns the whole idea with faint praise."

> *Relatively few women* are likely to possess the needed qualities and to feel the call to the office of the ministry; but *some* women may have both the will and the qualities …(therefore) in the view of the equal spiritual status of men and women in the Christian society … (the *church should not*) exclude women solely on the grounds of sex … the admission of women to the ministry may well enrich the church.[170] (Report author's emphasis)

I look up to see Faith rolling about on her bed laughing.

"Oh dear!" She gasps. "I see what you mean about 'faint praise.' We could add at the end of that paragraph, '…but we don't think so!' I wonder what kind of women they imagined the 'relatively few' would look and act like."

"The same committee made this statement also about how men are better suited to the ministry because they are, quote, "…more fair-minded and more independent in judgement. He is often able to make far reaching decisions and is thus a more natural leader. However, some women could learn to be leaders."[171]

"…but we doubt it!" Faith retorts, still wryly amused. "So little change at the time then?"

"Yes. Slowly, ambivalent attitudes changed for some, but Adair points out 25 years later that the church still remained ambivalent in 1991. Women's training followed a more pastoral bent and when women showed interest in postgraduate work, the church was surprised."[172]

"So, the church didn't change much of its structures even though a quite different group of candidates were being accepted?" Faith asks.

"Yes. That was also true when a large influx of Pacific Island ministry students suddenly arrived in the early 1970s too. That's a whole other story with great similarities. In connection with your question, this introductory chapter ends with a very relevant 1977 quote from two feminist writers – the writers would be sad to know this quote is still relevant today."

> Is it enough simply to be incorporated into the paradigm of ordained ministry, shaped by males for many hundreds of years, in hierarchical moulds, intended to exclude women? Or must women by their very presence re-shape the ministry into forms that are more open, pluralistic and dialogic?[173]

"Mmmm," murmurs Faith. She's commented on how 'male' the high school and university systems seemed to her after having been home-schooled by her mother for a large part of her schooling. She understands that paragraph.

"This also reminds me of an article I came across when I was researching this topic for postgraduate study. A scholar Mark Chaves wrote on what he called, 'The Symbolic Significance of the Women's Ordination.'[174] He reckons that if women are admitted to some position like minister or priest, it is more because the denomination wants to be seen getting on board with society's more liberal attitudes rather than because they are convinced about women being good ministers. This means when the new group get ordained, they find the attitudes inside the church have not changed much."

"Interesting. Makes sense." Faith nods. "That introduction helps to place what it was like in the 1960s as women started taking up the regular ministry. What did the researcher find? You might need to give me the edited version, as the family's going out for dinner in an hour's time."

"There's a summary at the back. Let me find it…" I flick through to the end of the report. "Oh yes."

"First, it's stated that she feels the Presbyterian Church is fortunate to have such great women ministers. But then she writes 'and secondly a profound sadness that the church as a body and as individuals can in the 1990s be the source of such pain.'"[175]

"She goes on to say that if what the women ministers bring to the church is going to be utilised, then 'structures, processes and attitudes' need to be examined at all levels of the Church. Some women are more interested in community mission than parish maintenance and others in postgraduate study. The researcher thinks new recognition structures might be needed for this. Also, she mentions that the call system disadvantages women."

I turn the page. "Here it's said that 'in many ways the women have identified a double bind. They need support in what has often been an alienating environment, but if they group together, it can be interpreted as elitism or separatist practice.'[176] It's all made more complicated by the fact that not all the women agree with each other and some feel left out of the group or not supported by the group."

"The writer picks up that some women have been surprised by how they have been able to serve and accomplish. They are happy to move slowly on matters of greater acceptance. But listen to this comment…"

> Whereas others are saying we can't wait any longer; we have the authority of God and want to get on with the job on equal terms. This second group of women see that they could easily be trapped into a feminised pastoral box which people are comfortable with. It would be much easier to survive by acquiescing to the stereotypical model by focusing on pastoral skills rather than the development of a critical philosophy of faith and theology. It is easier for women to 'domesticate' rather than to be prophetic or scholarly in ways that are strong.[177]

"Mmmm," murmurs Faith who has been listening intently. "So that's how it felt after 25 years. It's now what, over 50 years since 1965? Has any follow-up been done?"

"It has." I nod.

"Maybe they found things had improved?"

"We can find out next time we meet. Will your exams be over in a fortnight? Will we meet again the Thursday following exams? Will you be in town?"

"Yes, I've got a mid-semester research position, so I'll be in town flogging the books in a different way – and getting paid for it!" Faith replies. "Might need to arrange a different time with working and all, but I'll be in touch."

"Ok, have a good family dinner tonight!"

"I hope so," replies Faith as we each click 'leave the meeting' and the screen goes blank. I wonder if Faith will like the 50-year summary any better. I look at the last sentence in the report "…the energy put into effecting change is energy diverted from the central and urgent task of ministering."[178] Too right!

The woman came

A hymn about encounter

1. The woman came along that day
   for water from the well
   The other women had gone home,
   They didn't want to know her well
   She was left out, all alone,
   she was left out, alone.

2. She found a stranger sitting there,
   on her well's stony rim.
   He was a man, and she was not,
   she didn't think she'd talk to him
   He and her sort didn't talk,
   he and her sort don't talk.

3. But they discussed and argued long
   on water, life, and prayer.
   He challenged her, she challenged him,
   they met, connected then right there;
   Things would never be the same,
   they'd never be the same.

4. We do not know what encounters wait
   to meet us on our way.
   How strangers can reset our lives,
   how we can learn anew each day
   that the Spirit is within,
   the Spirit is within.

Words: Susan Jones, Progressing the Journey 2022
Music: Repton WOV 519(ii)

16 – Women of The Burning Bush after 50 years

During the next two weeks I notice a lot of stressed students walking about campus. Some of the older people in the congregation took up jobs at this time of year supervising examinations and they were busy too.

Then Faith got in touch. She explained her research job was 9 to 5 each weekday so Thursday afternoons were out, but how did I feel about Saturday morning ("Not too early," she added).

The Saturday after exams we meet at *The Cup*. Faith looks a bit pale but is smiling and her bright red T-shirt reflects an upbeat mood. 'I may be wrong, but it's highly unlikely,' it proclaims. Faith notices me looking at it. "My twin brought this home from his last holiday," she tells me. "He's got one the same!"

I laugh. "I don't think the girl I met at Jane's party would have worn that T-shirt in public," I say. "You've come a long way, Faith!"

Faith looks a little surprised and then agrees. "I think you're right. It seems to have happened naturally though," she replies. "I did feel when I was home that it seemed different from at the beginning of the year. We were so busy with the celebrations though, we didn't get time to talk much about religious stuff."

"How did you find the Gospel Hall on the Sunday?" I ask, very curious to know the answer.

"We didn't go!" Faith gives a wry smile. "We had so many relations staying and someone had to be taken to the airport on Sunday morning. I must admit I was a little relieved."

We talk a bit more about her research job which she was enjoying heaps and about the special commemorative service we'd held at my church that weekend. Saturday seemed to be a more relaxed time and I have almost forgotten why we are here when Faith brings us back to the point.

"Tell me about the Burning Bush women part II," she says. "Any better news than in 1991?"

"The report is online, so I'll send you the link, but here is a graph showing the timeline of when the women responding to the study were ordained." I click and scroll and turn the laptop so Faith can see the screen.

"I looked at the church's ordination records from 1965 to 2009. First deaconesses provided the numbers in the 1960s and 1970s, then there's a bit of a slump until Community Based Ministry Training started in the 1990s. A rough estimate shows women as 5% of those being ordained in the second half of the 1960s, 17.2% in the 1970s, 12.5% in the 1980s, 23.8% on the 1990s and 22.2% in the 'noughties of the new millennium.' Up till that point, we hadn't made a quarter of the numbers of ministers even though there are more female members in the church than males."

"Did women report feeling isolated without women colleagues near them? Those low numbers suggest that women would be sparsely scattered throughout the country," comments Faith. She sips her trim flat white. "Ah! That's good. Boy, did I miss coffee when I was home!"

"That's very perceptive of you, Faith." I comment in return. "There were a lot of comments about lack of collegial support."

"Are these women being received better than the women in the first 25 years?" Faith asks.

"In the summary the researcher says this, 'The overall impression is of a highly committed strong and resilient group of women who are passionate about the path to which they have been called.' She adds, however that there was '…still some dissatisfaction with the status of women in the church.'"[179]

"Hmm. After 50 years!" exclaims Faith.

"She does report that there was 'Increasing acceptance of women as competent ministers' but there were still areas of leadership in which women were poorly represented. That's positions like Presbytery Moderator and the national church Moderator and also senior minister positions."[180]

"What concerns were the conclusions focused on?" Faith had her head down, stirring the remaining froth in her cup so I couldn't gauge her reaction to the comments about leadership.

"Five areas. Here they are in these bullet points."

- The safety of women to say what they believe and feel
- The emotional and physical safety of women in the church

- The lack of women in training and leadership roles
- The need for women to be seen in places of leadership within regional and national bodies
- The need to address inequalities of systems which benefit some and exclude others.

Faith's head comes up as she listens to the list. "Some of those are pretty basic problems – safety? Emotional and Physical safety? That's very concerning. Is that what the recommendations focus on?"

I look through the following pages.

"Not quite, though close. The recommendation areas were developed by the oversight group after the report had been presented to them. They came up with..."

> The reform of governance and management... Identification and compliance with Health and Safety issues ...Identification and support for addressing issues specific to women ministers of Māori, Pasifika and Migrant ethnicity ... Valuing and Increasing the contribution of women in church leadership and training ... Mentoring women into and through ministry ...That training institutions demonstrate and teach gender equality.[181]

"You might like to download the document and ask your Aunt Hazel if she thinks these issues have been addressed in her experience as a woman minister in the church."

"Good idea," replies Faith "I've been meaning to get in touch with her and chew over some of what you and I have been talking about. She's in England on study leave at the moment, studying something called Fresh Expressions but she'll be home soon."

"There are lots of individual women's comments in the report which you may find good value. There's an ending paragraph which makes interesting reading."

> Women ministers in general are highly satisfied that they are where they are called to be and are able to make a difference to those who are the recipients of their ministry. There is evidence of commitment and innovation in their teaching and preaching and in their approach to service. Some women ministers work outside the confines of their parish and/or within secular institutions and all are committed to spreading the love of God.[182]

"That sounds encouraging," responds Faith. "It will be interesting to see what some of those safety issues are and what they meant about collegiality being thin on the ground. You were a minister during almost exactly these 25 years – what is your memory of it?"

I think for a moment. I had read the report with a sinking kind of feeling. One thing I had realised reading the various comments was that I was one of the woman ministers who had tried very hard – was trying very hard – to fit into the 'male' system. If I was honest, I looked around to see what behaviour 'worked' and did my best to comply with that. I supposed it was a continuation of the pressure I had felt as a little child to conform and comply.

Over the years as I worked in therapy, I found that was due to an early abandonment experience. So as not to be abandoned again, I worked hard to make sure I would be approved of and included.

I said something of this to Faith. She nodded with an empathetic look in her eyes. "I know what you mean about wanting to fit in and not to rock the boat. That was a very strong feeling for me when my twin Mark and I were running the young group. I got annoyed that he was listened to over me but didn't feel brave enough to protest. I figured since we were twins from the same family where we had always been treated the same, our ideas were equally valuable. I found they weren't thought to be that in the church. Did that kind of treatment make your ministry quite miserable?"

I think again for a moment before I reply. "Not miserable, but I frequently felt isolated. Other more conservative ministers laughed and joked together when we were in Presbyterian cluster groups. Particularly when you were the only woman minister in a local Minister's Association, the jokes were more blokey and 'in-house' than I was used to. Not crude, just like they were on another planet somehow."

"Mars, perhaps," quips Faith with that same empathetic grin.

"Maybe!" I chuckle back at her.

"I remember too one Presbytery meeting when a younger woman was present. She was an intern and I had known of her before. I was keen to say hello and talk with her, but I could sense complete indifference. It might have been theology, I was known by then as someone who spoke out on gay issues, or it might have been generational, I don't know. I remember feeling disappointed that there was obviously not going to be any collegiality there. It might have been my fault. I'm an introvert at heart and maybe I don't give welcoming signals back to people who want to talk with me!"

I hasten to add another thought. "I do enjoy the actual ministering. I particularly enjoy putting services together, some people call it curating a service these days. I also enjoy the thinking which you need to do before preaching. Latterly, I love networking and putting like-minded people together. Also, in the second half of my ministry I'm enjoying talking with people about how their faith doesn't work anymore and what can be done about that."

"Like you did with Hope."

"Yeah. That first book was all about that."

"And you work with a lot of gay young people too, I've heard from Charity about how you helped her work out what the church was doing."

"True. That experience produced book number two. I suppose I do more than I always remember, looking back. Thanks for reminding me. Ministry is a very ephemeral occupation when it comes to solid evidence of what you've done with your time. Perhaps I should have gone into coffee shop chaplaincy!"

As we laugh together, Faith catches sight of the over-size café clock and gasps. "Oh! I'd better go. I'm staying at Lisa's flat for the break and we're going grocery shopping. Thank you for meeting me on Saturday. I do appreciate it. All the best for tomorrow."

"Thanks, " I say. I am touched she has remembered that the service the next day had not only a baptism but also reception of new members as well as communion. "All the best with the shopping." I laugh, knowing she knows I know they will sort it beautifully. Faith laughs in return and grabs the brightly coloured shopping bags she brought in with her. "Bye!"

Thoughts on Psalm 131

Today I spent time with
a carload of young ministers,
strong, confident,
purposeful.
They seemed to have a goal
an aim to strive for.

Oh, they had frustrations, barriers, blocks to battle,
but the strength of purpose
of all
showed through.

They had attractive personalities ready to laugh at themselves
ready to pick up the meanings behind words
aware of nuances
expressions,
eager to serve even to the point of exhaustion.

They were all women like me.

I sat there and envied them.
Not the job, the study, the position,

 but the sense of purpose
 the identifiable vocation
 the common understanding
 the 'in-house' camaraderie
 they had together.

They had found their 'place.'
It was a place others could identify.
They know and are known as what they are.

What am I?
I'm to be,
but what am I to be?
or
is it who am I to be?
Just 'being' seems too nebulous.
I muse on it through the night,
then, in the morning
I am pointed back to my task

'have no lofty ambitions'
'do not look too high'
'enough for you to keep your soul tranquil and quiet
like a child in its mother's arms'

Mother God, you know the state of my heart and soul.
You know that above all
I desire to do your will
not my wishes.

Take my lofty ambitions
turn them into tranquillity and quiet
keep my eyes from looking too high
turn them inward instead.
Hold me in your arms, until I rest in you,
tranquil ... quiet…serene,
content to be with you.

And, patient God prepare yourself
to teach me this lesson
again and again and again

Susan Jones [183]

• • •

I note now that my readiness to disdain being ambitious was typical of the self-deprecation I fell into more frequently at that time.

When I printed and published the poem, in 1990, however, along with other reflections from an extended period of Chronic Fatigue Syndrome, I received an answer from one of the women who'd been in the carload of young ministers. These two poems together express some of the ambivalence of women training for ministry in the 1980s and 90s. (The ministry experiences of that carload of ministers would be reflected in the second report *Women of the Burning Bush*, rather than the first.)

Poem to....

Today I spent time with your poems,
I browsed, smiled, a-ha'ed,
felt,
shared them with a broken friend

One poem startles,
frightens.
It's about me
and my friends.

I remember that day,
it was hot.
In the cool of the evening
we stopped at Top View
and rested
in the green spaciousness
looked toward the mountains

We were so tired
weary of the struggle
bombarded by alien words
alien thoughts.

Some of us
had jobs to go to
some didn't.
All of us at sea
wondering if ministry ...
If.
Ministry,
the 'magic' word
so we make it a noun
be the minister?
Do we make it a verb
do the ministering
and who decides
what
and where?

That day
we had gathered
as a friend had hands laid on.
None of us had had hands laid on
in holy blessing

 anointing
 ordaining

Were we ministers?
Were we ministering in our teaching, our loving, our being
Did we have a place to stand?

You perceived us as a unit
you watched our 'in-house' camaraderie
a camaraderie born of desperation
and in that desperation
did we exclude you
were we unable to share who we really were?

That day
we rested
in the cool of the evening.
You were an important part of that
a locus of sanity in an alien world.

Since then
we have ministered
to others
to each other
most have had hands laid on.
And you,
you have ministered to me
you have emerged

 in your own right

Your being
is important to me.

Yvonne Smith.[184]

17 – *Women's inner voice*

Insights into my own experience in ministry brought to the surface by the Burning Bush report continued to haunt me over the next few weeks. Faith was on her break between first and second semesters and we had changed our arrangement to meeting when she returned to uni study. This didn't stop me thinking.

I could see ways in which adapting to the prevailing genre of ministry (a mostly male-conceived model) was productive. When the gender of the minister in front of you was different, I could see it helped if she did much the same thing your previous male minister had done. I could also see ways in which I had done the 'same' thing, but in quite a different tone or style.

I had to face however, that I had carried with me, for too many years, my own internalised misogyny. A world class snowboarder showcased on television recently had expressed hope her success helped girls beginning the sport to expect they could do well. She wanted them, she said, to be able to follow their own call to snowboarding without being put off by their 'internalised misogynistic voices.'

If a woman ventured into formerly forbidden territory marked as out of bounds for women because of misogyny, it is not surprising misogyny still monitors her movement within the new territory – either her own, or others.'

As a middle class, well-educated woman in an equalitarian country, I had my troubles, but intersectionality theory reminded any thinking feminist that add in race and class and difference in ethnicity and the troubles were compounded.

All maturing adults, female or male have the developmental task of working out what voices they will follow. There are parental cautions and warnings from childhood, authoritative and authoritarian voices of teachers, ministers and youth leaders. There are professional rules which accompany the acquisition of jobs and progress in careers. They jostle in our heads, some more deeply ingrained than others, depending on the importance of the person who has instilled them or the trauma of the circumstances.

It's well known to those entering contemplative lifestyles that once you manage to get to a quiet place, quieten yourself, and sit still for more than a minute, your mind suddenly erupts in chatter. All sorts of thoughts wrestle with each other for your attention. It may be as simple as the shopping list for the supermarket. It can be as earth shattering as how your relationship is faring. It can be the good old Protestant work ethic or Catholic guilt that asks you why you are sitting here doing 'nothing' when there is 'work' to be done.

I remember being relieved when Brother Laurence Freeman simply advised beginning meditators to keep on starting again when their mind wandered. He instructed them to pull their minds back to quiet stillness and begin again and again and again and again if necessary. (I found it was necessary). In a wider sense, however, thoughts wrestle for attention all the time in our day-to-day lives. More stillness in everyone's life would be a benefit, I thought, as a hymn floated through my mind.

'Let us reach down deep inside us'

A hymn about finding the Self within

1. Let us reach down deep inside us
   to the place where quiet reigns;
   Find the Self who lives inside us,
   knows our joy and knows our pains:
   Let our ego stand aside there,
   shadow sharing space with light.
   Let our inner selves rejoice
   at how Love shines in darkest night.

2. Wind and fire and earthquake pass
   but Spirit is not found in them;
   Still, small voice is hardly heard,
   but brings Love which does not condemn.
   In lives buffeted by windstorms,
   rocked by quakes and scorched by fire,
   stillness brings surprising solace
   as we find there, hearts' desire.

3. Sacred calm means minds can settle,
   hearts grow quiet, souls grow still;
   Busy thinking slows its rhythm,
   gives compassion chance to fill.
   Even long-forgotten scars heal
   as new balm brings a new way;
   Every space and every crevice fills
   as Love arrives to stay [185]

There is a special set of competing ideas attached to spiritual and religious activities. We have been told a lot about God and what the divine being expects. If we venture out of our cathedral, church, chapel, or local Gospel Hall of origin then we'll have heard many different versions of what the Holy One desires of us. The simplest perhaps is from the prophet Joel: "To do justice, love mercy and walk humbly with your God."

But put that apparently simple statement into your seething mind and there are many supplementary questions – what is 'justice' and 'justice' for whom? What does 'mercy' mean and what does 'loving it' mean and again, 'mercy' for whom? The word 'humbly' catches the eye also. What does it mean to be 'humble'? It was Charles Dickens who has his smarmy Uriah Heep say:

When I was quite a young boy," he tells David Copperfield, "I got to know what umbleness did, and I took to it. I ate umble pie with an appetite. I stopped at the umble point of my learning, and says I, 'Hard hard!' When you offered to teach me Latin, I knew better. 'People like to be above you,' says father, 'keep yourself down.' I am very umble to the present moment, Master Copperfield, but I've got a little power![186]

I remember as a teenager realising that I metaphorically treated young men the way a taller girl might treat a dancing partner, dancing with her knees slightly bent so she would not embarrass him – or herself. I thought that was a metaphor for humility. It was only later I came across this saying which I wrote into my commonplace book.

The true way to be humble is not to stoop until you are smaller than yourself, but to stand at your real height against some higher nature that will show you what the real smallness of your greatness is.[187]

Even this definition which comforted the teenage me, insists that there is a 'higher nature' against which we will look 'really small.' Maybe this definition is better.

Although humility is commonly equated with a sense of unworthiness and low self-regard, true humility is a rich, multifaceted construct that is characterized by an accurate assessment of one's characteristics, an ability to acknowledge limitations, and a "forgetting of the self."[188]

The problem though with this definition is the 'accurate assessment.' When have women had truly accurate assessments of their characteristics reflected back to them? When have we NOT been told we are too curvy, too loud, too bossy? When have we been told we are creative, helpfully assertive and smart in ways uncontaminated with envy or jealousy from women or from men?

Once your mother tells you not to get too bossy or you won't get married, you check yourself for a long time afterwards when you are feeling assertive in activities where potential partners are present.

With all the voices coming to us from the external world, it is very hard to decipher which is our inner voice, the voice of the Spirit of creation which resides in us, the sound of that divine spark within all humanity. When can we hear that voice when it is not drowned out by the socialisation messages, the critical strictures and the sarcastic put-downs?

David Tacey reminds his readers, "Everything Jesus said and did was about one thing: urging us to wake up to the mystery within our lives."[189] He rebuts the common idea of Jesus coming to the world to add to it, or correct us or save us.

> Jesus did not come to put in what God left out, or had taken from us at the Fall. All of this is ideology. Jesus taught how we could awaken ourselves to what God had already invested in our nature. He came to *remind* us that we are made in the image of God... Jesus reminded us of the pre-existing reality of God's abiding presence. This presence was "always already" there, as Derrida put it, and the idea that Christ *is* this presence is idolatry...Jesus did not change the nature of reality, or of God, which is the favoured view of the churches. He pointed to what already exists, not only in "Christians" but in all people. Like Socrates, he asked us to wake up to what is already present in our nature..."[190]

The rhetoric which little girls and young women, spinsters and married women hear throughout their lives tells them frequently they are 'not enough' in some way, or they are 'too much' in others. But Tacey is saying that right from our beginnings we have all that is needed for a spiritual life, we just have to wake up and discover it within ourselves.

Tacey reminds us Jesus said that 'the kingdom of God is within you.'[191] It is within us that we discover a meaningful life. It is within that we discover, "a new centre of authority in the personality." This is not to say that we are divine deep inside – to think this would be thoroughly narcissistic. On the contrary, "there is an interior life which is within, and part of 'ourselves' yet this is also radically other, rightly referred to as the 'not I.'[192]

Tacey argues that the East has a better handle on this reality of spiritual interiority than the West. This leaves us westerners to use the older term 'soul' to explain it.

> The soul is feminine in nature, whereas the spirit tends to be symbolised in myth and religion as masculine. It is the same for men as for women, and thus we are speaking about masculine and feminine archetypes in all people, not about stereotypes of social behaviour...The soul receives the life of spirit into itself,

and when this takes place, the human being is never the same... When spirit enters soul we are called back to the primordial source and made aware of something divine in our midst. Our essential nature is transformed, and we are reborn to a different reality...It is the most "natural" thing in the world for us to be penetrated by spirit and changed into the likeness of our maker but socialisation makes this appear "unnatural, crazy or weird."[193]

There are echoes for me in Tacey's words of the dissonance women often experience when they are wanting to express something of their inner convictions or dreams or desires. They seem crazy or weird to those who are not on the same wavelength, usually those who have not allowed their egos to be marginalised so a new self or 'soul' can take centre stage.

The territory of the soul is characterised by wholeness, a state of mind and heart which, in my observation, tends to come more easily to women once they lay aside the strictures of ego-driven masculine-approved rules.

The liberation within this is that it is not something generated by equally ego-driven feminist ideologues, but something which has been inside women (and also within men) from the beginning of human life on earth. This is not made up, but is being rediscovered.

> The soul institutes a "reign" that is governed by wholeness, and this can capsize the ego, which is wedded to one-sidedness and partial vision. The soul asks the ego to support a wholeness that it can barely comprehend. In this sense, God is not so much a theological abstraction, but a symbol for the unknown life in the psyche and cosmos. ...Through the individuation process, the soul unfolds in the personality and displaces the ego, and here we see the process of incarnation in action.[194]

Individuation, the maturing of the inner self, is an experience of what Jesus called the kingdom and what others call the 'new self.' This wakes up within our personality but has not been seen by us previously. It was already present but unregistered by the ego. "The ego cannot "see" it, which I assume is the real meaning of the miracles in which Jesus enables the blind to *see*."[195]

However put-down, ignored, neglected or abused a woman has been, this self is waiting to be discovered deep within. It is hard to describe, especially if the listeners are still ego driven. "The new self is a liminal reality that acts as a bridge between eternity and time and can only be described by paradox and riddles." [196]

This transformation/discovery process is not easy. Jesus uses the metaphor of being born again to express something of the pain of the birthing journey. It requires a leap of faith. While some of the old rules and restrictions have been irritating and worse, they are nevertheless familiar, and we get rewarded for continuing to obey them in our society. To break free and be transformed into a new person takes effort and courage. It also may surprise us – in a small quiet moment or a large life event. The need for being alert features in more than one of Jesus' parables.

> One cannot plan for this event or schedule it into one's activities for the new self or soul is an autonomous force and the ego can never know when the metanoia will take place. But the more alert one is to this possibility, the more likely it is that when it occurs, one will be prepared and able to cooperate with it. [197]

In the lead-up to our finding our own inner voice and beginning to speak our own language, women begin to realise they have been living not in a world of full and complete reality, but within a particular paradigm. It might be the paradigm of conservative religion. It may be the paradigm of success within a patriarchal free market system. It may be a paradigm of devoted motherhood. It could be the paradigm of unexamined heterosexuality.

Slowly anomalies appear in our paradigm-of-origin. At first, we bat them away, seeing them as distractions one should not entertain for long. Then the anomalies begin to join up. The central arguments of the paradigm begin to be undermined. A life event or reflective moment may then complete the disillusionment. We have an 'aha' moment or what both church and society call an epiphany.

We might get a glimpse of how life is within another paradigm and want that reality more than our current one. Satellite TV and smuggled videocassettes reaching over the Iron Curtain into communist countries challenged acceptance of the communist way of life. It is not dissimilar to the way printed pamphlets, carried village to village during the 16th century Protestant Reformation challenged the thinking of average people. It is very like gains women made in the 19th and 20th centuries which led to other gains in years ahead.

It is so too in private lives. A woman sees through what she thought was an inevitable track for her life. She sees through the brutality of her partner which she had rationalised as love. She realises that study is an option for her too. "One day you finally knew what you had to do, and began, though the voices around you kept shouting their bad advice..." begins Mary Oliver's poem 'The Journey'[198] which visualises the moment when a woman's life is transformed because she leaves the old paradigm and, despite obstacles and fear, walks towards a new one.

Starting anew, beginning a life where you intend to listen and obey only your inner voice, is not easy. A battle ensues between the ego and the new self.

The ego, for women, is the part of us that has been trained well by the world. It keeps us organised so we will be seen as compliant, successful, loving, good, the kind of woman "everyone" likes. The ego does not understand the new priorities of the self. "...the ego is unable to see the point of this wholeness.... The ego's values and attitudes are contradicted and reversed by the new self especially in the early stages of transformation, when the ego doesn't 'get it.'" [199]

What urges us to begin this transformation can be a very small event, sometimes as small as a mustard seed.

> In the course of any life, a person is often alerted to the reality of the new self by seemingly insignificant events. Perhaps it is something that someone says, or a random image that arises in conversation. Perhaps it is a moment of synchronicity when one feels a connection between one's inner life and the world; insignificant to others and almost not worth telling, but it sets off a spiritual journey that leads to the awakening of the new self. ...We are predisposed to be alerted to the new self, and hence the intuitive faculty of the personality is in a state of readiness to external and internal suggestion. The possibilities of initiation are endless, and it is not necessarily an encounter with clergy or scripture that gets us moving.[200]

Well-known scripture passages take on new meanings when this lens is applied to them. The tiny mustard seed becoming a great tree. The acts of seeking, knocking and asking. What is asked for will be given, what is knocked upon will be opened, what is sought for is found. Jesus' distinction about treasures on earth rusting and being eaten and stolen, compared with the treasure of the heart which does not rust, and cannot be stolen from us.

As well, we are reminded that the gate is narrow and the way is hard. Not everyone will take this route. Even among women who have suffered the same trauma and hurt, you may not find them rediscovering their inner self, that internal strength, that small quiet voice. They may not want to take the risk.

When the new self is re-discovered however, life is available, life which is abundant and full. We discover that far from needing to be perfect as we have been told for centuries, we are to rather reach for 'completion', for wholeness.

Or, as Tacey puts it "Jesus' words should be read in this sense: 'You must allow yourself to arrive at an end state; or be brought to completion.'"

This gives a whole new approach and perspective to the idea of religion – not a controlling of our morality, not a forcing of the ego into acceptable behaviour, but a spiritual transformation of our deeply inner self which has been there all the time and only needs to be rediscovered. It is particularly good news for women because it is clear that within them also is this self, waiting to be rediscovered and listened to, to be lavished with care and attention and nourished with tender loving care.

> The primary task of religion is not to appeal to the ego to do what it cannot do, but to activate the second self, by rituals, exercises and psychological transformation. Modern religion is not spiritual enough if it believes that change can come about by preaching to and commanding the ego. The challenge is to lead people into an experience of the spirit, and allow it to change the person from within.[201]

Reading Tacey several years after I first devoured his book – understanding it contained important words for my own journey – I see now that women need to look at the ego somewhat differently from men.

In a patriarchal society, ego carries a connotation of pride. It is true the ego is our organising principle. It holds our personality together. Its rationality and logic help to form useful frameworks for our lives. It is not our ego which is the problem, but our attachment to it. It is this attachment which prevents so many from pushing the ego aside to discover the self within.

The ego for women however is not always about pride but often rather its opposite, self-deprecation, putting yourself down, minimising what you are and what you have done.

If the over-weaning sin of males is pride and for women it is not, this has big theological implications. If it is considered that almost all theology and doctrine have been fashioned by male minds, it follows that their conclusions may not fit women's experience. Valerie Saiving Goldstein looked at this issue in the 1960s.[202]

> It is my contention there are significant differences between masculine and feminine experience and that feminine experience reveals in a more emphatic fashion certain aspects of the human situation which are present but less obvious in the experience of men. Contemporary theological doctrines of love have, I believe, been constructed primarily upon the basis of masculine experience... Consequently, these doctrines do not provide an adequate interpretation of the situation of women nor, for that matter, of men...[203]

She adds a rider to this which shows her view of the state of women in 1960.

> For the temptations of woman as woman are not the same as the temptations of man as man, and the specifically feminine forms of sin – "feminine" not because they are confined to women or because women are incapable of sinning in other ways but because they are outgrowths of the basic feminine character structure – have a quality which can never be encompassed by such terms as "pride" and "will-to-power." They are better suggested by such items as triviality, distractibility, and diffuseness; lack of an organizing center or focus; dependence on others for one's own self-definition; tolerance at the expense of standards of excellence; inability to respect the boundaries of privacy; sentimentality, gossipy sociability, and mistrust of reason -in short, underdevelopment or negation of the self. This list of specifically feminine sins could be extended. All of them, however, are to be understood as merely one side of the feminine coin.[204]

Whatever you think of the specifics of Saiving Goldstein's list of feminine 'sins', her writing demands that we re-think preachers decrying the sin of pride from the pulpit. Are they are speaking appropriately to both genders? It may be that a devout woman who's had all the spirit crushed out of her, is listening. She may conclude the small voice inside urging her to leave her marriage right now, is merely a sinful pride in her own knowing.

Consequently, it is important that women consider their ego with some suspicion. They should listen to its voice sceptically, since for many women the ego has been trained to think in subservient ways. It has been trained to have her look to others for her self-definition. It has her trained to regard her concerns as trivial and her need for self-awareness as rebellion. This type of socialised ego definitely needs to be pushed aside. The still small voice within can then be heard and can be allowed to increase in volume and urgency.

This still small voice within is not a creation of greedy and aggressive radical-thinking women. It has been within the female soul from birth. It needs rediscovery, not creation. It needs encouragement, not disguise. It needs us to notice it and pay attention, no matter how loudly our own ego or other's egos protest.

How was I going to put all that in a nutshell when I next talked with Faith? I ask myself the question as I check my watch. Ah. I sigh gratefully. Time for my evening meditation. I need it. My still, small voice had had to compete with too many loud thoughts today.

I reach for the candle and my phone, turning to the meditation timing app, and pick up the notebook containing my selection of lead-in prayers and affirmations. Some are liturgies I'd originally written for use with groups and have responses in bold font. I simply change the 'we' to 'I' when I use them in solitude, like tonight. Which one is most appropriate today?

The familiar actions begin the quietening process.

I feel the spirit's peace beginning to settle me.

Stillness threads its way through my body.

I begin.

We have a journey to make
An inner journey circling deep within in labyrinthine style.
We do not need external armour
But internal preparation which protects and guides
as we step on the journey the ancients followed,
continuing it in our time.[205]

• • •

The cosmos can be very, very large
and can be very, very small.

From supernovae and giant nebula in the universe's skies
To quarks and gluons at the atomic level
Its realities baffle and defeat scientific minds
Its beauty defies the skill of artists and poets
Its scale amazes the human mind.

Who are we that any divinity in the world
might be mindful of us or visit us?

Yet we are loved, welcomed and accepted into this world
This world which stretches from visible stars and planets,
to invisible particles and electrons. Amen.[206]

• • •

We trust in Life which never ends.
a flowing, underground aquifer of life,
refreshing and nourishing all who root themselves
in its cool clear water.
We yearn for greening to spring forth
from this Source of Life.
new growth unfolding in human hearts,
despite the drought-stricken deserts which lie around them
and the heart-stopping, bitter cold of evil greed.

We trust that deep down inside us
the aquifer of life flows unendingly,
unpolluted and magnificent,
delicately whispering its loving way
when our wounds need the salve of fresh hope.
We seek the grace to plant ourselves
beside and in this sacred stream of living water
so we too may bear fruit in the season to come.[207]

• • •

We affirm the value of the wild
in people and animals
and plants.
We affirm the importance of all having opportunity
to roam and grow and travel, unhindered and unbound,
to feel wind rushing and water flowing
to feel the rising heartbeat as difficult summits are scaled
and risky journeys undertaken.

We affirm the need of the wildness within us
to have its freedom,
that we do not censor the creative impulse
or quash sudden intuition or divert unusual thought
only to be mannerly and polite.
We affirm the risk inherent in following Jesus
on those wild journeys where he calls us onward,
where we may not find a place to lay our head
nor private nest or den for a hiding place.

We affirm the need to befriend our inner wildness
so we can live and work and play with others
in harmony, not monologue, in dialogue not monotone,
adding zest to our communal life,
each sparking life from the other.
We affirm a person's right to be individual, eccentric,
or unusual,
and pursue their own path in life.[208]

18 – Being Woman in the World

A couple of weeks later, Faith and all the other students were back into their second semester studies. She told me she had chosen a biblical studies paper on hermeneutics ("I've practiced spelling it!" she quipped), a second philosophy paper and a literature paper focusing on the poetic imagination. They sounded like a fascinating mix.

When we first met after the break, I had filled Faith in on my musings about inner voice for women. She listened attentively and asked perceptive questions when something got too complicated to grasp easily. I was very struck by a comment she made as a response.

"You know, had you told me I could trust my own inner voice months ago when we first started talking, I would have thought you were being quite unchristian. I would have thought you were talking about your or mine own wishes and wants and desires and were dressing it up as the voice of God, or God's plan for me."

"I realise now that what I have taken to be God's voice is that trained ego you've just been describing. Some of it is probably truly God, but a lot of it is stuff from my parents just being protective parents. Other voices in there," she taps her head as she continues, "are from the Assembly and I can recognise the difference in that kind of voice more easily now. There are still more voices which just simply kept me in my 'place' well, the 'place' other people thought young girls and women should be if they were going to be good Christians."

"I find I have more trust now, that if I do it carefully, I may be able to hear that still small voice and begin to trust it."

I nod, fascinated by this glimpse into the workings of Faith's mind having heard everything over the past few months.

Faith is on a roll and she carries on talking in a wondering kind of tone.

"I think it was the still small voice that got me the courage to email you and set up an appointment. I'd been having a real tussle with all the thoughts in my head. You know you've got a radical reputation with people like my parents and I've spoken to some evangelical Presbyterians who are not thrilled with your stance over the position of gays in the church."

I grimace inside, but try to keep my face impassive.

Faith ducks her head a little. "Did you know? I thought if you didn't you perhaps should. Forewarned being forearmed as it were." She flushes with embarrassment.

"I suspected it. I guess I haven't had it completely confirmed before." I had known it was inevitable. You couldn't bring up controversial topics at your church's national gathering and have them voted down without making some enemies, I supposed. It didn't feel good though.

"Well my point is that you were not the person whom others would have thought I should talk with. But that small voice inside wouldn't let the idea go away and I felt so good once I had made contact. Despite the guilt and the fear, there was also a feeling I was doing the right thing."

"What would you call that feeling?" I ask, curious to know how Faith would describe a feeling I had had myself many times before.

"I don't know…. calm…. a kind of knowing ….even…perhaps… serenity?" Faith looks a little surprised at the word. It was almost like it had popped out of her mouth without her thinking it first.

"It's good to sit with that feeling and reflect on it, so you'll recognise it next time. When you have a difficult tussle with what to do and you make a choice, look for that feeling. It's a kind of non-verbal inner voice. We sometimes would call it a gut feeling. It kind of feels like the weather might be stormy but your ducks are all lined up and swimming through the turbulent water in their row."

"Yeah! A lot like that!" responds Faith.

"When you think about the women we have talked about – some of them will have had that feeling too when they did a difficult thing. Think of Tamar when she decided to dress as a prostitute and waylay Judah. She must have been so nervous and scared, yet she had an inner conviction that it was the right thing to do."

"And she was vindicated in that later by Judah!" Faith exclaims.

"Yes. The same with Rahab and Ruth. They did hard things, but must have been sure they should do them. How many other voices inside them would be telling them the opposite – "Stay home, Ruth! Go back home like Orpah!" and "Send those spies away, Rahab. You're being watched all the time by the city guards. Don't risk it."

"But they tussled their way through and made it in the end."

"Yes, can you think of any others who might have got through to hear that small voice?"

"There's Vashti and Esther – they risked a lot because they though the principle of what they were doing was important."

"Yes going in to see the king without invitation was death in those times, yet they both did it. You're right, they must have heard that still small voice."

"And," carried on Faith, "Hagar didn't have any decision to make because she was thrown out by Sarah, but when the angel 'spoke' to her, do you think that was actually her still small voice telling her everything would be OK even though it looked hopeless at the time?"

"Maybe. That's an interesting thought. Perhaps, when Jesus was being tempted in the desert before he started his ministry, his ego was speaking the devil's lines and he was answering out of his gut and small voice."

"That's so helpful. Let me see, who else?" Faith thinks hard and flicks over the pages of the notebook she usually scribbles her notes in.

"What about those three women in Luke 8 who leave home and follow Jesus? Your poem brings up lots of good reasons why they would meet opposition to that idea, but they did it. They followed, probably got a bad rep for it too, but they did it."

"And see how important Mary Magdalene, out of that group, became in the early Jesus follower groups and how even now we are encouraged by her being entrusted with Jesus' message for the other disciples."

"That's true," says Faith, "those are the positive stories. What about the *Texts of Terror* type women, though?"

"I was thinking about them the other day when the news broke about that young Iranian woman who was beaten and killed for not wearing her headscarf properly."[209]

"Masha Amini?" Faith asks. "That was terrible. I joined the protest on campus that the Iranian students were holding outside the Vice-Chancellor's office."

"Remember Phyllis Trible said she wrote *Texts of Terror* because of similar everyday experiences contemporary women had had which she heard about?"

Faith thinks for a moment. " Yeah, I remember now. One woman called herself a Hagar."

"And remember that case where two children were found cut into pieces in a suitcase in a storage locker just last month? That reminded me of the unnamed concubine story."[210]

"Yes. That was terrible too. So, what does all that mean?"

"Well, there's no hint that Jepthah's daughter or David's daughter Tamar or the anonymous concubine or Hagar deserved what was done to them. It maybe is to the credit of the biblical writers and compilers that they left these discreditable stories in the canon of scripture. Even though most of this list of women do not seem to get justice, they are recorded. Is it a warning about how brutal life can be? Or a lament for the waste of lives? Even in a patriarchal society perhaps someone had a conscience about the loss of female lives?"

"I guess it is for us now to protest such deeds and defend women who are helpless victims," suggests Faith thoughtfully.

"Yes. It's good, for example, that you were at the Iranian protest. That's why I advocate for gays in the church even though others think my actions will split the church. They don't of course, admit their own exclusive attitudes might be part of the reason for the general fall in church numbers."

We sit in silence for a moment. I couldn't tell what Faith was thinking but in my mind there were a parade of cases I knew of where women had been beaten, tortured, raped and killed, not always with any redress or justice.

I continue. "What we can know positively from our conversations are a couple of things. First, there is a lot of evidence of female images being used for God in the Bible. That, along with Phyllis Trible's interpretation of the simultaneous creation of the man and the woman, puts woman absolutely as an equal peer with man. It also makes brutal treatment of women a far worse crime than it already is. We are not second class human beings, we are equals and equally part of the image of the divine."

"I hadn't thought of putting those two facts together before. That does make sense," comments Faith, smiling.

"Secondly there's also the question of women as leaders in faith matters and religious groupings. Contrary to the general suppression of and ignorance about leadership roles women took as disciples and apostles and as leaders in the emerging church during those first few centuries, they were leaders and sometimes very influential ones. As well, the interpretation of "women keep silent in churches" was not written by the original Paul so does not carry his personal authority. It also seems it may have been a specific instruction in a real context which was about something other than teaching and leading. So, the Bible does not prohibit women as leaders in the church."

I pause, then continue. "There is more cause here for lament, however, for women who were discouraged or prevented from taking up leadership positions, women who were not chosen because a man was available, women who got a leadership role then were treated badly, women who were abused and vilified and misrepresented for taking an unusual role. We need to take the time to do that lamenting as well as celebrate the women who had led and still lead and will lead in the future."

Faith has been listening carefully. Slowly she speaks. "That is good to hear. So often what I hear or see is subtle and nonverbal lack of encouragement. No one has actively opposed me, but they just haven't encouraged me – like the way the elders encourage Mark, but not me in the youth work back home."

"And there, in our local Gospel Hall, all I see all the time are men taking the lead, so why would I think I could do it, or Hazel could do it? It's true that statement you told me weeks ago, 'you have to see it to be it.'"

I nodded. "You know, at the beginning of the 1980s, when I was in the U.S., I heard a young black woman lawyer speaking about her life. She said that what she missed most was older women role models in the law. She had no models just like her to learn from or to imitate. No one who looked like her was in the law offices and the courts at that time. It made me realise I had wrongly assumed that when the civil rights legislation was passed in the US in 1964, everything came right for black people in the States. It might have given them the rights they deserved as human beings but it would still take time (facing quite a lot of opposition still) for black students, for example, to study law and then become qualified lawyers in the system. If the Act was passed in 1964 and I was listening to that young women in 1980, it was only 16 years that she had had to get to her present position. Not time for her mother's generation to become lawyers too. She was, along with others, a true pioneer, having to work it out herself."

"It's like that for all the firsts, I guess," replies Faith. The first woman prime minister of a country,[211] the first female Governor General,[212] the first chief Judge of the District Court,[213] the first Chief Justice,[214] the first minister in a denomination or the first woman bishop. That must require a lot of self-belief."

"And a lot of support from others too," I add.

We pause for a moment, thinking of different women who broke the glass and the stained-glass ceilings[215] in our world.

"We need another drink," I say suddenly. "What do you feel like, Faith?"

"Chocolate please," she replies. Hot chocolate is her go-to drink when the work gets heavy, I've noticed. "Right," I say and disappear to the counter.

I notice as I stand in the queue waiting to order that Faith is staring into the middle distance, still and quiet. She looks pensive, but also… excited?

When I return she bursts into speech.

"The other thing we haven't mentioned is women's inner voice. I found that really enlightening. That we have an inner voice which can direct us to what is right and real for us, not into paths which others have decided as best for us. I found it very liberating that the soul voice is feminine in both men and women, so it's not something like wishful thinking from women who don't want to listen to men. It is me here," Faith presses her hand to the centre of her chest. "It is the real me. If I can let the trained ego voice recede and listen hard, I can find out my own path and my own direction. That is so important. And I love that it was important for Tamar, daughter in law of Judah and important for Rahab and Ruth and Mary. And I lament that it wasn't possible for those women who got overpowered by men like Tamar, David's daughter and Jepthah's girl and Hagar and the unnamed concubine. But I can learn from that and guard my own truth."

"Has it helped to find out where misogyny springs from and the basic reasons for its existence?"

Our hot chocolates arrive, adorned with marshmallows.

"Thank you," we both say absently, intent on our conversation.

"It does help, because realising that the resistance I meet isn't actually about me but is generic and about women in general, or rather about men in general, is a great help. If I can learn not to take it personally and not to agree with it myself deep down inside, then I am freed of that opposition holding me back. I can decide how much to push, whether I want something hard enough to push through or whether I will leave that battle to fight one which is more significant and vital."

I nod, scooping up a marshmallow and tasting its sweetness. Faith had got it. She might lose that certainly from time to time, but she had learned now that she was entitled to be a woman in the world the way her inner voice would lead her. She had gained enough discernment to start her on the path of sifting out the false, socialised voices within her and seeking the quiet sure voice deeper down. She knew her path might not win majority approval among friends and family, among enemies and opposition, but if she was sure it was the right path for her, she must take it for her own integrity and inner fulfilment.

It was like a jury being urged to make their decision based on whether they were sure, beyond reasonable doubt. Women could be sure of themselves in the world, they could be confident beyond reasonable doubt that they were following their right path – if they spent time searching for, listening for that inner voice which carries divine truth, that inner voice at home in their own soul. I smiled back at Faith over the chocolate foam. We would have many more conversations about this and other issues, but for now, we had reached a point where we had confirmed a deep truth about being woman in the world.

Poems of Lament & Celebration

Lament for Everywoman

I lament

the girl baby born into poverty and addiction
the little girl who hides away from predators
in a dark bedroom
the girl student who is not coached or encouraged
like her brothers
the female adolescent trained to wear her hijab properly
– or else

I lament

the teenager schooled to be compliant so boys will like her
the girls deprived of leadership opportunities
the young woman keeping her knees bent so as not to be
taller than him
the female student missing extra tuition for that special exam

I lament

the office worker dodging groping hands
the partygoer whose drink has been spiked
the lawyer noticing the partnerships always go to the men
the unsuccessful candidates who find all the mayors are
 white and male

I lament

the ease with which women can become
the handmaidens in church
the language which does not situate women
as divine or human
the preaching which assumes both genders think and
feel the same
the regulations which exclude lesbian women
from church leadership

I lament

women stuck in singledom
women stuck in unsatisfactory marriages
women afraid to come out as different
women in violent and abusive situations

I lament the disappointment, pain and trauma
experienced by these my sisters.

Celebrating Everywoman

I celebrate

the girl baby born into love and sufficiency
the little girl who plays hide and seek
without fear of consequences
the girl student who is coached and encouraged
like her brothers
the female adolescent free to dress as she chooses

I celebrate

the teenager allowed to be assertive
the girls given leadership opportunities
the young woman standing tall and proud
the female student given extra tuition for that special exam

I celebrate

the office worker working in a collegial atmosphere
where she is valued
the partygoer confident her drink will not be spiked
the lawyer finding that partnerships are open to women
as much as men
the successful candidate who finds women can be mayors

I celebrate

the ease with which women gain positions of responsibility
in church
the language which allows all to be included,
women and men together
the preaching which caters for genders
which think and feel differently
that regulations can be changed

I celebrate

women enjoying singledom
women in marriages which are better than only satisfactory
women unafraid to come out as different
women in violent and abusive situations who get support and
courage to leave
I celebrate the achievement, love and happiness
experienced by these my sisters
and yearn that this may be so for all.

Appendix 1
Other Women from the Genealogy
of the Christ in Matthew 1

Rahab

Unusually, it was your house
but then yours was an unusual profession
for an ancestor of the Christ;
hospitality your trade
a hospitality which took many forms
and, this night,
sheltered two Israelite spies.

You knew the risk how easily the guards on city wall
could monitor comings and goings
could see
when there was a coming without a going.

Why did you shelter them?
Oh, there's that long theological discourse
some editor has put into your mouth
but when had you time to read theological tomes?

Was it self-preservation?
That instinct for survival
which had served you very well already?
A yearning for a better life, perhaps?
Something those spies said
which caught your imagination?
Whatever the motive, the risk paid off.
a grateful nation took you to their heart.

Rahab
harlot
hotelier
householder
became mother
whose son begat a son
who also befriended a foreign woman,

a woman who begat a son
whose son's son
is known down years of history

But so too are you.
your scarlet cord
is for us a thread of hope
that we too can escape the ruins of our lives
even when all tumbles down about us
if we dare to take the risk.

Ruth

Ruth,
so grey, life
all of a sudden.

Alone now, three widows, destitute;
two of you Moabite women,
but one, the eldest, yearning for her homeland.

You know she must go even if to die there
In that land far away, foreign to you.

Your choice is meagre
trudge weary miles to Bethlehem
or go back home to father.
Exile or diminishment?
Meagre as it is
you choose deliberately exile
with the mother you have come to love.

Of the journey the words tell us nothing.
How did you survive it?
The loneliness the energy-sapping days
the anxiety and fear.
"They came to Bethlehem" is all we know.
You only know the cost.

What humiliation did you feel
as you joined the group of gleaning women
dusty, hot, prickly work
aching back?
throbbing head?
learning the skill of avoiding lascivious labourers'
groping hands.

Boaz, drawn by what -
Your graceful walk?
Your quiet dignity?
Your devoted work?
– grants you a privileged place.

We in twentieth century western times
delight to scent a fairy tale
"*First Glance across a Cornfield*
would title a romantic fiction
to our satisfaction

Was it love?
Or was it dutiful obedience to a beloved mother in law
that found you lying at the dark edge of the threshing floor
ringing with drink-sodden laughter
creeping forward in the dark to lie with Boaz.

What relief to find the man was true
and you had found an ally in this male world
one who could speak for you
who would negotiate and win your case.

One who, with you
made a son for Naomi;
a son who sired another son
whose son in turn became king.

You, foreign woman,
yet loved, respected, married in Israel
great grandmother of King David
later to rule this land;
ruler of the fields near Bethlehem
where widows glean for grain.

And was it that in time to come
David stood on palace wall
surveyed his fields about the town, pointed and said,
"There!
There she gleaned for grain.
Right there!
My great-grandmother Ruth."

Mary

Mary, do you know why Matthew did it?
Why he included the five of you
you, all of you, in his genealogy of the Christ?

What point was he trying to make?
What do you, young woman of serene reputation
and gentle fame
have in common with
Tamar – apparent seducer of her father-in-law
Rahab – harlot and spy-shelterer
Ruth – propositioner of respectable Boaz
Bathsheba – did she seduce or was she raped by her king?

The male double standard overemphasizes sexuality
in the stories:

    Tamar's propositioning of Judah

       Rahab's membership of the oldest profession we know

         Ruth's creeping into Boaz' bed

           Bathsheba's brazen bathing on the roof

But wait, let's reframe, maybe the headlines
could read like this:

WIDOW CLAIMS JUSTICE FROM FATHER-IN-LAW
HOUSEHOLD SAVED THROUGH WOMAN'S COURAGE
FAITHFUL DAUGHTER BETTER THAN SEVEN SONS
WOMAN SURVIVES INSTITUTIONAL RAPE

"Read all about it!"

What an honour to mix in this company
of strong, determined women,
who knew their rights, took risks,
toiled in foreign fields, survived violence and loss.

So we might not ask what they have to do with you
(pure, unsullied as the stereotypical virgin story goes)
but what qualities fit you to mix with them?
Matthew groups you in strong sisterhood
five foremothers amongst the list of men
five of the women who begat the Christ.

Was it to tell us that in Jesus' veins runs
the courage of Tamar, Rahab's risk-taking spirit, the
determination showed by Ruth mingling with the resilience of
Uriah's wife?

And what of you, Mary?
What blood-inheritance do you offer this special child?
Faith needed to face an unbelieving fiancé
stamina needed for along journeys on a donkey's back?
Or
Something deep inside, beyond description;
a something that enabled you to face that ghastly hill
to be present in the midst of horror
to wait there despite inner fear.

In such a way
Tamar faced the only way she could right the wrong
and Rahab chose the danger of espionage.

In such a way
Ruth faced the unknown in the shadows of the threshing floor
and Bathsheba survived the horrors of violation and loss.

An inheritance fit for a Christ, an impeccable bloodline,
a first class pedigree, this legacy
rich with courage and risk-taking, determination, resilience
and a certain something that survives all kinds of horror.

Something like.... like ...
like an indestructible sort of love.
Something like that.

Something very like Love.

Appendix II

'Jesus was fortunate'

A hymn about friends and stillness

1. Jesus was fortunate to have good friends
   Martha, Mary and Laz,
   The siblings lived in Bethany
   a suburb of Jerusalem,
   a home that welcomed him in love,
   a home that offered love.

2. One night he came, bringing more friends too,
   a band of hungry men.
   It was a stretch to feed them all
   and Martha found it quite a strain,
   She found Mary useless in the main
   her stillness was no gain.

3. Jesus suggests a new approach
   more quiet, and more still.
   He says that is the better part,
   and Martha ponders in her heart
   if his comments were the truth
   Were his words ringing true?

4. We know that Martha took those words that day
   and changed her way of life;
   later, when first her brother died
   she spoke truth which only could come
   from the Spirit, deep inside,
   the Spirit, quiet and still.

5. We may have strengths of usefulness
   and many handy skills;
   but we find how the Spirit leads
   when we can pause and listen, still,
   for the Spirit deep within
   the Spirit quiet and still.

6. Give thanks and praise for all who spend
   much time in care and cure.
   We honour them and also pray
   they find their own still, quiet time
   to hear the Voice within,
   and find Love's quiet ways.

Words: Susan Jones (2022), unpublished hymn
Tune: Repton WOV 519 (ii)

Endnotes

1 Hope's story can be found in *Wherever you are, You are on the Journey* (Philip Garside Publishing Ltd, Wellington 2021)

2 Charity's story is told in *We Are All Equally Human* (Philip Garside Publishing Ltd, Wellington 2022)

3 Susan Jones, to be published in forthcoming *One Step at a Time*. Originally published in *What was it Like?* (JBCE Melbourne, 1993)

4 New English Translation (NET)

5 Catherine Keller, *The Face of the Deep: A Theology of Becoming* (Routledge 2003) chapter 5

6 Keller, 2003 chapter 5

7 "In *Protestant Thought: From Rousseau to Ritschl*, the great Protestant theologian Karl Barth refers to the German philosopher, G.W.F. Hegel (1770-1831), as the "Protestant Aquinas." Barth mentions that he has some theological differences with Hegel, but wonders why Hegel did not become for the Protestant world what Aquinas was for the Catholic world." https://www.thecatholicthing.org/2013/10/23/hegel-the-protestant-aquinas/ Accessed 6 October 2022

8 https://www.mothergodexperiment.com/ Accessed 29 July 2022

9 https://thepracticelondon.org/poetry/poems-of-transformation-the-journey-by-mary-oliver/ Accessed 29 July 2022

10 https://reflections.yale.edu/article/seize-day-vocation-calling-work/merton-prayer Accessed 6 October 2022

11 NET

12 NET

13 NET

14 NET

15 NET

16 'Eve and Adam: Genesis 2-3 Reread' Phyllis Trible Copyright 1973 by Andover Newton Theological School. All rights reserved. Used by permission. https://www.law.csuohio.edu/sites/default/files/shared/eve_and_adam-text_analysis-2.pdf, p. 2

17 Trible 1973, pp. 1-2

18 Trible 1973, p. 2

19 John Dominic Crossan *Who is Jesus?* (Louisville Kentucky: Westminster John Knox press, 1996) p. 79 cited in David Tacey, *Religion as Metaphor: Beyond Literal Belief* (Transaction Publishers, New Brunswick, US & London, UK 2015) p. 32

20 "The term "depth psychology" was coined at the turn of the twentieth century by Eugen Bleuler, a professor of psychiatry at the University of Zürich and director (1898-1927) of the Burghölzli Asylum in Zürich, where C. G. Jung began his career as a psychiatrist. It has become used by Freudians and Jungians to indicate those psychologies that orient themselves around the idea of the "unconscious."" https://www.pacifica.edu/about-pacifica/what-is-depth-psychology/ Accessed 8th September 2022

21 Edward Edinger, *Ego and Archetype*, (Shambhala Publications, Inc., Boston, MA., 1992) p. 18

22 Edinger (1992), p. 21

23 Edinger (1992), pp.21-22

24 https://thepracticelondon.org/poetry/poems-of-transformation-the-journey-by-mary-oliver/ Accessed 8 September 2022

25 Review of *Against Our Will: Men, Women, and Rape* quoted in Rutherford, *Alexandra* (June 2011). *"Sexual Violence Against Women: Putting Rape Research in Context." Psychology of Women Quarterly.* 35 (2): 342–347. doi:10.1177/0361684311404307. S2CID 145146774

26 https://en.wikipedia.org/wiki/Rape_culture Accessed 6 October 2022

27 https://en.wikipedia.org/wiki/Rape_culture Accessed 6 October 2022

28 https://www.dictionary.com/browse/misogyny. Accessed 13 August 2022

29 https://nzhistory.govt.nz/women-together/theme/religion Accessed 13 August 2022

30 Rev Dr Ruth Page (tutor) 1975-1979; Rev Nan Burgess 1983-1995 (Acting Principal) 1989-1990; Rev Dr Judith McKinlay 1991-1996; Rev Marie Ropeti-Uipeli 1991-1995; Rev Dr Sarah Mitchell 1991-1996; Rev Dr Mary Huie-Jolly (1997-c. 2005); Rev Dr Susan Wernstein 2011-2006; Susan Jones *Governing for Theologia* PhD thesis University of Otago, NZ 2006 and Register of New Zealand Presbyterian Ministers, Deaconesses and Missionaries 1840-2015: https://www.presbyterian.org.nz/archives/page143.htm Accessed 11 October 2022

31 Rev Lynne Baab, (Adjunct, 2008-2016); Rev Dr Susan Jones, (2006-2014); Dr Rosemary Dewerse Thornton Blair Research Fellow, (2017–2018); Rev Nikki Watkin (0.3 position) (2020-present)

32 https://en.wikipedia.org/wiki/Misogyny Accessed 6 October 2022

33 https://en.wikipedia.org/wiki/Misogyny Accessed 6 October 2022

34 https://en.wikipedia.org/wiki/Misogyny Accessed 6 October 2022

35 Jones, (2022)

36 https://en.wikipedia.org/wiki/Misogyny Accessed 6 October 2022

37 Gilmore, David D. *Misogyny: The Male Malady.* (University of Pennsylvania Press, 2001) pp. 1-16. ISBN 0-8122-3589-4

38 https://www.amazon.com/Misogyny-Malady-David-D-Gilmore/dp/0812217705 Accessed 17 August 2022

39 Gilmore 2001

40 Gilmore 2001

41 Sander L. Gilman *Misogyny: The Male Malady* (review) *Bulletin of the History of Medicine* (Johns Hopkins University Press Volume 76, Number 2, Summer 2002) p. 406 https://muse.jhu.edu/article/4868 Accessed 17 August 2022

42 Gilman, 2002 p. 406

43 Gilman, 2002 p. 406

44 Anita Diamant *The Red Tent* (Picador USA, New York, 1997)

45 Carol A. Newsom, Sharon H. Ringe, Jacqueline E. Lapsley, eds. *Women's Bible Commentary*, (Westminster John Knox Press, 2012 3rd ed.)

46 Rev Dr Prof Judith McKinlay

47 Phyllis Trible *Texts of Terror: Literary-Feminist Readings of Biblical Narratives*, (Augsburg Fortress Publishers, Minneapolis, USA, 1982). Trible makes a close literary reading from a feminist perspective of four stories about women: Hagar, Tamar, an unnamed concubine, and the daughter of Jephthah.

48 Miriam Therese Winter, *WomanWord: A Feminist Lectionary* and *Psalter: Women of the New Testament* (1990), *WomanWisdom: A Feminist Lectionary* and *Psalter – Women of the Hebrew Scriptures: Part 1* (1991), *WomanWitness: A Feminist Lectionary and Psalter: Women of the Hebrew Scriptures, Part 2* (1992) (The Crossroad Publishing Company)

49 NET

50 NET

51 NET

52 NET

53 NET

54 NET

55 NET

56 NET

57 NET

58 These poems are intended to be part of an anthology forthcoming in 2023 entitled *One Step at a Time*

59 See Appendix 1 for 3 of these poems

60 https://en.wikipedia.org/wiki/Harvey_Weinstein_sexual_abuse_cases Accessed 6 October 2022

61 https://en.wikipedia.org/wiki/Jeffrey_Epstein Accessed 6 October 2022

62 https://en.wikipedia.org/wiki/Clinton%E2%80%93Lewinsky_scandal Accessed 6 October 2022

63 NET

64 2 Samuel 2:5

65 https://www.theoi.com/articles/important-facts-about-king-midas-daughter-marigold/ Accessed 7 September 2022

66 Also Cheryl J Exum 'Raped by the Pen' *Fragmented Women: Feminist (Sub) versions of Biblical Narratives* (JSOT, 1993)

67 Genesis 19:1-18 New International Version (NIV)

68 Phyllis Trible *Texts of Terror* Kindle 40th anniversary edition, 2022, p. 2

69 Trible Kindle 2022, Introduction, p. 2

70 https://www.learnreligions.com/davids-many-wives-in-bible-117324 Accessed 7 September 2022

71 https://en.wikipedia.org/wiki/Sons_of_David Accessed 6 October 2022

72 2 Samuel 13: 14-15.

73 Phyllis Trible *Texts of Terror* Kindle 40th anniversary edition, 2022 p. 48

74 Trible Kindle 2022 p. 49

75 Trible Kindle 2022 p. 51-52.

76 Trible Kindle 2022 p. 56.

77 https://www.helpauckland.org.nz/sexual-abuse-statistics.html Accessed 11 September 2022

78 https://www.police.govt.nz/advice-services/sexual-assault-and-consent/myths-and-facts Accessed 11 September 2022

79 Susan Jones, 'To the wilderness so hostile', *Progressing the Journey*, (Philip Garside Publishing Ltd, Wellington, NZ., 2022), p. 53 Sung to the tune Cwm Rhondda (With One Voice #478)

80 *The Canterbury Tales* is a collection of 24 stories written between 1387 and 1400 by Geoffrey Chaucer.

81 AD = Anno Domini, In the Year of our Lord to distinguish from B.C which means Before Christ. A less semitic way of putting it is BCE – Before the Common Era and, after the birth of Jesus, using CE for Common Era – the time when both Judaism and Christianity exist together.

82 "The Jesus Seminar was founded in 1985 by Robert Funk. The group of about 50 critical biblical scholars and 100 laymen worked under the banner of the Westar Institute,[1][2] active through the 1980s and 1990s, and into the early 21st century. They published *The Five Gospels* (1993),[4] *The Acts of Jesus* (1998), and T*he Gospel of Jesus* (1999). The work of The Jesus Seminar continued after the Funk's death (2005). Two seminars followed: The Seminar on God and the Human Future and The Christianity Seminar. The latter's first report in 2022, is *After Jesus Before Christianity: A Historical Exploration of the First Two Centuries of Jesus Movements.* Westar publishes a bi-monthly magazine, *The Fourth R: An Advocate for Religious Literacy.*" https://en.wikipedia.org/wiki/Jesus_Seminar Accessed 18 September 2022

83 Erin Vearncombe et al, *After Jesus Before Christianity* (Westar Christianity Seminar Harper One, New York, NY, 2021) p. XVII

84 NIV

85 To be published in *One Step at a Time* forthcoming 2023

86 Dan Brown, *The Da Vinci Code* (Anchor Books, Random House, N.Y., 2003)

87 Adapted from: https://www.womeninthescriptures.com/2014/05/list-of-all-women-in-new-testament.html Accessed 12 September 2022

88 To be published in *One Step at a Time* forthcoming 2023

89 Appendix III

90 *Mary Or Martha?: A Duke Scholar's Research Finds Mary Magdalene Downplayed By New Testament Scribes.* A 12th century Greek manuscript in Duke's library helps religion doctoral student Elizabeth Schrader argue her case https://today.duke.edu/2019/06/mary-or-martha-duke-scholars-research-finds-mary-magdalene-downplayed-new-testament-scribes.

91 Judi Fisher, Janet Wood (eds) *A Place at the Table: Women at the Last Supper* (Joint Board of Christian Education, Melbourne 1993)

92 Painting by Margaret Ackland, *The Last Supper*, 1993, Acrylic

93 p. 115 in this book Also to be published in One Step at a Time forthcoming 2023

94 Being mentioned in dispatches refers to a soldier's name being included in reports written by superior officers to send to high command. What was 'mentioned' was their brave or courageous acts in facing up to the enemy. The early Jesus followers were in a warlike zone in those early centuries. Both men and women mentioned in the letters or epistles which came after the Gospels were brave as they stood out for their conduct in dangerous times.

95   https://www.womeninthescriptures.com/2014/05/list-of-all-women-in-new-testament.html Accessed 12 September 2022

96 Vearncombe et al,2021, p. 101

97 Vearncombe et al, 2021, p. 102

98 Vearncombe et al, 2021, p. 102

99 Vearncombe et al. 2021, p. 102

100 Vearncombe et al 2021, p. 104

101 Vearncombe et al 2021, p. 105

102 Vearncombe et al, 2021, pp. 6-9

103 Vearncombe et al, 2021, p. 9

104 Vearncombe et al, 2021 p. 11

105 Vearncombe et al 2021 p. 24

106 Vearncombe et al 2021 p. 25-26

107 Vearncombe et al 2021 p. 27.

108 Vearncombe et al 2021, pp. 29-30.

109 Vearncombe et al 2021 p. 99

110 Vearncombe et al 2021 p. 100.

111 Vearncombe et al 2021 p. 318ff

112 https://www.britannica.com/topic/list-of-Roman-emperors-2043294 Accessed 18 September 2022

113 https://www.britannica.com/topic/list-of-Roman-emperors-2043294 Accessed 18 September 2022

114 One camp (led by Arius) held that Jesus the Son and God the Father were of different essences, and the other camp (led by Athanasius) held that they were

of the same essence. https://thebible.evangel.site/did-constantine-corrupt-the-bible/ Accessed 18 September 2022.

115 https://www.learnreligions.com/when-was-the-bible-assembled-363293 Accessed 18 September 2022

116 https://www.learnreligions.com/when-was-the-bible-assembled-363293 Accessed 18 September 2022

117 https://www.cbeinternational.org/resource/priscilla-author-epistle-hebrews/ Accessed 13 October 2022

118 Bird, *Romans* (The Story of God Bible Commentary) (Grand Rapids: Zondervan, 2016) cited by Marg Mowezko https://margmowczko.com/junias-junia-julia-romans-167/ Accessed 18 September 2022

119 Dunn, *Romans 9-16* (Word Biblical Commentary, Vol 38B) (Dallas, TX: Word, 1988), 894m cited by Marg Mowezko https://margmowczko.com/junias-junia-julia-romans-167/ Accessed 18 September 2022

120 https://margmowczko.com/ Accessed 18 September 2022

121 https://margmowczko.com/ Accessed 18 September 2022

122 Richard G. Fellows and Alistair C. Stewart *Euodia, Syntyche and the Role of Syzygos: Phil 4:2–3* from the journal Zeitschrift für die neutestamentliche Wissenschaft https://www.degruyter.com/document/doi/10.1515/znw-2018-0012/html Accessed 18 September 2022

123 Vearncombe et al 2021, p. 108

124 Vearncombe et al 2021, p. 114

125 Vearncombe et al 2021, p. 114

126 Vearncombe et al 2021, p. 114

127 p. 11 in this book

128 "'…then the male is God.' So wrote Mary Daly in a – perhaps the – classic text of early feminist theology, *Beyond God the Father* (Beacon, 1973). Daly's argument in the book was that the predominantly masculine imagery deployed for God in Judaeo-Christian traditions inevitably led to a patriarchal society in which women were multiply disadvantaged; the proper ethical response, in her view, was to reject all Judaeo-Christian religious traditions as demonstrably immoral and so unworthy of belief." https://shoredfragments.wordpress.com/2012/02/05/if-god-is-male/ A blog by Steve Holmes, a Baptist minister, presently employed to teach theology in St Mary's College, St Andrews, Scotland.

129 King Charles III's heir is William and then William's son George succeeds. The line of succession now goes to the child born next (whether they are male

or female), but the first born of William's family is male. Only if something happened to George before he had children, would his sister Charlotte become queen.

130   A statement by Marian Wright Edelman, a lawyer and activist in the US who heads up the Children's Defense Fund. https://en.wikipedia.org/wiki/ Marian_Wright_Edelman Accessed 19 September 2022

131   https://www.mpp.govt.nz/assets/Reports/2020-stocktake-of-gender-Maori-Pacific-and-ethnic-diversity-on-public-sector-boards-and-committees.pdf Accessed 19 September 2022

132   Virginia Ramey Mollenkott *The Divine Feminine: The Biblical Imagery of God as Female* (Crossroad N.Y, 1987)

133   Bridget Mary Meehan *Delighting in the Divine Feminine* (Rowman & Littlefield, United States 1994)

134   Rosemary Radford Reuther *Sexism and God-talk: Toward a Feminist Theology* (Beacon Boston 1993, p. ix)

135   Catherine Chrisp *Travelling with Sophia: Encountering the Feminine Divine* (The Women's Resource Centre, Ellerslie, N.Z., 2002)

136   Mollenkott 1987, p. 36

137   Mollenkott 1987, p. 37

138   Mollenkott 1987, p. 37

139   Mollenkott 1987, p. 42

140   Mollenkott 1987, p. 78

141   To be published in *One Step at a Time* forthcoming 2023

142   To be published in *One Step at a Time* forthcoming 2023

143   Chrisp (2002), p. 65

144   T.S. Eliot, from "Little Gidding," *Four Quartets* (Gardners Books; Main edition, April 30, 2001) Originally published 1943.

145   https://nzhistory.govt.nz/women-together Accessed 20 September 2022

146   Religion, Enid Bennet 1993 https://nzhistory.govt.nz/women-together Accessed 20 September 2022

147   Bennet 1993

148   Bennet 1993

149   Bennet 1993

150 Bennet 1993

151 Audrey Scobie was the first woman Moderator of the Synod of Otago and Southland. Nola Stuart was the first woman Convenor of the PCANZ Council of Assembly

152 Mrs Joan Anderson C.B.E., M.A.

153 Very Rev Margaret A. Reid-Martin, B.Sc

154 Very Rev Margaret E. Schrader Dip R. E.

155 Very Rev Pamela Tankersley, B.Sc, DipTchg, BD

156 Rev Rose Luxford, B.A. B.D.

157 Millie te Kaawa QSM https://gg.govt.nz/images/millie-te-kaawa-qsm-whakatane Accessed 11 October 2022

158 https://en.wikipedia.org/wiki/Sarah_Mullally Accessed 20 September 2022

159 Vivienne Adair, *Women of the Burning Bush: The report of a Survey of Women Ministers in the Presbyterian Church of New Zealand after 25 years of Ordination* The Presbyterian Church of New Zealand, Wellington, 1991. (Until 1990, the Church was the PCNZ. Aotearoa was added in 1990 to make it the PCANZ.)

160 Waddell was a very important figure in social reform. He was the first president of the Tailoresses Union. https://teara.govt.nz/en/biographies/2w1/waddell-rutherford Accessed 24 September 2022

161 Rev Gibb cited in Adair 1991, p. 2

162 Adair 1991, p. 3

163 Adair 1991, p. 3

164 Adair, 1991, p. 40

165 Adair, 1991 p. 4

166 Kupu Whakapono accepted by the GA2010. It means confession of faith or 'speaking faith'

167 https://brethrenhistory.org/History.htm Accessed 24th September 2022

168 Adair, 1991, pp. 4-5

169 Adair, 1991, p. 5

170 Adair, 1991, p. 5

171 Adair, 1991, p. 5

172 Adair, 1991, p. 6

173 Ruether & McLaughlin cited in Giles, K *Women and their Ministry* Dove 1977, p. 8

174 Mark Chaves The Symbolic Significance of Women's Ordination *The Journal of Religion* Vol. 77, No. 1 (Jan., 1997), pp. 87-114.

175 Adair, 1991, p. 62

176 Adair, 1991, p. 63

177 Adair, 1991, p. 63

178 Adair, 1991, p. 63

179 Vivienne Adair *Women of the Burning Bush still burning 25 years on* PCANZ 2018, 95. https://www.presbyterian.org.nz/about-us/research-resources/research-papers/women-of-the-burning-bush-still-burning-25-years-on Accessed 13 October 2022

180 Adair 2018, p. 95

181 Adair 2018, pp. 98-101

182 Adair 2018, p. 97

183 Susan Jones *One Woman's Journey: First Steps* (Self-published, Gore N.Z., 1990)

184 Unpublished poem, used by permission.

185 Susan Jones *Progressing the Journey* 2022. Tune: Gaelic Traditional Melody. Arr © John Bell. Faith Forever Singing 10(i)

186 https://www.theguardian.com/books/2015/feb/17/baddies-in-books-uriah-heep-david-copperfield-charles-dickens Accessed 11 October 2022

187 Phillips Brooks (December 13, 1835-January 23, 1893) was an American Episcopal clergyman and author, long the Rector of Boston's Trinity Church and briefly Bishop of Massachusetts. He wrote the lyrics of the Christmas hymn, "O Little Town of Bethlehem." https://en.wikipedia.org/wiki/Phillips_Brooks Accessed 28 September 2022

188 Abstract, Tangney, J. P. (2009). Humility. In S. J. Lopez & C. R. Snyder (Eds.), *Oxford handbook of positive psychology* (pp. 483–490). Oxford University Press

189 David Tacey *Religion as Metaphor: Beyond Literal Belief,* (Transaction Publishers New Brunswick N.J., 2015), p. 107

190 Tacey, 2015, p. 108

191 Tacey, 2015, p. 107

192 Tacey, 2015, p. 110

193 Tacey, 2015, p. 110-111

194 Tacey, 2015, p. 113

195 Tacey, 2015, p. 113

196 Tacey, 2015, p. 114

197 Tacey, 2015, p. 115

198 http://thepracticelondon.org/poetry/poems-of-transformation-the-journey-by-mary-oliver/ Accessed 28 September 2022

199 Tacey, 2015, p. 115

200 Tacey, 2015, pp. 117-118

201 Tacey, 2015, p. 125

202 The Human Situation: A Feminine View Author(s): Valerie Saiving Goldstein Source: *The Journal of Religion*, Vol. 40, No. 2, (Apr., 1960), pp. 100-112 Published by: The University of Chicago Press Stable https://www.jstor.org/stable/1200194 and https://www.sjsu.edu/people/jennifer.rycenga/courses/gsr/s1/Saiving_Article.pdf Accessed 28 September 2022

203 Saiving Goldstein (1960), p. 101

204 Saiving Goldstein (1960), pp. 108-9

205 Susan Jones, 'Gathering to Consider the Inner Journey' *Progressing the Journey*, (Philip Garside Publishing Ltd Wellington, NZ, 2022), p. 64.

206 Susan Jones (2022b) 'Gathering for Cosmos Sunday' p. 65

207 Susan Jones (2022b) 'Affirmation of Faith' p. 72

208 Susan Jones (2022b) 'Affirmation of Faith...' p. 80

209 https://www.dw.com/en/protests-in-iran-after-woman-dies-in-police-custody/av-63186795 Accessed 11 October 2022

210 https://www.theguardian.com/world/2022/aug/18/new-zealand-suitcase-human-remains-two-young-children-auckland Accessed 11 October 2022

211 "Dame Jennifer Mary Shipley DNZM PC (née Robson; born 4 February 1952) is a New Zealand former politician who served as the 36th prime minister of New Zealand from 1997 to 1999. She was the first female prime minister of New Zealand, and the first woman to have led the National Party." https://en.wikipedia.org/wiki/Jenny_Shipley Accessed 11 October 2022

212 "Dame Catherine Anne Tizard ONZ GCMG GCVO DBE QSO DStJ (née Maclean; 4 April 1931–31 October 2021) was a New Zealand politician who served as mayor of Auckland City from 1983 to 1990, and the 16th governor-general of New Zealand from 1990 to 1996. She was the first woman to hold either office." https://en.wikipedia.org/wiki/Catherine_Tizard Accessed 11 October 2022

213 In 1989, Cartwright became the first female Chief District Court Judge, and in 1993 she was the first woman to be appointed to the High Court. https://en.wikipedia.org/wiki/Silvia_Cartwright Accessed 11 October 2022

214 On 17 May 1999, Elias was sworn in as Chief Justice of New Zealand, the first woman to hold that position in New Zealand. https://en.wikipedia.org/wiki/Sian_Elias Accessed 11 October 2022

215 https://en.wikipedia.org/wiki/Stained-glass_ceiling Accessed 11 October 2022

Other books by Susan Jones
from Philip Garside Publishing Ltd

Wherever You Are, You Are On The Journey:
Conversations in a Coffee Shop Book 1

Do you feel there is more to Christian faith than is told on Sundays? Are you questioning whether the firmly held beliefs you grew up with are going to be useful in the next stage of your life?

Don't panic! You have simply reached a transition point in your faith journey.

Hope and her minister/mentor Susan chat about deepening & re-enchanting faith at their local café.

(Print and eBooks now available.)

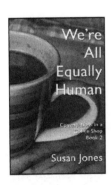

We are All Equally Human:
Conversations in a Coffee Shop Book 2

Charity, a young lesbian church goer, attends her church's national conference, and finds herself hurt and upset by the swirl of the 'gay debate' in the Church. She comes home puzzled and worried.

Charity and her minister plunge into coffee shop conversations about this issue.

(Print and eBooks now available.)

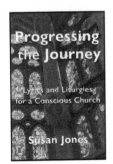

Progressing on the Journey:
Lyrics and liturgy for a conscious church

Words for 40 new hymns, that can be sung to well known tunes, which address contemporary issues and celebrate the church year. This book also contains a wealth of responsive prayers and liturgy for worship.

Includes: Gatherings, Creeds, Affirmations, Communion liturgies, Blessings, poems and two Reflections.

(Print and eBooks, and PowerPoint slide sets now available.)

Printed in Great Britain
by Amazon

15889123R00127